THE BLACK BONNET

BOOK TWO IN THE DARKER CITIES TRILOGY

ELOISE REUBEN

SHARPENING THE QULL

Cover Design by Damonza

Edited by Amy Teegan

✿ Created with Vellum

ABOUT THE AUTHOR

A lover of old cities, history and travelling, Eloise is an Australian living in the United States with her husband and young daughter. She is drawn to worlds long gone, and loves thrilling stories with gritty characters and lots of heart.

Join Eloise's mailing list at eloisereuben.com

CHAPTER 1

LONDON. 25TH JANUARY, 1849

essie traced her fingers over the small book in her hands. Its gold leaf title glimmered beneath the passing lanterns as their carriage rumbled along the dark streets of Marylebone. The icy air stung her cheeks as the sloe gin she'd sipped after dinner still fizzed in her belly.

"Will yer teach me to read?" she asked of Kyran as she flicked through the musty pages.

"Of course. If you wish."

"Mrs Whitley were kind to gift it to me. I've never owned a book. What's it about?" She passed it to him, watching as he expertly scanned the pages.

"It's a collection of poems."

"Poems." She said the word carefully. "Like ballads. Folk songs?"

"Yes. Like that."

She took the book back, enjoying the way the pages felt through her gloves. "I tried to learn my letters once but numbers was always the thing, weren't it? Paying rent. Counting pennies."

Kyran smiled, stifling a yawn. It had been a long evening

filled with business talk and just enough jovial chatter to call it a social engagement. He wished to flee London the moment Ruby was well enough to travel, and he'd been working day and night to spark investment interest in Boston. Tessie could see the strain of it in his kind eyes, the greying at the edge of his blonde sideburns.

"Was it a wasted dinner? Do yer think Mr Whitley will invest after all?" she asked.

Kyran rested his chin to his knuckles, the cuff of his suit crisp and white against the shadowed background. "He is interested but it's quite a leap for him. We must wait and see."

Tessie relaxed back in her seat as the West End terrace homes passed by the window. The charming brick facades peeked through the fog as the horse's hooves echoed over the cobblestones. This corner of London still felt so very far from the Old Nichol slums. So very far from the quiet evenings she and Finn had spent in their small tenement, their bodies weary and bellies empty. If it wasn't for Kyran sitting beside her, and the ache beneath the taffeta and silk of her dress where the blade had pierced her skin, she might have believed it had all been a dream. But it had been real. Every bit of it.

Not three months ago she had sold ginger cakes at Spitalfields market. Rising each morning to greet her customers on their way to the docks or stables or warehouses, playing her part in the ever-turning cycle of East End life. Her dresses had been threadbare and her boots muddy and old, while here in Mayfair with Kyran's soft sheets and fancy clothes, that life felt so very far away.

The Angel of Bishopsgate was her father. The truth of that statement still sent a shudder down her spine. It was he who had caused it all, all the pain and separation, all the fear that stained her veins, the angst and heartache. It was he who had sent her to Kyran on that rainy November night to deliver a message - a message meant to kill her and strike a devastating blow against her estranged mother, Aileen. Instead, she had gained a brother. Kyran, just like her, wanted nothing more than to be free of his father's shadow.

While it felt like time had been spinning around her, they were only now entering the last week of January. It had been just over a week since the Angel had released Finn from prison. One week since she'd been able to wrap her arms around him and relax her breath. It had been one week since they'd made their promises and deals with the Angel.

Dear God. The promises she'd made. They were promises that let her reunite with Finn, and had Kyran and Ruby on their way to Boston, but the thought of how much it might cost them now left her floundering in dread.

"I want to enjoy this. All of this. I want to learn. But ... it ain't real, is it? Not yet." She looked down at that book in her hands, but a small token of a life she and Finn imagined would always be outside their reach. Didn't they deserve a chance to be free? Hadn't they earned it?

Kyran tilted his head understandingly. "You still haven't told Finn?"

She lowered her eyes, smoothing the creases in her white gloves. No, she hadn't told him. She had tried all of twice, though the words had quickly fallen away. She couldn't so easily shatter the comfort and relief still warming their bones. Perhaps if she waited long enough the need to tell him might disappear completely. She hoped so badly for that to be the truth, and yet the drumming in her chest grew louder with each passing day. Deep down she knew her time in this city was running out.

As they rounded the park on the home stretch for Mayfair, a carriage pulled beside them in the otherwise empty street. Their driver flicked his whip, urging his horses on.

"Are they trying to go around us?" Tessie asked, a pang of concern tugging at her chest.

Kyran leaned forward to see; he rapped his fist on the siding and called through to the driver. "Let them around. Slow down. Let them around."

The driver slowed, but instead of passing, the carriage cut in front of their horses bringing them to a shambling and chaotic halt. One horse reared up and the driver lurched forward to calm it.

"Bloody mad. They're going to hurt someone."

Tessie pressed her face to the freezing glass, clenching her hands into fists. "What is it? What's going on?"

Kyran's expression fell and all at once she knew the answer, the breath seizing in her throat. "He's come for me. He's come for me, hasn't he?" She'd known he would. The Angel of Bishopsgate would call in his debt. But not now. Please, not now.

Before she could speak again a face appeared at their window. Tessie pulled back in fright. The sharp edge of his top hat gleamed in the moonlight and the whites of his eyes glowed. Castor Adams was looking right at her, a casual smile grazing his lips as he pulled open the carriage door, allowing a bluster of winter air to engulf them.

"He will see you."

Tessie sat pinned to her seat. "Out here? Right now?"

"Come with me."

"We're on our way home...We're—"

"Castor, stop this," Kyran interjected. "If he wants to see her, we'll follow you to the house. We—"

"I will drag you out if you don't come yourself." He spoke directly to Tessie, his gaze firm as he offered his hand to assist her down the steps.

Tessie felt the weight of her dread plunge through her. Not now. She wasn't ready. Please not now. She looked to

Kyran, unable to insist on anything else. His eyes narrowed with concern and he exited ahead of her, pushing Castor's hand out of the way. Tessie stumbled down the carriage steps after him, her skirts catching on the doorway so that she hastily pushed them through.

The bitter wind outside whipped against her, forcing her to fold her arms in a futile attempt to stay warm. Ahead in the dark carriage, Arthur's shoulders cut an imposing silhouette in the window and her heart pounded in her ears. There he was, the Angel of Bishopsgate. Her father. The man who had tried to have her killed. The man, who it seemed, commanded all of London. The door kicked open. The smoke from his cigar billowed out.

"It's time." Arthur's gruff cockney accent shot through the smoke before his face became clear. Tessie forced herself to step closer. Her thoughts raced so rapidly she couldn't get a word out. Arthur pressed his lips into a thin line. "I said, it's time."

"We're only just recovering. We need to rest. We need…" Her breath plumed out in front of her as she faded away, still unable to make out Arthur's face.

"You came to me, remember." Arthur shifted forward, pressing his large frame through the door so that he propped one foot on the step. He leaned in close, his piercing blue eyes as sharp as ever. "You stood in my house and spewed your promises and plans. You got your man, didn't you, darlin'? Now you'll come good or…" He broke into a smile as if he relished the threat left unspoken. He drew on his cigar and let the cloud of smoke consume Tessie.

"Yes, but…" Tessie clasped her hands into fists. "It won't work. My mother will never listen to me. She—"

Arthur's arm shot out, his fingers squeezing Tessie's throat with such force the air froze in her lungs. "You will get your mother out the way or she'll be at the bottom of the Liffey with stones in her belly. Do you understand?"

Tessie's knees buckled, her hands clawing at his grip, but it made no difference.

"Or you and your man can join her."

"Stop!" Kyran rushed forward but Arthur only tightened his grip before releasing her with a violent shove backwards.

"She's fine," Arthur said, waving his hand as if the fuss was ridiculous. "She's fine."

Tessie spluttered for breath, her knees on the icy stones as Kyran helped her up. Aileen Fisher would never step aside, no matter how Tessie may plead. There had to be another way.

"What if I can't do it? What if I can't get her to let go?"

"You have seven days."

Tessie's heart seized. "Seven days? But it's two days travel just to get there." That wasn't enough time. It wasn't nearly enough!

"It's only for *him* I'm entertaining this bloody charade." Arthur's pale eyes darted toward Kyran as he pointed. "Rest assured, darlin', if I don't hear from you by then I'll grace Dublin's shores myself to squeeze the life out of you and your mother."

"Why?" Tessie demanded with frustration. "Why must yer hate her so? For all these years?" The question cried out from her belly. What drove his hatred so deep that it spanned the Irish Sea and drew them all into its path?

"Hate?" The word rolled in Arthur's mouth, a half-snarl, half-grin forming on his lips. "Believe me, hate ain't the half of it." With that, he slammed the carriage door. "Seven days, girl. Better move."

CHAPTER 2

Tessie leaned forward, breathing fog onto the glass. Curled into a chair by the window, she sat in the early morning quiet watching Finn's broad shoulders steadily rise and fall on the bed. She had returned late with Kyran and had no desire to wake him.

As much as she wished to crawl in beside him, her mind whirred with the mad fog of Dublin - and her mother, the Black Bonnet. She could already feel her strength. Formidable and ferocious, ready to crash through her like a tidal wave. And on the other side, stood the Angel of Bishopsgate, his hand ready to squeeze the life out of her. She was impossibly caught between them. How could she survive this? How could she survive and not lose all they had worked for?

Tessie slid open the top drawer of the dresser and quietly rifled her fingers through the contents. She was looking for something. She held out a small figure of St. Brigid in her palm, the very same from Aileen's nightstand. Closing her fist around it, she brought it to her chest.

It had been St. Brigid that carried her prayers for Finn and triggered their deals with the Angel, but Tessie had thought little of Aileen's parting gesture. She'd imagined her carelessly tossing it inside the coin purse before rushing her to the quay and away from Dublin. It had been a goodbye. A final thrust of distance and separation. Tessie looked down at the figure, tarnished and old. Maybe it had been a blessing. A well-wishing. Or maybe it had been nothing at all. Whatever it was, now it held all of Tessie's hopes. Please, may her mother listen. Please.

Outside the door, she heard soft thudding footsteps and the rustling of a skirt. Tessie hurried to drop her blanket and leap back into the bed. As she did, Finn instinctively wrapped his arm around her and pulled her close.

It was only young Anna come to re-light the fire as she did every morning to stave off the icy chill, but Tessie wasn't yet ready for interaction. She kept her eyes closed and her breathing steady as she heard the soft shuffle of coal being tipped from the basket and the light wisp of Anna's match. The familiar smell filled the room and Anna quietly exited, leaving the room empty and still again.

"Are yer scared of the fire girl?" Finn's voice roused, croaky and deep in her ear.

"No."

"She won't hurt yer," he teased. "And if she tries, I'll stop her."

"Hush yer mouth." She jabbed him playfully with her elbow, trying to shrug away the anxiety in her belly.

"Easy does it. I'm still fragile." The rawness of Finn's bruises had faded, but beneath the skin the tenderness lingered.

"I'm sorry," she said, reaching for his side. She knew she'd done no actual damage, and touched her fingers to a rough graze along his collarbone, wanting to feel the warmth of his skin. As his dark hair flopped over his eyes, he stretched towards the window, eyeing her blanket by the chair.

"Yer couldn't sleep again?" He swept his hand over her cheek, resting his thumb on her temple. The small familiar scar above his left eye caught the morning light, faded and pale beside the fresh ones still healing. She thought to others he must look a menacing figure, but she knew his heart. "It's all them thoughts going on up there."

Tessie wondered what he could see in her eyes. She could not remember any other secret she had ever kept from him. Could he see this one brewing within her? If he did, he said nothing.

He pulled himself from the sheets to stand and raised his arms high in a stretch. "I thought to go with Mickey to Queenhithe this morning. We're to try for a day's work."

"Yer only escaped the hangman a week ago. Yer needn't rush back out so soon, yer know."

"The world stops turning for no one, least of all me, Tess. And I'll go stir-crazy in this house if I sit about any longer. My hands'll turn soft and all." He looked down at his chest, inspecting old bruises and grazes. "I'm just about healed up."

"Aye, but..." Tessie trailed away. "We're not in need of money is all." She was stalling, trying to form the words she needed to burst this most splendid bubble.

"Yer have some money. Kyran and Ruby have money. I don't have money."

"There is plenty left from my mother. That is ours."

"I'd arrive in Boston with money I earned myself. I'll not rest on another man's coin, Tess. Or a woman's. There is worth in this body still."

He was looking forward to Boston, so they all were. She had dreamed of it just the other night, the street scene vivid in her mind though she had never laid eyes on it. She was there with Finn, together in the New World stretching out before them, just as they had spoken of many a night cocooned by the fire, in bed, or counting their meagre coins at the table in their tenement in the Old Nichol.

She'd told Finn almost everything of their compromise with the Angel - that he'd agreed to release Finn from the Old Bailey's cells if she could bring Kyran to see him. That Kyran and Ruby were to go to Boston, establishing a branch of the Angel's shipping business in the New World. But that's where the telling stopped.

She and Finn wished to go with Kyran to forge a new life for themselves across the ocean, away from all they'd left in Dublin, and all they'd struggled through in London. It had felt so impossibly out of reach. Yet, after everything Arthur Crabbe, the mighty Angel of Bishopsgate, had put them through, they were here with their dream at their fingertips. There was just one thing standing in their way - it stuck in Tessie's throat.

Across the room, Finn splashed water on his face and dried himself before pulling a fresh shirt over his head. "And I need a new one of these before Ruby has her way and takes me shopping. She'll have me dressed like a bloody toff before yer know it."

Tessie managed a smile. "But yer would look so fine in a suit, so yer would. Yes, sir. Mr O'Shea, sir."

He tossed his dampened facecloth at her and she ducked beneath the covers, laughing. "No. It'll be Queenhithe for me this morning. Get this body moving. It's good for a man to work."

He sat to pull on his boots as Tessie felt a swirl in her stomach. She was about to break the spell.

She cleared her throat. "Finn. There's something more I need to tell yer." She heard her voice, deep and strange.

"Something I haven't yet told yer." She rolled onto her side, propping herself up on her elbow and reaching her fingertips towards him on the quilt. "I should have told yer already. I should have told yer when yer first returned to me and for that yer will have to forgive me..."

Finn frowned, the colour fading from his face. "What? What is it?"

"I thought I had more time. I thought..." She swallowed, turning her eyes to his.

"What is it, Tess?"

"I made a deal with him. With Arthur."

"To have me released. Aye, I know. Yer told me that."

"No. There is more. He told me..." She paused again. "They're going to kill her."

"Who?"

"My mother. The Angel is going to kill her."

"Aileen?" He frowned. "I don't know what yer mean, Tess."

She pulled herself free of the covers and stood, gathering herself. "He has given me seven days to get her out of the way, to have her step aside in Dublin and make way for his plans or he'll wipe her out himself. He'll kill her. And if I don't go... If I don't go... he'll kill me." She instinctively felt her neck where his grip had choked her.

Finn held his shirt, still unbuttoned in place. His warm eyes creased, processing the flood of information. "I don't understand. Everything is fine and we're going to Boston."

"No." Tessie looked around the room, searching for the right words. "No. I don't know what I was thinking, except I would have promised him anything. And I made the deal. I did. I said I'd go to Dublin to get her out of the way for him. This all started because he was to send me home in a coffin to taunt her, hurt her, I don't know, but he was trying to win. He still wants to win and he'll use me to do it one way or another."

Finn lifted his fists in the air as if to punch the wall, but instead clutched them to his chest in frustration. "Can they not fight their own battles? Must they involve us? Use us? Suck us dry? We are to go to Boston. This is it. We are going."

Exasperation shone in Finn's eyes. He was holding desperately to their plans. It was she who had stopped them going before, that night in the Nichol before Moses came for her. Finn had wanted to run and again, she still stood in the way. It was cruel.

"I must go to Dublin and I must leave today." Tessie swallowed; she felt the pressure deep in her chest.

"Today? For Christ's sake, Tess. Today?" Finn sat back on the bed, hunching over and running his hands through his hair.

"If I knew any other way. Any way to resist him, or a way to run where he would not follow..." Her words fell away. "But I don't. I don't know what else to do. Except to try. I cannot imagine she will listen to me and it may all be for nought. She will not easily surrender to the Angel, nor any man. But I will have tried."

"Yer have to leave for Dublin today?"

Tessie crouched in front of him, her hands on his knees. "If I can just talk to her, perhaps it will all fall into place. I don't know what else I can do but speak to her, try to make her see sense. I'm so sorry."

Finn raised his head. "Don't apologise to me, Tess. Not for that man or for trying to do what's best. The wrath of that man will span the oceans."

She looked at him, her eyes longing to see the warmth and welcome she needed.

His shoulders sank. "Come here." He reached out and pulled her to him. "If yer tell me we must go to Dublin, then to Dublin we must go. We'll go and we'll speak to her."

"Yer will come?" Tessie searched his expression, knowing

what returning to Dublin would mean for him. His eyes held a shadow for that city, and for all he'd left behind there. She knew stepping foot on its shores again would not be easy for him.

"We will not be apart again, mo chara, not after everything we've been through."

Tessie squeezed his hand. "But what about Madochée? She'll follow yer. Yer know she will." That girl had followed Finn's every move since the moment he'd noticed her crouched in a dank corner of the city's most notorious slums. He had needed her help and she had saved him in more ways than one. She was his little shadow now, and even as she embraced Mickey and the others, it was Finn who anchored her to stay.

Finn cupped her cheek with his hand and let out a lengthy sigh. "Aye. She won't be shut in by closed doors, that much is true. Even if I ask her to stay, she's never listened to me before." He gave a wry chuckle and Tessie well knew she was an independent and resourceful little girl.

"What about Mickey? Would she stay with him?"

Finn shook his head. "He was to work at Queenhithe today and every other day to save for Boston. He'll not be around to see to her."

"Well, she will stay if yer here. Yer needn't come. I can speak to my mother. I can do it-"

"No. We'll not be separated again. Especially not for anything involving the Angel."

"Then what if she tries to follow and gets lost? She'd be out in the streets again, all alone. We'd never forgive ourselves, Finn."

Tessie watched as he twisted his fingers through her auburn hair, his brow creased in thought. "Yer are just planning to talk to your mother, aren't yer? If we bring her with us, she can stay with me while yer deal with your ma. I'll be close if yer need me. But..." He paused again. "We can better keep Madochée safe if we know where she is."

Tessie buried her face in his neck. It was all so hard and fraught with risk. She wished for Boston - for that life they had waited for. They would get there. They had to. They deserved to. They just needed to do this first.

CHAPTER 3

Finn lingered in the entrance hallway knowing Mickey was waiting just outside on the steps. He heard him whistling his early morning tunes, filled with his usual enthusiasm for the day. They had planned the day's work at Queenhithe together. It was a smaller dock than either of them were used to, and quite a walk from Albemarle Street, but they had been eager to stretch their muscles again to something productive and real. He hated to let Mickey down.

Finn's stomach hadn't stopped cramping since his conversation with Tessie. The very idea of returning to Dublin sent waves of nausea surging through him, but he wouldn't leave her to go alone, even if it meant returning to that city.

His final days in Dublin had been heavy and broken. He could scarcely fathom the boy he had been back then. He still thought of his brother, Tadhg, in his quiet moments. He'd been so young and Finn hadn't protected him. Hadn't been able to save him from that damn city. Sometimes fond memories climbed out of nowhere, stirred up by menial daily tasks or a whiff of something in the wind. Other memories were not so warm, and the thought of standing in the place where he had lost Tadhg flooded his mouth with a sour taste. But they were going, their dreams would wait, and he would bear it all for her.

Squaring his shoulders, Finn finally pulled open the heavy door and saw Mickey propped against a step. The winter sun was out and bright, though it gave no heat and a heavy frost still gathered on the hedges. A careful-footed paperboy skidded by on the icy footpath just as Finn approached and Mickey scrambled for a penny in his pocket.

"Here, lad." Mickey leapt after him and quickly flashed open the front page. "Look see." Everyday Mickey read the papers and filled them all with more stories of grand and outlandish opportunities in the New World. Only in America could they dream of owning land, or any life so different from the one thrust on them by this dark city, and the one before it.

"What's it now?" Finn didn't even look. "Free gold now? They hand it to yer fresh off the boat, I bet?"

Mickey's brow furrowed as he skimmed the page. "More folk are leaving for the Americas every day. More Irish. More from all across Europe. They're taking our place, brother. We need to get on board or we'll miss our chances."

Mickey's energy always went up a notch when he spoke of their plans as if that place would give them a life so golden he could barely contain himself. It could be infectious, but this time only regret and dread rose in Finn's chest. He rubbed his eyes.

"We can't go with yer, brother. Not right now, anyway." Finn let his hand drop to his side, words failing him. "I'm sorry to tell yer."

"Nonsense." Mickey's jovial expression fell as he realised

Finn wasn't playing around. "What do yer mean? What do yer mean yer can't go? We've talked about it."

"I mean we're to go to Dublin first." Finn said it with finality, and he wasn't sure why. It needn't be a long trip after all, but it felt like a heavy blow.

Mickey's bright eyes widened into a scowl. "You're going back to Dublin? Why on earth would yer go back there?"

He couldn't hide his grimace as he answered. "Aye. Tessie must go. And I'll not leave her side. Not after these last months apart."

He braced awaiting Mickey's reaction. He knew that while Dublin plunged his heart into foreboding, it held something else entirely for Mickey.

"My boy is in Dublin. You'll be near my boy." Mickey's voice caught in his throat. His eyes grew shiny as he rolled the newspaper tightly in his hands.

"Aye."

"Why, though? Why are yer going back there?"

"Tessie has business with her ma. That's all. We'll be back as soon as we can."

Mickey nodded, his gaze dropping to his boots as he held a fist to his mouth.

"Come with us then, Mick." Finn stepped towards him, bracing his shoulders. "See your boy again before yer go to Boston."

Mickey shoved his hands in his pockets as if suddenly noticing the icy wind that blew against him. "I can't do that, brother."

"Of course yer can."

A light smile teased Mickey's lips. "It's not as easy as popping in. His grandparents, they...the family...there's a lot of other stuff I left behind too...mess like. I might have only left Dublin a few months ago but it's been longer still since I've been in their good graces and longer still since I seen

Connor. That city don't want me back, let me tell yer." Mickey struggled for the words and punched his fist to his chest in frustration.

"You're his da, Mickey. Whatever yer have done, yer deserve to know yer boy."

Mickey's eyes shone. "Aye. But does he deserve to be burdened with a da like me?"

"They can't keep yer away from him."

"I've been so bleedin' stupid is all. And her spoons—"

"Ah. Forget the damn silver spoons. They're gone. Yer can't do nothing about them. And he's yer boy, Mickey. Yer don't need any damn spoons to see him."

Mickey waved his hand in front of him as if chasing away a bug. "Argh. I got no business being there."

"It'll only be a few days if all goes well. Tessie needs to have a conversation or two with her ma. Then we'll head back."

"That city has a way of getting its claws into yer, drawing yer in." He mimed strangling with his hands out in front of him.

"I know that to be truth."

"Best have an exit plan, brother. And stick to it."

Mickey tucked the newspaper under his arm and started south, but stopped when Finn didn't follow. "Yer not coming to work now either?".

"We leave now. This morning."

"This morning?"

"Aye. Straight after breakfast."

Mickey scuffed the toe of his boot into the icy slush at his feet and looked down. "No work for yer then? Is everything free in Dublin now, brother?"

Finn shrugged in apology. "Ha. More likely we'll be paying a shilling for a bleedin' potato."

"You'll be mudlarking for your supper, so yer know it."

Mickey shook his head. "And yer are just now telling me? Right now before yer leave."

"I've only just found out myself. Come, eat breakfast with us. Queenhithe shall be there tomorrow if yer want it."

Finn watched Mickey's stocky frame as he stretched his shoulders. To think this man's path had collided with his own just by chance, yet he'd stuck by him. Mickey had been willing to charge into the Angel's home alongside him, sat in that prison cell and lamented together about life and loss. If it weren't for Finn, Mickey would already be in Boston, striving for that fortune he dreamed about. He may have lost Tadhg years ago, but he had found a brother in this man.

CHAPTER 4

*M*ickey's feet wouldn't yet carry him inside. He stood on the steps, still and quiet, until his knees buckled and he knelt on the path. The thin sheet of frost prickled his knees with dampness, but he didn't get up. Could he be so easily shattered by one little word? Dublin. They were going back to Dublin?

Connor was in Dublin. Innocent little Connor, with his Ciara's eyes. The waves of shame kept coming and he covered his face.

It was Boston that called his name. It was there that he could put things right. He'd make his fortune and pay back Ciara's family the money for the farm. He'd return triumphant for his boy.

It was a good plan, wasn't it?

But…Dublin.

That word choked in his throat. Finn and Tessie were going right now, this morning, and he wasn't ready. He wasn't ready to go back. He wasn't ready to face them.

"What do you see?" Young Madochée watched him from the door in one of the white cotton play dresses Ruby had bought her. Though she had yet to fully embrace the dress code of upper class London, and Mickey could see her old trousers poking out the bottom. They'd all become accustomed to her Haitian-Creole accent filling the halls, and her resilience gave them strength and hope every day. If this young girl of only seven or eight could survive Jacob's Island alone, surely they could withstand anything.

Mickey lifted his head, realising he was staring at the street.

"Nothing, Mado. Yer need a coat if yer to come out here."

Ignoring him, she stepped closer and joined his gaze, her ebony skin glowing in the morning light. "Did they tell you? Did they tell we go today?"

"Aye. They told me."

"We go to the Dublin city."

"Aye. Yer will like that, hey?"

"On the boat. Do you come too?"

"I don't think so, Mado. Not this time."

"Mr Mickey!" She said it as if to scold him. "You will come too."

He hung his head, feeling a pang of guilt stab him deep in the chest.

"But why, mister?"

"I need... I need to work..." He tried to keep his voice light but trailed away, dropping his eyes again to the pavement. It was all too hard to pretend. He felt he had a brick in his heart and let out a long breath. "What if my Connor is better off there, Mado? Better off without me?"

"Connor?"

"My boy, Mado. He's my boy." He tossed a pebble across the street in front of him, watching as it skimmed beneath a passing carriage.

"He is your boy," Madochée echoed, and crouched to follow the pebble as a clopping horse kicked it along. Mickey considered her slight frame against the backdrop of the street.

She had told them many stories of how she'd come to be separated from her mother. Many stories of the ships she had travelled on, the shores and shipyards she'd visited in an endless search. It was hard to separate the real from the tattered imaginings of a young girl just trying to make sense of how she ended up alone. To her, the most obvious answer seemed to be that she was invisible, so her mother could not see her no matter how she had searched.

Mickey bit down on his lip. What stories would his Connor tell himself? How would he make sense of having lost his mother, and his father leaving him for the New World?

"If yer mother wasn't perfect… I mean, would yer still want to find her?" Madochée looked as if she might speak but looked away. "I mean, even if… even if she made mistakes?"

Madochée shrugged. "Like if she was… wrong?"

"I guess." Mickey trailed off and shook his head. "I've made a mess of things, Mado." Wasn't Connor better off without him?

"I will always try to find her. Always. *Pou toutan*. Always."

Mickey took a deep breath and looked to the sky, letting it all swirl up inside him. "Always."

CHAPTER 5

The soft winter light filtered through the dining room window as Tessie gulped her hot tea, willing it to settle the urgent flutters in her stomach. The breakfast table across the room displayed an impressive selection of eggs and toast, fresh fruit and cold cuts of ham and pork, though she'd hardly been able to fill her plate. In contrast, Finn piled his high with eggs and ham, and heaped so many teaspoons of sugar into his tea that Tessie lost count.

"I'd say slow down, there's food in Dublin, you know, but I'm not sure that's true right now." Kyran took his seat, a forced smile accompanying an ever-optimistic tone. Draining his cup, Finn hardly seemed to register the comment and Tessie hid a smile of affection for him as she too sipped her tea.

"Your attempt at humour, my dear?"

Tessie looked up to see Anna pushing Ruby in on a wheelchair. Kyran stood, wiping his mouth in haste.

"Ruby. You shouldn't be out of bed."

Ruby waved her hand in dismissal, her smile as warm and magnificent as ever. "Nonsense. If this is their last meal before they go, I won't spend it listening to voices waft up the stairs. Anna, please set me a place."

"Yes, ma'am."

Ruby flicked back a stray curl from her neck and flashed her green eyes around the table. She had been recovering from the Angel's stab wound since the night of the ball and the colour had only just started returning to her cheeks. A grimace teased with any sudden strain of movement, and Tessie could see it was only sheer determination that held all Ruby's charm and effervescence in place.

"We would have come to yer before we left," Tessie said, though it filled her with hope to see Ruby up and about, even if it was just for breakfast.

"Of course you would have. But it's no fun being shut away from all things living and alive. I need activity around me. I keep telling Kyran. Besides, whatever awaits you in Dublin I will send you with my blessing."

"Aye, we will need it, I'm sure." Tessie let out a long breath, pressing her hand to her temple. "On any other occasion a week might seem plenty of time, though right now it feels like every moment is slipping through my fingers."

She could scarcely calm her breathing for the anxiety brewing within. Their train left from Euston Station in less than two hours. From there they would take the steamer from Holyhead and she felt the panic of urgency bubbling in her belly. It felt like they had already wasted so much time even though there was nothing else they could have done. They would be on the earliest train.

The door opened again and this time Madochée and Mickey joined them. Seeing Ruby, Madochée broke into a run towards her. "Miss. You feel better." She patted her hand to Ruby's cheek and Ruby squeezed it warmly.

"Oh, my dear. A little stronger every day."

Madochée bounced towards the breakfast table and took a piece of toast, biting into it as she returned to her seat besides Mickey who sat without filling his plate at all.

"Are yer sure yer won't come, Mick?" Finn urged, despite Mickey's expression.

Tessie could see the news had affected him. He usually prattled with quick wit and enough morning enthusiasm to drive them all to irritation. She didn't know the extent of his situation in Dublin but could only assume the news had triggered something sombre within him. She'd never seen him in such a mood.

"I can't." He kept his eyes on his empty plate.

"Yer boy—" Finn started.

"Let's not talk of it, brother."

Tessie put her hand on Finn's forearm, urging him not to press further.

"We'll not pressure yer, Mickey. We don't expect to stay long in Dublin but yer are welcome to join us if yer heart compels yer to."

Mickey only nodded, and Tessie cleared her throat and turned to Kyran.

"Can yer think of anything yer know that might help us persuade Aileen? Anything about my mother's war with Arthur? Do yer know what happened between them?"

Kyran sat back in his chair. "They've been at each other's throats for as long as I can remember. Both stubborn. And vicious." He pulled his fob watch from his waistcoat. "I've rarely understood my father's values. Perhaps if I did, I'd have an answer for you."

"I just wish I understood what started all of this. Though perhaps it makes no difference now."

The table succumbed to silence as they each retreated to their thoughts. Whatever treacherous history existed between the Angel and Aileen, they'd all had to navigate its tangled legacy. And they were far from being in the clear yet.

"Come. We must go if you are to make your train." Kyran stood from the table.

Tessie set down her fork and nodded at Madochée. "Yer can fetch your coat if you like."

Needing no further encouragement, Madochée dropped from her chair and ran from the room.

"Are you sure you won't let us drive you?" Kyran stood up and moved behind Ruby's wheelchair.

"A cab will do us fine. It doesn't feel the occasion for a big sendoff. The less fanfare the better."

"Very well."

"I shall be thinking of you often. Know that." Ruby smiled and reached across the table so that Tessie could squeeze her hand. They quickly moved to peck each other's cheeks and Finn and Kyran shook hands.

Beside the front door, their hastily packed luggage awaited. No fancy trunks, just a small travel bag each, enough for a change of clothes or two. Tessie had told herself packing light was an act of faith. If they prepared for it all to go smoothly, surely it could only help steer it in that direction.

Mickey had already left the room as the small gathering moved to the front entrance. Kyran's butler hailed a cab and the footmen packed their bags into the carriage.

"Travel fast and safe, my dears. I hope your mother listens and it will all be as quick and painless as can be." Ruby's cheerful voice carried on the wind.

With Madochée's gleeful smile, Tessie might for a moment have believed they were off on an exciting adventure.

"Send word as soon as you can," Kyran said.

"Yer know I will." Taking Finn's offered hand, Tessie

hoisted herself into the cab and settled into her seat. As Finn and Madochée joined her, she closed her eyes and her mouth went dry. They were on their way.

As the horses drew around the corner and their speed increased, Madochée suddenly lurched forward. "Look! He's coming. He's coming!"

Tessie followed her gaze to see Mickey's stocky frame sprinting with all his might after them. Finn leaned out the window calling for the driver to stop.

Out of breath and flushed, Mickey pulled at the door and Madochée slid across the seat, making room for him. Without a word, he slipped in beside them — his decision made.

CHAPTER 6

The steamer slipped beneath a low-hanging canopy of evening cloud as the warehouses along the Anna Liffey wrapped around them. A dreary mist rose off the water as if Dublin itself was breathing fog into the freezing winter air. Behind the grand facade of Georgian buildings, dark alleys and soot-covered tenements lay in wait, and that's where Tessie's mind wandered — to where her mother would be this very moment.

Tessie had barely spoken a word throughout the two-day journey. Her thoughts were lost in a swirl of what the next few days might hold for her and her companions. It had only been a matter of weeks since this city had torn at her edges and left its scars. She and her mother had parted with finality. That moment carried with it a painful echo, and left both a full and empty space hollowed out inside her — an everlasting yearning for something she could not speak words to. What kind of welcome could she expect now after all that had happened? She had not imagined herself back here, not to see her mother again, nor to revisit the place of Faye's death. Faye. Her name was like a bruise deep within her chest. She'd barely allowed herself time to think of her. To grieve for her. To feel the shame for her part in it, though it tremored always just below the surface.

Over the weary hours of travel, she'd welcomed the distraction of Madochée's face pressed to the glass at every new cloud or splashing wave in the distance. Mickey, not unlike her, had hardly been still for a moment, repeatedly getting up to smoke on the deck and shuffling his feet whenever he tried to sit. And Finn, his was a different sort of energy. One glance at him and she could see the clouds in his eyes — the sadness and grief being pulled up from the depths with every surge forward, bringing them closer and closer to the city of his birth. What were they doing here? Tessie couldn't quite get it straight in her head. She had to be here. She'd had to come, hadn't she? But what of her friends? What of Finn?

The steamer bumped and swayed as it hit against the dock. Her companions stirred from the numbness of travel, stretching their limbs from their hard, wooden seats and setting their eyes on the beckoning scene outside. A strange low-pitched scream pulled Tessie from her thoughts, hitting her in the pit of her stomach.

She rose quickly, joining Madochée at the window. "What was that?"

"I don't know." Finn too stood and moved to the doorway, peering out at the deck. More yelling. More shouts. Something was happening out there.

Mickey pushed through the gathering crowd of passengers on the deck to get a better look and returned with an even darker scowl across his brow.

"There's some kind of fracas down there. Come, we need to get off."

"A fracas? A fight?"

"Aye," he said, and swung his bag on his back to lead the way.

They silently gathered their things and filed after him, Tessie's heartbeat quickening in her ears.

Out on the deck, an icy gale off the Anna Liffey struck them with all the gritty bluster of a cold welcome. She expected nothing less from this merciless city, but it was the rumbling in the crowd below that had her nervous. Dublin in January was bleak. She'd known it before, though now a scent of danger stirred through it, thicker with every cry and shout. Tessie's eyes danced across the gaunt faces trying to determine the centre-point of turmoil, but she couldn't. It was hunger — nagging and ugly. It was everywhere.

"My God," Tessie whispered low.

A cluster of bony figures, clad in nothing but rags, stretched out their limbs towards them. Finn lifted Madochée to the safety of his shoulders as they rushed down the gangplank. Tessie could hardly believe her eyes. She had known poverty most of her life. She had known hunger. But this... *this,* was something else.

She had stood in this very spot only months earlier and had not seen the extent of it. Had the stench of it grown? Or had she been too cocooned in her problems to notice? Too protected within Kyran and Ruby's world of luxury? Whatever it was, she saw it now. A city emaciated and harsh, the low murmur of starvation simmering from every corner and crevice.

"Keep moving. Keep going." The unease choked in Finn's voice behind her.

She could feel it too. Any moment this chaos could break loose upon them, unbridled and angry. She knew the madness that hunger could drive in a person. Her guts twisted and lurched — they had to get out of here.

"Over there."

Mickey pointed across the yard to safety, but the bodies were pressing in against them now. They were fighting against the tide, a suffocating haze of hunger. Hands grabbed at her skirts and Tessie knew what they saw. Someone well-fed. Someone with wealth. She knew how the injustice of it burned. She'd known it well - hunger and cold, her fingers frozen and numb, her stomach so hollow it ached and screamed for anything. She wanted to tell them how much she knew it. How much she would save them if she could. But they were one beast of desperation and had no ears for hearing.

A man beside her fell hard. The crowd swallowed him up, ransacking his bags in frenzied haste. Up ahead, strange figures looted a cargo stack, igniting a mad flurry of screams and cries. The crowd surged forward, dragging Tessie and Finn along with them. Bodies clashed as the harbour's security rushed in with batons raised. Children scattered. Women screeched. Tessie held her breath as a crate toppled and burst open, the rush of grain sparking a stampede.

"Here!" Mickey hollered, yanking them all forward into a protected doorway between the warehouses. Finn lifted Madochée off his shoulders and Tessie held her close to her skirts and covered her ears, letting the frantic burst of chaos rush past them.

"When did it get so bad?" Tessie asked, her voice cracking.

"It's the farmers and field workers pouring in from every corner of the bleedin' country, now. Their farms are dead or gone. They have nowhere to go. Meanwhile, they're still loading grain back to the mainland. Shameless bastards." Mickey spat on the ground in disgust.

"What do yer mean?"

"While we are here starving, the food we do grow is getting sent back to the English. We grow it, they eat it. Enough to make yer sick."

Tessie shook her head. "This must happen every night."

"Hence the security. But don't be fooled. They're here to protect the grain, not the people."

"Let's get out of here," Finn cut in, urging their eyes away from the fray.

Tessie nodded toward her mother's place.

"North. Head north."

They cleared the chaos of the harbour and broke out onto the main streets. It was almost four o'clock, and while the crowds had thinned to regular families and workers returning home for the evening, a dark ache lingered amongst the stragglers gathered on the corners for warmth, and in the hungry overflowing outside the churches. The smell of frying fat mixed with the odour from the gutter and she couldn't shake the chill in her spine even as she pulled her heavy cloak tight around her.

She directed them towards Capel Street and nodded toward an old hotel on the corner. "They have rooms. Yer should all hole up here. I'll go on alone."

Finn dropped their bags at his feet. "Now? You'll not rest and eat first? It's been a long couple of days, Tess."

Tessie shook her head. "We can't afford to wait. Every moment that passes we're running out of time."

"Then I'm coming with yer."

"Yer don't need to, Finn"

"After what we've just seen, I'll walk with yer just the same. Mickey can stay with Mado."

"Aye. Of course." Mickey said.

"Alright." Tessie discretely pressed a coin into Mickey's hand, wary of prying eyes and gestured again at the hotel. "Can yer get us two rooms? Will yer do that?"

He nodded.

"Why can't I come?" Madochée asked.

"Go with Mick and get some rest. We'll be back in no

time." Tessie managed a smile and touched her hand to the girl's cheek. She'd grown to love that little girl and all at once felt panic at having brought her here. "You'll be safe with Mick."

Mickey heaved Finn's bags up on top of his own and steered Madochée toward the once-grand hotel. Tessie and Finn watched them cross the busy street and go inside. Her heart raced as she turned in the direction of Capel Street. She was here now, with a job to do.

"Are yer ready?" she asked Finn. She took a slow breath, forcing it deep enough to stretch her ribcage and lift her heavy chest.

"I am, mo chara. Are yer?"

CHAPTER 7

essie led Finn through the alleys of her childhood. She diverted from the main street to slip between the wash-lines strung between the tenement windows and leap over refuse left to rot.

"This is the first time we've been together in this city." Tessie allowed herself a moment of reflection as she reached out to squeeze his hand. They had both been born right here in Dublin's northern streets, yet had never crossed paths until after they had fled its shores. "I wonder how close we came to meeting?"

Finn managed a smile. "Not too close, I hope. I'd be kicking myself to have gone a moment longer without yer than I needed to." He winked at her quickly then focussed his eyes ahead. She could see he was nervous.

As they rounded the tenement block on their right, Tessie's gaze struck the place where Faye had lay dying. She jolted to a stop. She had known it was coming, though staring at the same cold stones where Faye's blood had run, the weakness in her knees forced her to crouch. Pressing her hands to the ground, the memory of Aileen cradling Faye in her lap swelled up, burning the back of her throat. For a moment she thought she might vomit, but she coughed and swallowed it down. This was no time for grief.

Taking a deep breath, she raised her eyes to Aileen's door, not twenty paces down. Even from this spot, she could see the windows were boarded up, jagged edges and nails jutting out as deterrents. The front door was secured by a single board nailed across it.

"Oh, my God." Tessie rushed forward to stand in the shadow of that old dilapidated building, a heavy lump in her chest. "I'm too late. How can I be too late?"

The sign above the door still displayed a faded Black Bonnet sign, but the building was only an empty shell. Pangs of dread tumbled through her as she rushed down the side alley to check the back entrance. There, the windows too had been boarded over, though the kitchen door stood untouched. What was going on? Picking up her pace, Tessie drew away from Finn and banged loudly on the kitchen door.

"What is it?" Finn asked.

Tessie held his eyes as she banged again. A light shuffling moved behind the window but quickly went quiet.

"Hello?" she called. "Open up. Who is there?"

Nothing. Then a shuffle sounded at the window.

She lifted her fist to bang again as the door swung open and a young woman with long blonde hair glared back at her. Bright blue eyes lit up with sharpness and scanned the intruders at the door. Tessie recognised her immediately. It was Siobhan, one of Aileen's girls.

"Oh. It's yer. Yer've got some nerve, ain't yer?" she said, casually.

Tessie cleared her throat, a flutter of relief rising in her breath. "Is she here?"

"Is who here?" The woman leaned on the door frame,

taking her time to scan Tessie from her hair to her boots. "We were glad to see the back of yer. What do yer want?" Siobhan folded her arms against a dress that had once been extravagant. Its bright pink stripes and red ribbon had long since faded, though its frayed edges were still pretty against her pale skin.

"Why is the door open?" A voice called from the darkness, and a tall man with a light tan complexion appeared behind her. His rich brown eyes held on Tessie with only a slightly warmer expression than Siobhan's.

"She's the one I told yer about." Siobhan unashamedly pointed in her face.

"What? Aileen's girl?"

"This is'er. That's her."

The man raised an amused eyebrow, looking her over again. "Yer don't say. Ha. Bessie?"

"Tessie," Siobhan corrected. "Tessie, ain't it?"

Tessie felt her face burn and sunk back a step or two. "That's right. Just tell me if she's here."

"Who?"

"Stop. Yer know who."

Siobhan smiled. She was enjoying needling her. "The only one who cared a lick about yer ain't here. Yer got her killed, didn't yer? Ain't no one here waiting around to see yer now."

"Come now," the man beside her interjected, intrigued by the situation. "Aileen's daughter, hey." He was searching Tessie's face. "Aye. I can see it. I can see her in there. Fancy that, now."

Finn stepped forward, nudging a protective shoulder into the conversation. "Is she here or not? Stop mucking her about."

"Step back, brother!" The man's warm demeanour dissipated, his eyes holding fast on Finn.

"Or what?"

The man's face spread into a wide grin. He had an unusual manner. Aloof and warm with an air of strength he could flex at any moment. "Or yer'll regret it, friend."

Tessie pressed between them. "Stop it, both of yer. If Aileen doesn't want to see me, she'll throw us out, won't she? But let us in. If she ain't here, we'll wait."

That was if Aileen was still here? Tessie searched their eyes for confirmation. Was Aileen still in the city? Was she even still alive?

The man looked down at her, then back and forth from Finn, and the heat faded from his eyes. She was no threat to him. He had to know that.

"I'm her bloody daughter. Let us in. Please."

He stepped away, clearing their entry. "Let her in, Shiv. Let her in."

"Sam!"

"Let her in for Christ's sake. What's the harm in it?"

Siobhan narrowed her eyes disapprovingly. "Go on then, m'lady."

She moved, but only ever so slightly, leaving her foot across the frame so that Tessie and Finn had to step over it.

Inside, an inadequate candle spluttered on the table and Tessie gestured for Finn to take a seat beside her. The place seemed empty but for the two of them, though she could barely see into the front room or very far up the stairs. What had happened here?

Tessie waited a moment and took in the scene, wondering if either of them might explain without prompting. But they didn't. Siobhan hovered at the stove; the only other light source in the room. On it, a large pot bubbled with something Tessie assumed was edible, though its aroma was less than appealing. Sam quietly observed them, perhaps wondering if she too might explain her presence without his asking.

"I never saw yer when I was here before," Tessie broached, as the man rolled himself a cigarette. "Sam, is it?"

"Never yer mind about him," Siobhan said without turning around. "Never yer mind about anything."

But Sam placed his hand on her arm as he too lowered his frame to the table. He lit his cigarette, hunching his shoulders to stop them hitting the rafters sloping low into the corner. He might have moved his chair, though he kept himself at just the right angle to spring into action at any moment.

"I was away. Taking care of something for Aileen." He pulled a small knife from his pocket and casually spun it on the rough table surface. It seemed a mindless action, as if fidgeting with a button or biting his nails.

"Where is everyone? Where are the other girls?"

Tessie could barely understand the change in mood. Where there had been life, it was now vapid and dark. Something had gone very wrong. The Angel had said Aileen was almost through, but how, when only a month ago she was strong as ever?

"Stop asking questions. Don't tell her nothing, Sam. She don't deserve to know nothing." Siobhan leaned back on the kitchen counter, her manner a complex blend of childish petulance and worldliness.

"Aileen sent them away," he said, dipping his eyes from Siobhan. She made a noise of disapproval and turned back to the stove.

"Sent them away?" Tessie couldn't understand. What about her men? Had Aileen given up? Could it be possible Tessie's task here could be easier than she thought? "But why? Why the boarded-up windows? I don't understand."

"Well, yer wouldn't, would yer?" Siobhan interjected.

"What's happened here?"

"What's happened? Yer've got to be bleedin' joking with us."

Tessie didn't know what she meant. "Where is Aileen? Where is she?"

"Oh, she'll be here," Sam assured her. He leaned back in his chair as if ready to watch it all unfold.

Before Tessie could speak again, the door opened, and she let out a quiet gasp. It was Aileen.

CHAPTER 8

*A*ileen stood in the doorway, her wild hair waving down her back like a banner and her hatchet tucked safely in her waistband — just the way Tessie had left her. Staunch. Shoulders strong and proud. Aileen's sharp eyes took in the scene, a candlelit silhouette around her dark green dress. Tessie could see her exhaustion, her years of conflict evident in her scowl, but there was something else there too. A slight droop at the edges of her mouth, though her lower lip stiffened at the sight of Tessie. She shot a loaded glance at Siobhan and Sam as she chopped her hatchet into its place on the overhead beam. Her eyes moved over Tessie, but she spoke not a word.

Tessie stood to speak, but her mother turned her back and spoke into Sam's ear. Siobhan craned to hear, rolling her jaw defiantly at Tessie. Sam listened intently, a solemn frown pinching his brow as he rubbed his hands together, eager and read to go.

"We have a good few days to get through yet. If there's anyone spare put them along the river." Moving to the stove, she warmed her hands, then lifted the ladle from whatever Siobhan was cooking and slurped loudly. "Christ, girl. Tastes like shit and river water."

Siobhan's mouth dropped open. "Well, yer try making coddle with nought but turnips and pork bones."

"That ain't coddle then, is it?" She tried another sip but gave up, dropping the ladle into the liquid. "Put some fucking salt in it for Christ's sake."

"I ain't finished yet." Siobhan begrudgingly grabbed for the salt and shook the empty tin over the pot. "And we're out."

"Fancy that." Aileen lit a cigarette and leaned back on the counter, taking her time to inhale and exhale her smoke over the room as if it had already been the longest of days. "So, what is it?" She turned to Tessie but didn't meet her eyes, instead inspecting a minor wound on her finger. "What do yer need? More information? More money? What?"

"No. I just came...I just came to see yer."

Aileen scoffed, finally squinting her fierce eyes at Tessie, a grimace taking hold of her jaw. Tessie felt it stir within her. She knew her mother's moods. "Don't trifle with me, girl."

"I wouldn't come all this way to trifle."

"Wouldn't yer? I don't know what yer'd come all this way for. Last time I seen yer, yer were tangled up in the Angel's mess. Who knows what calamity yer dragging back in this house?"

"This is Finn." Tessie gestured towards him quickly, wondering if her mother might soften seeing she'd found the man she'd told her about.

"I gather enough who he is, thank yer." Aileen rolled her eyes over him without the least bit of interest. "Warms my fucking heart, so it do. Now, I could smell bullshit before I even opened that door, and the stench, girl, is coming from yer."

Aileen propped her foot upon the chair beside her and pointed her cigarette at Tessie.

"Alright then." She tried to swallow the hard lump in her throat, and shooting a sideways glance at Finn, she sat down at the table grasping for composure. She hadn't expected the warmest of welcomes, but her mother never ceased to rattle her. "I did come to see if yer were alright. That's the truth. But…" Tessie had thought over and over how to condense the story of all that brought her there, but the words failed her now. "I have…I also come with a warning."

A low rumble rose out of Aileen. "Ahhhh. Now we have the heart of it. A warning from who?" Her eyes turned to slits as she roughly stubbed out her cigarette. It was serious now.

Tessie swallowed again. "From him."

Aileen's jaw locked as she searched Tessie's face, slowly nodding as she took it all in. "If I'm not mistaken yer were just here running for yer life. And now here yer are on his bidding?" Aileen spat on the floor at Tessie's feet. "He's your da, after all, my love."

"I said I've come to warn yer," Tessie said with more conviction. "I'm not here on his bidding. I want to help. I came to help."

Siobhan scoffed. "Look at the fancy girl from the across the sea come to help us."

Tessie threw her a sideways glance and held fast on Aileen. It was her reaction she needed, not Siobhan's. As her words hung in the air, though, she felt incredibly small.

"In what world do yer live in that I need yer bleedin' help?" Aileen's voice grew low and harsh.

Tessie's face burned. She had to hold on. She had to believe she'd come for good reason.

"Yer do not understand what he has planned. He—"

"Look around," Siobhan said. "Yer think we need yer

warning? Yer think there is anything yer can do for us that we can't do for ourselves?"

"He's sending an army to root yer out. Yer will be overrun."

"Will I? So little faith in yer old ma. Yer know what he can do with his army, darlin'?"

"Yer need to stop this madness. This is real. It will end at some point. He's only given me this time. One week to—"

"To what? Clear a path to get what he wants. If yer think we're gonna bend over for him the way yer clearly have then yer have been away too long, my love." She leaned in close and turned to Finn with a salacious glint in her eye. "I don't bend that way."

Tessie clenched her fists, digging her nails into her gloves. She'd known it would be near impossible to get her mother to listen. Why should her mother care that she too was under threat? Why should she believe that Tessie cared about the outcome? They didn't trust her. The truth of it sunk heavily in her bones. Why should they? And how on earth could she earn their trust in now only five days?

Finn stepped forward. "She has been through hell, yer know. She's here because she wants yer to make it out alive."

"Then she should have thought twice about coming. She's here to weaken me, boy. And yer'd know that if yer thought about it for one God-forsaken moment." Aileen leaned in and tapped the side of Tessie's temple. "Am I stronger with yer here, daughter? Or am I weaker?"

All eyes were on her, waiting for her answer. Tessie clenched her jaw and turned back to Finn. She didn't have an answer. Not yet. She needed time. Time to understand what was going on here. Time to earn her way in. "He wants yer gone. I just want everyone to be alright. There has to be a way—"

"Get her out of here." Aileen threw her arm up at Finn in disgust. "If she's got no sense in that thick skull of hers, yer take her with yer."

Finn looked torn as he turned back to Tessie. He hadn't wanted to come in the first place, and she knew that leaving was exactly what he wanted to do, but Tessie couldn't. Why were these windows boarded up? Why had she sent everyone away but Sam and Siobhan? Was her mother merely pretending to hold on? No, she couldn't leave yet. Even if they loathed her for it.

"Yer go," Tessie said to him. "Go back to Mickey and Madochée for the night. I'll join yer tomorrow."

Siobhan laughed, and Aileen shook her head, turning away in exasperation.

"And leave yer here with them? No way," Finn said through clenched teeth.

"I'll be alright," Tessie said. "I need to stay here. Yer go."

Finn turned his back on the room, locking eyes on Tessie. She nodded slightly. She would be alright here. She just needed time. Her eyes pleaded with him for just that. *Trust me.*

Finally, Finn took a deep breath, relenting. "Nothing better happen to her," he said to the room. He paused on Aileen, though her expression remained unimpressed.

"Only thing she's in danger of here is her bleedin' self." She stood with one hand on her hip as Finn left them alone. "Might as well go with him, darlin', for all the...*help*...yer will be here."

"I won't go. Not yet." Shaken as she was, she held her voice steady.

Aileen looked her over, then turned to Sam with a begrudging expression. "Make sure her man gets wherever it is he's going."

Without a word, Sam ran after him.

"Yer not really letting her stay?" Siobhan protested.

"Hush." Aileen pursed her lips. "She can find a room upstairs. See if I care."

"Not my room." Siobhan held up her fist. "Yer stay out of there or I'll beat yer fancy tail."

CHAPTER 9

Upstairs, Tessie stood at the landing holding a lantern toward the short corridor before her. Aileen's room overlooked the staircase, but it was the only open door at the end of the hall that drew her attention.

"That's Faye's room." Siobhan stood behind her, the accusation ripe in her voice.

"I know whose room it is."

Tessie moved closer and ran her hand along the door frame, feeling Siobhan's eyes hard on her back. Small offerings had been left along the mantle and window, Tessie assumed by the other girls — small twisted bundles of ribbon fashioned into roses and crosses, other trinkets made from lace pulled from the hems of their skirts or boot laces. Tessie's eyes stung at the lonely stillness in the room, untouched and empty but for memories and musty linen.

"Yer think yer better than us." Siobhan's sharp tone interrupted her thoughts, her tone a horrible mismatch for the swell of emotion in Tessie's belly.

"No. I don't think that."

"Aye, yer do. Got yerself a good-looking man and a fine

dress. Come here offering us lowly folk yer help." Siobhan said, her otherwise pretty jaw twisting into a sour grimace.

Was that really what she thought? That she didn't belong here? That she was different? "I was born here. Right in this house."

"And I bet yer shout that from the bleedin' rooftops, don't yer?"

Tessie thought to speak but instead turned to the window. The high emotion and exhaustion from her journey crashed in around her now. She wanted to be alone.

"No one ever spoke of yer, yer know. Some light whispers of a daughter who was once here. That's how little mark yer left on this place." She was trying to hurt her now.

"Well, this place left a mark on me. That's true enough."

"That'll get no pity from me."

"I haven't asked for yer pity."

"And we haven't asked for yours."

Tessie took a deep breath. She didn't want to quarrel. She hadn't come here to fight. She wanted to ask about the boarded-up windows. She wanted to ask about the empty house, but Siobhan's expression held a firm boundary. She'd get no information from her. Not about that.

"What happened to Faye?"

Siobhan held her gaze before picking up one of the lace trinkets and twisting it in her long but rough fingers. "We buried her, of course, what yer think? She had her a proper Catholic funeral up there at the Prospects. Aileen paid high for it and all. Some prime dirt right there under a tree on the hill. Makes me laugh at all the richies up there, never knowing they're resting next to a whore they wouldn't have given the time of day. She was better than all of them. Every single one of them. We was all there, lined up in our best dresses. All of us. And where was yer?" Siobhan flashed her eyes and squared her shoulders.

Where had she been? The question fluttered through Tessie, the realisation quickly settling in. As far as Siobhan knew, she had gotten Faye killed and vanished like a coward. It didn't matter that Tessie had her own story to tell, and it didn't matter if Tessie shared their grief. Faye was gone, and it was all Tessie's fault.

"We was there," Siobhan repeated, her confrontation gathering steam. "But where was yer?"

Tessie held her glare, trying to find a shared anchor to speak to. "I had to go."

"I'm sure yer did. We had nowhere else to go though, did we? Where was we to go?"

"I didn't want to go. I didn't want to leave her. But I couldn't stay. I couldn't—"

"No. Yer left. And now yer are back with wise words about a world yer don't even understand. With yer good intentions. Yer helping hand." She swung her arm up, holding her fist out in front of her as if she wanted to throw a punch. "Well, no one believes that. Not in this house. Not even if yer swan in here in finer dresses than we got."

A burst of anger flared in Tessie's chest. She didn't care about her bleedin' dress. "Thump me if it'll make yer feel better, but I loved Faye. I loved her like a sister, just as yer did. Think what yer like about me, but I've come here because I care about my mother. And yes, I care about yer too. I couldn't care less about this dress."

Siobhan held the defiance in her eyes, assessing Tessie's words. "Give it to me then."

"What?"

Siobhan put her hands on her hips. "Give me the dress if yer really care none about it."

It was a dare. A challenge. Tessie felt it swell up inside her as she looked down at her skirt.

Beneath her travelling cloak was a simple outfit that

paled beside any of Ruby's dresses, but it was good quality, clean, and more importantly, new. Tessie remembered well enough the rough fabrics of her work dresses, the waxy texture of over-worn material, smooth with wear and soaked in the musty odours of the streets. This simple dress had been as far from her reach then as it was now to Siobhan. She could have it. She could have them all if that's what it took to prove herself.

Siobhan watched, her nostrils flared but her venom faltering as Tessie held out her coat for the taking.

"If you want it, take it. It's yours."

Siobhan hesitated, but realising Tessie was serious quickly snatched it.

"Give me yours."

"Mine?"

"Or what am I to wear tonight? My petticoats?"

Without further protest, Siobhan and Tessie stripped down their layers and stepped out of their skirts, exchanging one for the other. Tessie turned so that Siobhan could tighten the ribbons at her back, before smoothing her own dress jacket along Siobhan's shoulders. When they'd finished, they lingered in awkward silence, looking down at the tips of their boots peeking out beneath their fresh hemlines.

Siobhan's chin quivered with an ill-hidden smile as she ran from the room to pose in front of a tarnished mirror in the hall. They were similar sizes and it did indeed fit her well. She looked smart, and Tessie felt herself soften towards her as she too stepped forward to see her reflection in Siobhan's buoyant outfit. With her honey-auburn hair against the candy-pink hue, she felt all rosy and bright, but it didn't matter.

"Yer needn't worry. I had it washed this week." Siobhan half-smirked, turning to admire her profile.

Tessie, though, had turned her attention to the rooms

behind her. Her head heavy with the day's travel and all that had transpired in the dark kitchen below them. She needed to lay down. She couldn't make sense of any of it without rest.

"Take that one." Siobhan pointed at the room opposite, pushing open the door. "It was Peggy's. She weren't the cleanest but it'll do for the saviour girl from across the sea." She was teasing now, and Tessie hoped they had struck a tenuous truce.

"Just wait till Sam sees me." Siobhan sauntered away, taking Tessie's lantern with her.

Tessie peered into the dark room before her, only just making out the pale cover on the bed in the corner. That would do just fine.

CHAPTER 10

The streets outside were quieter now, voices drawn in from the cold to the burning fireplaces and stoves indoors. Those without a place to go lined the shallow eaves of the back alleys and Finn was overwhelmed at the sheer number of them. He kept pace in front of Sam as they traced his path back to the hotel. The cold bit through his coat as he pressed back toward the river and he could already feel the sharp grit of the city digging into his skin.

"I can take it from here," he said, though a shudder twitched on his shoulders at who or what might jump from the shadows. These were not his streets anymore, after all.

"I'll stick with yer all the same."

Sam strode with his hands in his pockets, nonchalant and calm, though Finn noticed his eyes constantly scanning. One man dipped his hat from the alley.

"Evening, Sneak."

"Evening," Sam replied.

And another. "Hello, Sarge."

"Evening."

"I thought yer name was Sam," Finn asked.

"It is."

"Why do yer have so many names?"

"Because I do a lot of things."

Sam was well-known, that was clear enough. But known for what? For all Finn knew, he accompanied him only to do him harm. Finn kept him always in his periphery, even as he turned away from him down the alley on his left — but Sam continued straight.

"Not that way."

"It's quicker." Finn hadn't forgotten everything about this city.

"Not if yer factor in the mob we'll run in to on the way."

Finn looked toward the dark tunnel waiting and turned around to follow Sam this time.

"If Tessie is harmed—" he started.

"She won't be," Sam spoke with confidence.

"She better not."

Sam didn't argue. There was something in his expression that felt sympathetic to Finn's concern. Even as it settled his nerves, he stopped. Finn needed more. They didn't have time to play games. They didn't have time to guess at intentions or hold back their own. He had to take a risk. He turned to face Sam, seeing his height was much taller than his own. He wasn't used to men towering over him, but Sam did. He searched his eyes in earnest this time. "Tell me true. Is she safe there tonight?"

The light smile never left Sam's face, but it wasn't filled with malice or mischief. "She'll be fine, brother."

"Do yer give me yer word?"

"A man's word ain't worth the shit on his shoes these days, but if it'll make yer feel better."

Finn held his expression and took a step closer, pressing him. He needed more. "It's yer word I'm interested in. What kind of man are yer? What is yer word worth?"

The subtle smile left the corner of Sam's lips. He squared his shoulders and held Finn's eyes. "I might be the last man in Dublin whose word yer can count on. I promise yer, she will not be harmed. " He spoke the words clearly and deliberately. Finn was sure he saw honour in him, though prayed to God he was not being deceived.

"Then I tell yer the truth. She means yer well. All of yer. If yer have any sway with Aileen at all, yer have to make her listen."

To that, Sam folded his arms and couldn't hold back a smirk. "Make Aileen Fisher take heed of the Angel?"

"We do not have the Angel's protection. We carry a warning and urge Aileen to take action to save herself. Please. We don't have his protection. Make her listen or we are all here to die. We didn't come back here to do that."

"Then there must be another way."

"There is no time."

"There's got to be. No one knows Aileen's mind, but I can tell yer this. She won't lay down to anyone. Especially not to him. She'll die first."

Finn's heart sunk. He'd seen her gruff and battle-scarred, though whether that made her a woman of conviction he didn't know. "Even if she takes yer with her? Is that really alright with yer?"

Sam gave a light shrug of resignation, his smile reappearing with the shine to his eyes.

"How can yer be so free about it?"

Again, he shrugged. "Come on. Let's get yer where yer going?"

IN THE HOTEL ROOM, Finn lifted the lid on a bowl of stew left to go cold.

"Mr Mick didn't eat it," Madochée said matter-of-factly as she swung her legs off the edge of the bed.

Finn helped himself to it as Mickey paced by the window.

"Will yer not sit and eat, man? I can order up another."

"Yer have it. Yer have it." He waved his arm dismissively before sitting briefly then returning to peek through the edge of the curtains. "He is just over the river, beneath one of those God-forsaken rooftops."

"Yer will see him tomorrow. We'll go together in the morning, whatever yer want."

"I can't wait till morning. I ought to go now. Before it's too late."

"What do yer mean before it's too late?" Finn put down his tepid broth and moved to the window, joining Mickey's gaze across the rooftops.

"Now that I'm here I can't believe I ever left him. How could I do it?"

"Yer did what yer thought was best at the time, Mick."

"I feel like something bad is going to happen if I wait."

"Alright, but is rushing over tonight a good idea? Maybe get some rest."

"I won't get any rest. Look at me." He clutched his chest and pulled the collar from his throat as if it was choking him.

"Well, eat. Then we'll wander down there for a bit. Walk off some energy."

"It's been months. He'll have teeth now. Almost two." Mickey laughed. "Imagine that. Mouthful of chompers. Probably talking. Who's he been calling da? Will he even remember me?"

Finn gripped Mickey firmly on the shoulder in a reassuring squeeze. "We'll see him. Tomorrow. Yer will see him. And he'll know yer."

"It has to be now. I have to go now." Mickey grabbed his

coat from the bed and before Finn could say anything else, he ran out the door.

"Mickey!" Finn hollered, but there was no stopping him.

Finn turned to Madochée, but she too was already pulling on her coat.

"Quick, mister. Quick." She darted past him out the door.

"Wait," Finn called after her. "Yer stick with me. Bloody wait."

OUT IN THE cold Dublin night was the last place Finn wanted to be, but he raced after Mickey as he gripped Madochée tightly by the hand. Memories rose in the bluster off the Anna Liffey, but he had no time for ghosts of the past. This was a terrible idea. He could feel the dread bubbling up inside him as he strained to keep up. Perhaps he was overthinking — his dread for Tessie and Aileen infecting everything else. He wanted Mickey to get his son back. Of course, he did. Maybe a happy father and son reunion was just what they all needed. But it didn't feel that way. It didn't feel that way at all.

Mickey led them south until they were striding past a string of Georgian townhouses, double-story with neat, matching doors and tidy brown brick. He stopped on the street in front of a specific red door, though as Finn finally caught up to him, he could hardly tell it apart from any of the others.

Mickey's chest rose sharply beneath his bundled coat as he pulled the cap from his head and scrunched it in his hands. He looked like he was about to speak. Finn searched for something useful to say, but then they heard it — a baby's cry.

Mickey clapped his mouth shut, a torrent of distress

furrowing his brow. Without another word, he ran towards the house.

"Mickey," Finn hissed after him. He watched in alarm as, instead of knocking on the door, he pushed it open and went inside.

"Oh God. Mickey!" Finn strode after him but stopped at the threshold, watching helplessly as Mickey moved down the hallway towards the cries. "Please, come back."

But his friend couldn't hear him anymore.

Finn looked frantically back and forth between Madochée, still outside, and Mickey's disappearing silhouette, as a woman stepped into the hallway. Her hair pulled back into a sensible knot. She was already in her nightly dressing gown and had a proper middle-class look about her. Seeing Finn and Madochée on the step, her mouth dropped open.

"Yer will get out of here!" She shooed them away as if nothing more than pests when her eyes moved to the open room across the hall where Mickey had gone. She hurried after him.

"Jesus and Joseph!" Finn heard her curse, but it wasn't fear in her voice. It was anger. "Michael Bell. How dare yer burst in here! It's near the dead of night."

"He's my boy, Dana. And calm yer hellfires, it's barely eight o'clock."

Finn pointed at Madochée to wait at the doorstep and moved inside to see Mickey clutching baby Connor tight to his chest — the baby squirmed but his crying ceased.

The woman reached to take him. "Give the child to me."

"Get back, Dana."

"Yer are upsetting him. Look at yer."

"Like hell I am, I could hear him screaming from the street."

"I said give him to me."

"Stay back." Mickey bounced Connor on his shoulder, delight filling his eyes as he peered into his son's face.

Dana's brow stayed pinched as she trailed Mickey around the room, her arms outstretched.

"Yer weren't to return here. That was the agreement," she said.

"The agreement were wrong and yer know it."

"We paid good money for that farm, Michael. We paid yer out. Yer can't be here. Yer can't." Her voice was both shrill and croaky as she pressed her point.

"Blow the money, Dana. The blight ain't my fault and yer'd never have done it if Ciara were still alive. Never."

"It doesn't matter now. Yer can't be here. I'm telling yer to go." Dana's eyes held on her grandson. She cared for the boy; Finn could see that. But there was something else in her tone. Something urgent. She wasn't just concerned, she was scared.

"Eamon will be here any moment. I won't tell him if yer go now. I promise I won't."

"Let him come. I won't be run off this time, Dana. I won't be."

"Yer own child doesn't know yer. He'll never know yer. And truth be told he'll be better off not knowing yer. Badness surrounds yer, wherever yer go. That was our fear for our Ciara and look what happened to her."

"Is that what yer telling my boy?" Mickey was going red in the face. "That his da is full of badness?"

"He's a baby, Michael. He doesn't understand but he'll come to know it. He'll know the truth that all around here knows."

"And what's that?" Mickey gripped his boy tightly, his eyes lighting up and shiny.

Dana pinched her lips and did not answer.

"I loved Ciara, and she loved me. Yer should tell him *that*.

That's what yer should tell him. That his da loved his mother and that it broke his heart to be away from him."

"It's yer stupid dreams and melodrama that killed our Ciara."

"Influenza killed her. And she shared those dreams."

"It would kill her again. And again. And this here sweet boy too. Get out!" She screamed now. "Get out, Michael! Eamon is coming. Get out!"

Eamon? Who on earth was Eamon? There was something wrong. Finn felt the unease filling the room. What was it? Why must they hurry? Finn turned to check on Madochée at the door only to find her right behind him.

"Dammit, go back—"

He moved to grab her as a loud whipping sound cracked down with such force that Finn flinched as if he had been struck. The room went silent. All eyes turned to the back where a young man stood, his ornate walking stick lay outstretched across the table.

"Mickey bleedin' Bell," he said with a snarl. Even in a smart maroon frock coat and peacock-blue waistcoat, he looked disheveled. He had light scruffy hair and chapped lips, complete with a sore, red ring around the edges. Two men flanked him in attire far less lavish, but their fists and scowls at the ready just the same. "Who let yer in here?"

"Eamon." Dana moved in front of Mickey and Connor as if to protect them. "He's just leaving, so he is."

But Finn saw no such intention on Mickey's face, only indignation and disgust.

"Back from the rebellion are yer?" Mickey quipped, not deterred by the young man's theatrics. "What happened? Stub yer toe and run home? Get chased off by a cow?"

Eamon moved forward, a menacing glower just for Mickey. Finn thought one of his eyes widened larger than the other. "I was doing something for this country. What have yer been doing, Mick? Running? Like a scared little scamp. Like a fucking schoolboy. We got Irish starving all over. Dying in the streets. And yer ran. I don't forget my Irish blood."

"Christ Almighty, yer think yer fooling anyone? Yer don't care about the starving. Yer don't care about anything or anyone. Now, I'm here for my boy. Connor is coming with me."

"Yer boy?" Eamon smirked, a dismissive snort choking in his throat. "Yer boy belongs here, Mickey. That's what was decided, right? My ma is to raise him."

"Not anymore. He belongs with me and I'm taking him."

"Things have changed around here if yer haven't noticed, Michael Bell." Eamon held out the lapels of his frock coat, trying to intimidate him. "Tread careful. Yer in my house now."

Finn's heart beat fast as he noticed Madochée watching with wide eyes. It wasn't safe here. He moved her behind him, nudging her towards the door.

"I'll tread my way out of here right now alright, but I'm leaving with him."

"No!" Dana shrieked.

"Get out of the way, Ma." Eamon thrust her to the side, having eyes only for Mickey. "Yer not listening."

"Eamon, don't." Dana's voice held with shaky parental authority. Even she was nervous.

Finn's mouth went dry. What was Eamon capable of if his own mother was on edge?

Mickey didn't budge. Eamon flung back his coat and pulled out a pistol. The breath caught in Finn's throat as he saw the first hitch in Mickey's expression. Eamon brandished the pistol as if making sure all could see it and pay him the proper respect. He pointed it at Mickey, his two sidekicks flanking him.

"This here was John Blake Dillon's pistol. Ain't it a beauty?"

Mickey swallowed. When he spoke, his voice was firm. "I don't know who that is, brother, and I don't care."

"He fired it in Tipperary running from the English pigs. I could shoot yer in the chest with it right now in honour of the fallen." Eamon's expression was sullen and grey. The light in his eyes vanished.

"Eamon don't," Dana cried, running to claim Connor from Mickey's arms and this time Mickey let her take him. The moment drew out long and hard with the pistol aimed dead at his face, Eamon's dangerous eyes bearing down. Finn held his breath. There was nothing he could do.

Then Eamon laughed, light and easy, as he pulled the pistol back and pointed it in the air. "Yer see how things have changed, Mickey Bell. Best yer see it quickly. Or do I need to prove it to yer more?"

Anger rippled over Mickey's face though he lifted his hands in the air and took a step back. "If Ciara could see yer now, she'd turn in her grave, brother."

"No, she wouldn't. My sister would see the courage in me. The strength. I've done more for this family than yer ever could."

"At what cost? Yer are nothing but a fraud. At least I'm true. I don't pretend to be anything but what I am. The farm was real work. Honest work. And that's what I'll teach my boy."

Eamon flashed a lopsided grin. "We'll teach him to win. Not to cower like a dog."

"Mickey. Let's go." Finn's voice was low and urgent.

Mickey threw one last desperate glance at Connor, now quiet in his grandmother's arms. The pain on his face struck Finn hard but they had to back out now. They had to go.

"This isn't over, Eamon. I'll be back, yer hear me. I'll be back to get my boy."

"Not if I get yer first." Eamon blew a kiss into the air.

Mickey's face twisted with revulsion but he turned and ran. Gathering Madochée from the front step, Finn followed him. Finn gripped Madochée's hand tightly and though she struggled to keep up, she didn't complain. They ran and ran and didn't stop until they finally rounded the canal bridge outside their hotel. Their lungs screamed for air.

"That's Ciara's brother? That's her brother?"

"Aye. He's grown some stones since I seen him last. Maggot. Weasel bastard. The thought of my son being around him..." Mickey spat on the ground. "I ought to have grabbed him and run."

"If yer had, yer'd have a bullet in yer back right now."

Mickey shook his head. "He hasn't got the bullocks."

"I don't know about that." The look in Eamon's eyes had given Finn chills. "He looked well bleedin' mad to me."

"He is mad. Dana's scared of him. But he ain't never been anyone. I don't know whats given him the bollocks to show out, but I know one thing. I'll put this right. Some way or somehow I will do it. For Ciara. For my boy. For all of it. Yer will see."

Movement on the stairs woke her. Tessie's head hurt, and only the faintest light seeped through the boarded-up windows. Whoever it was down there made no attempt at being quiet. Laying back on the lumpy mattress, she listened as they clattered pots onto the stove and thumped on the floorboards. Around her, the creaks and moans of the old house spoke to her too. She held her breath, wondering if she was still enough if she might feel the house swaying in the wind, shifting on its foundations. How long could this old place stand? Was it just the will of Aileen Fisher, and the strength of the Black Bonnet, holding the rickety building together? Or would it all collapse the moment she left?

Standing to uncoil her donated pink dress from where it had wrapped around her, she reached her hands high, stretching to the ceiling. All night she'd thought about being more comfortable in her petticoats, but her limbs had been too heavy with exhaustion to properly rouse. It had been a suffocating sleep of dread and dreams. Instead, she'd lay with the dress's heavy boning digging into her ribcage. She now felt bruised and out of breath, aching with every movement. She had other dresses back at the hotel with Finn if she needed them, but for now, she had more pressing matters to attend to.

When she reached the base of the stairs, she peered into the darkness of the front lounge room. Someone had pushed the sofa up against the door and the quilt that had wrapped Faye's body was still slung over its back. Even in the dim light, Tessie could see the bloodstains aged and faded where they had tried to scrub them out. The space felt cold without the girls to fill it and a shiver rolled down Tessie's spine. She'd never seen it so lifeless in all the years she'd spent in that house.

As she moved into the kitchen, she found Sam standing over the stove keenly watching a kettle as it threatened to boil, a fresh oat cake toasting on the griddle beside him.

"Morning." Tessie cleared her throat.

His eyes creased with amusement at the sight of her in Siobhan's dress.

Tessie shrugged. "It's a long story."

"With Shiv it usually is." He expertly flipped the oatcake and shook the pan back and forth as it sizzled, its warm nutty flavour filling the room. "She'll make a deal for the air in yer lungs if yer not careful. She were right chuffed with yer's so I wouldn't be expecting it back anytime soon."

"It's hers to keep if it means that much to her." Tessie took a seat at the table, pressing her hands to the cool surface, something about it grounding her to this place.

"Did yer sleep alright?" he asked, a smooth Dublin accent rolling off his tongue.

"I suppose. Did yer see Finn to the hotel?"

"I sure did. He's a good bit worried about yer, ain't he?"

"Aye. We have a lot to lose."

"I don't blame him. Most of this bleedin' country is

scrambling to leave and here yer all are come back the other way. But who am I to say what's what."

Sam set her a teacup and saucer with quaint pink roses, more civilised than one might expect in this place. He added a chipped green cup for his own, before setting the teapot on the table and serving their tea.

Away from here, Tessie would never have picked him for a man of this life. Softly spoken with warmth to his eyes, Sam held himself with sturdiness; he seemed to be the dependable type. Why else would Aileen keep him around? He didn't seem to be shifty or soured like the others around here. There was something solid in his eyes. Something quiet and safe. It made her feel at home.

"Can yer tell me what's happened here, Sam?"

"What do yer mean?"

He knew exactly what she meant — he had to. Or was this state of turmoil so normal that he hadn't even noticed it?

"Yer don't need me to tell yer this place looks different from a month ago. Why? Is she...is she alright?"

He smiled broadly and gulped his tea back in one go. "I don't recall anyone ever wondering if Aileen Fisher were alright."

"I know she won't listen to me. I know none of yer trust me. But..." She ran her fingernail around the edge of the teacup. "Will she really survive this?"

Sam's eyes flashed in thought and she wondered how much he was at liberty to tell her. If he was as loyal to Aileen as he seemed, it wouldn't be much. He moved towards her, topping up her tea even though she had barely touched it, then piled three teaspoons of sugar into his own. "Things changed with Faye. That much I will tell yer."

Tessie felt her breath catch in her chest. "With Faye?"

"Aye. They sure did."

"What things?"

He rolled his eyes and moved away from her again. He was holding out on her. "Hard to say, really."

Tessie felt her frustration well up. Would they never let her in? She waited, hoping he would embellish further, but quick footsteps sounded at the back door. When it opened, Siobhan stepped inside, her eyes finding Tessie as she dumped a sack of meagre groceries on the counter. Seeming pleased with herself, she removed her coat, revealing Tessie's navy skirt and blouse beneath. She swaggered towards Sam and flung her arms around him. Kissing the back of his neck, her eyes glanced back at Tessie as if the display was entirely for her benefit.

"Aren't yer all pretty in pink?" she teased. "What are yer talking to my Sarge about?"

Tessie looked down at her tea. "Sarge? He's just being a good host."

"We call him Sarge. Yer can call him Sam like everyone else."

Tessie shook her head. "Alright. Sam then."

"Either is fine," he contradicted, but Siobhan shot him a warning look.

"Know why we call him Sarge? Sergeant?"

"Why?" Tessie went along with it even though it seemed unimportant.

"Go on, tell her Sam."

"Why don't you tell the story, Shivy, if yer want her to know."

Siobhan looked mildly disappointed he didn't wish to brag on himself, but undeterred, she spun around in Tessie's navy skirt, her blonde hair whipping with it.

"Yer see his skin, don't yer? Sam's da was in the East India Company Army. An officer, so he was. A military man. Big wig. He went off to India and married himself a wife. He married her first day he seen her, so he did. Ain't that right, Sam?"

"That's the story." He shrugged as Siobhan moved behind him and twisted her fingers in his hair.

"We call him Sarge on account of his da. And because he would look so handsome in a uniform."

Tessie smiled, though Sam didn't seem that taken with the story. "Are they here in Dublin? Yer ma and pa?"

Siobhan let out a long sigh as if Tessie had sucked all the fun out of the story and rested her hand sympathetically on the back of Sam's neck. "His ma died on that ship from India giving birth to our Sarge. And his da…who knows? He went mad, didn't he, Sam?"

"That's the story," he repeated.

Siobhan was about to speak as the kitchen door flew open again and a rough wind swept through, teasing the flame beneath the griddle. Aileen entered, solemn eyes scanning the room.

"What's this, a breakfast party? Yer all finished what I asked?"

Siobhan pushed herself away from Sam and moved back to unpacking her groceries. "I been and started, ain't I?"

"Have yer been and finished is the question." Aileen splashed her face with water and sat at the table opposite Tessie.

"It's barely light out. And someone's gotta keep us fed. I been down to see Father Joseph. He snuck me out three pound of flour."

"He better sneak his way to the mercy of Father John if he gets caught. That there flour is for the poor."

"What is we then?"

"It's for the *real* poor."

"Ah." Siobhan waved her hand dismissively. "How'd yer think we been eating this past week. He's too young to be a

Father anyway and I think he likes me. He likes it when I knock on the back door early in the morning, so he does."

"God save us all from yer early morning visits, Siobhan Gallagher."

"There's a church on the corner what'll feed yer if yer convert Protestant." Siobhan had a glint of teasing in her eye. "How many times yer converted now, Sam?"

"I'm no souper," he scoffed. "But their stew sure is tempting. They be bubbling those big bastards out there for all to see and smell. I don't blame a man who caves. And I'm sure the Lord understands a man can only eat so many oatcakes." With that he smacked his fresh cooked oatcake in the centre of the table, pressing his spoon down on it so it broke into large chunks.

Aileen lifted her boot to the table to fidget with the laces before taking a large piece of oatcake for herself. She glanced at Tessie. "I expected yer'd be gone. Or yer man come to fetch yer."

"I told yer. I'll not go before I'm satisfied."

"We're in the middle of a famine and a turf war, love. Ain't no one leaving here satisfied. And these two have work to do." She spoke to Siobhan and Sam now and pointed back at Tessie. "Don't let this one follow yer on yer rounds. Stay focussed on what I told yer. It's important."

"Aye. Delivering eggs to Mr Ponham is sooo important." Siobhan rolled her eyes.

Aileen moved to clip her across the ears but Siobhan was quick enough to scoot out the way. She laughed triumphantly.

"It is if it keeps Mr Ponham loyal, ain't it?"

"Even if they use it to bake an offering to—" Siobhan bit her tongue, but Tessie saw Aileen's eyes seethe in warning.

Bake an offering? What on earth was she going to say?

And why wouldn't she say it? Tessie tried to glean more, but Aileen quickly and deliberately changed the subject.

"What of the drop off?" she asked Sam. "We need it to clear all the way through, yer hear. I want it set in stone. Nothing left to chance."

"I got it. I understand," Sam said.

They were preparing for something. Tessie thought it must be a delivery, but she could feel the stakes were high. Sam's demeanour was calm but she could sense the tension laced just beneath. The pressure was on. There could be no mistakes. Aileen repeated her orders, pacing back and forth.

"Is there anything I can do?" Tessie insisted. "What can I do?"

They all fell silent and Aileen sighed, her mind focussed elsewhere. "Stay out of the way, girl."

"I'm here. I can be useful. Make use of me."

Silence again.

"Why don't yer visit our Faye?" Siobhan chimed in. It was another dare. Another challenge. "If yer care as much as yer say, yer ought to go. I told yer where to find her, didn't I?"

"Yer did what?" This time Aileen got her, kicking her sharply in the shin.

"Ouch," Siobhan whined, rubbing the spot. "That hurt."

"Not as much as it'll hurt if yer don't learn to shut yer bleedin' gob. Last thing we need is her gallivanting about up there." Aileen raised her voice. "Christ Almighty, Siobhan. Are yer listening? Are yer thinking up there?" Aileen shot her a stern look, pointing her finger in warning.

Siobhan bit her lip, her face solemn, and held up her hands in surrender. "Aye. I am. Alright. I'll shut it. I'll shut it."

"Yer better, girl. I'm not above sending yer away with the others. Yer know it. Don't push me no further. Don't do it."

Siobhan nodded quickly in promise, though as soon as Aileen turned her back a slight smile returned to her face.

She darted her eyes at Tessie. She couldn't help herself, Tessie thought.

"I'll be at the Cleary waiting on yer, Sam." Aileen eyed each of them, one last stern affirmation. Satisfied she had made her point, she broke off another chunk of oatcake and slammed the door behind her as she left.

Tessie felt a tug to follow, but the stern telling-off left her planted to the seat. What had just happened? What had she missed? Something had just played out before her, but what?

Siobhan raised an eyebrow at Tessie as if daring her to ask. "She's just trying to put yer off."

"To put me off what?"

"Visiting Faye."

Tessie couldn't make sense of it. "Why shouldn't I go? Why wouldn't she wish me to?"

Siobhan spoke with her mouth full of crumbling oatcake. "She doesn't think yer can handle little old Paddy Mac, that's why."

"Paddy Mac?"

"Shiv..." Sam warned her. "That's enough now."

"He's just a lad what thinks he controls that part of town now. Gotta go through him to see Faye—"

"Shiv!"

It was Sam's turn to scold her. What? What was she not supposed to hear? There had always been small gangs and factions springing up throughout the city, but they were never strong enough for Aileen to pay them any heed. Tessie could barely contain her curiosity. What was different about Paddy Mac?

Siobhan shrugged off Sam's warning. "I'm sure she can handle him." Then she lowered her voice and turned toward Tessie. "He certainly wouldn't be enough to stop me paying my respects. I'd go with yer if Aileen didn't have me a list of errands." Siobhan dusted the crumbs from her hands. "But suit yerself, saviour girl."

Tessie looked to Sam as the challenge curled in her stomach. He avoided her eyes and offered a dismissive shake of the head before Siobhan wound her fingers around his shirt buttons. He was too loyal to provide any clarification and she didn't press him on it. But had he been scolding Siobhan for goading her, or was it the mention of Paddy Mac? Why should he matter? The name hummed unspoken in her mouth. *Paddy Mac. Who was he?*

CHAPTER 12

Finn stared up at the water-marked ceiling as the sounds of their Dublin hotel moved about him. People in the hall dragged their luggage along the carpet, and attendants banged doors as they stripped rooms and moved the food cart along the creaky floorboards.

The sounds were hardly different from those he might hear in London, and yet, there was a distinct scent in the air. A detectable aroma that made it so very Dublin. Part of it was comfortable and familiar, but the rest fell upon him in shudders of discomfort. He'd known those streets below him very well. He and his brother had walked by the river almost every day. Indeed, the square where the cobbler had struck him as he ran away with his coins was only two streets away. He wondered if the cobbler was still there all these years later. Were the same shopfronts facing the square? Or had famine made the city unrecognisable?

Finn swallowed hard and sat up, wondering whether to call upon Tessie or wait for her to return. He'd not wanted to leave her there with those people, but he had to trust her. He sighed and fell back on his pillow. On the other side of the wall, he heard Madochée clunking around.

"Yer alright, Mado?" He knocked on the wall.

"Don't come in. I'm using it," her small voice called back.

He threw his blankets back and moved past Mickey who still snored loudly. His bed was a wreck, as if he'd tossed and turned all night — poor sod.

Finn used the chamber pot and splashed his face in the basin before moving to the window to peer down at the street. The scene was exactly as he'd imagined. Carriages and farm wagons lumbered past, as city folk and paupers gathered on corners. A bell-ringing priest held up a sign, relentlessly calling over the crowd for them all to repent. The blight was a sign of God's displeasure, he said. And there, directly in front of the hotel, Finn saw two faces he recognised. The sight of them plunged a sickness into his belly. They were the two men from last night, Eamon's sidekicks — scowling at the hotel entrance and slouching against a lamppost.

"Damn it." He pulled the curtain closed and moved to Mickey's bed, shaking his shoulder. "Wake up, Mickey. Wake up."

"What?" Mickey, sleeping with his chin jutting upward on the pillow, shook him off. "What is it?"

"He's bloody well had us followed — that's what. Come see for yourself."

Mickey moved sleepily to the curtain where Finn pointed for him to look down and across the street.

"See them? That's his two ruffians. The ones from the house," Finn urged. "They've damn well followed us. Who is this guy?"

"I don't know anymore. I swear I don't."

"Well, I'll not sit up here like bait. And I'll not be threatened into a corner."

"Damn him!" Mickey kicked the side of the bed.

"Mado, pack up yer stuff," Finn called through the wall.

"Why?" She opened the adjacent door and rushed into the room in a long nightgown and her black hair in fizzy disarray.

"We'll be leaving."

"But I smell breakfast. I'm hungry."

"We'll get something on the way. I promise. Go."

Madochée instead followed Mickey to the other side of the window. "It's them. Bad men. Bad men right there." Madochée didn't seem deterred and squinted down at them with a scrunched-up face. "We can be invisible."

"Yes, Mado. Please dress and gather yer things. Go on."

Madochée skipped past him, swinging the door closed between the rooms. Mickey slung his bag on the bed and shoved his belongings back inside. "Where will we go?"

"To Aileen's for now, at least to tell Tessie we've had to move. We'll decide from there."

Mickey was spying down at the street again, watching the men pace back and forth below. "They want to scare me outta town. Well, they're wasting their time. Maybe I should just go down and tell them so."

"I don't think they're after a friendly chat, Mick."

"Aye. But there will be a reckoning soon enough — that much I can tell yer."

"I'm ready!" Madochée announced returning in a fresh day dress, though her hair was still in disarray.

"Put yer bonnet on, Mado." Finn straightened his own cap before seeing Mickey had lost focus. He picked up Mickey's boots and thrust them at his chest. "Come on, Mick. Who knows who else is watching us? We don't want to be caught off guard, not with Mado here with us. If yer want a reckoning, then yer choose the time and place. We'll not be pounced on unawares."

Mickey pulled on his boots as Finn opened the door.

"We'll head out the back through the kitchen. Come on."

Finn's heart pounded as they wound their way through the long corridor and out the back way. Many a ruffian had crossed his path and he wasn't usually one to run, but this felt different. His anxiety mixed with the sour scent of a city in distress. This place would bring them nothing but pain, just like it always had — he could feel it in his bones. They just had to wait long enough for Tessie to get her job done. He hoped they could last that long. He wanted out of this place and off this island. The sooner the better.

CHAPTER 13

Tessie had wanted to visit Faye. Of course she had, but this was far from the way she'd imagined. She'd wanted to wait until all of this was over so she could go in quiet reverence and pay the moment its proper respect. Faye had been her friend. She didn't deserve a rushed and panicked visit squeezed between the turmoil of Aileen and the Angel. But here she was, striding north, having absconded as soon as Sam and Siobhan had left on their errands. If Paddy Mac could somehow help her understand, then she had to try.

Making her way along Bolton Street into the cool morning air, the church bells rang out a call to Mass. The echoing sounds sent her heart racing - each toll a reminder the Angel's wrath drew closer with every passing moment.

Tessie still knew these streets well enough to move with haste and confidence, and she picked up her pace. She had spent her childhood traipsing every inch and they hadn't changed so very much. In the alley to her right, she and Faye had made a game with string and a ball. Up ahead at the crossroads, she had been standing on the corner when a fishmonger's cart dropped a parcel right at her feet. She had run all the way home as fast as she could only to find it was nothing but fish heads. Aileen had laughed but dumped them in the stew, even as Tessie felt decidedly shortchanged.

Then right up ahead, there was the building of dark red brick. The sight of it shot a bolt of grief up her legs. It stood out against the mottled stone walls and grey tiles of all else around it. The wrought-iron gates loomed silently at the entrance just as she remembered them. It had been nine years since she'd stood before the North Dublin Union, the workhouse, and for just a moment she thought if she looked down she might see her old grey uniform hanging from her shoulders.

Tessie wrapped her hands around the cool bars thinking of the people inside picking oakum exactly as she had done, their fingers raw and bloody as they stripped old rope into fibres and strands.

For better or worse, before the workhouse, her world had been filled only with Aileen. Here, she had felt alone for the very first time. Here, she'd had to fend for herself. Here, she'd decided to run. To get out. To fight. The instinct rose up in her with a familiar burning sensation. How different her life might have been if she hadn't run from that place.

As she walked onward, a family crossed the street in front of her, a young woman clutching a loaf of brown bread to her breast. Tessie assumed they were headed to church and followed them. Another couple appeared behind them, the woman carrying an entire baked cake on a plate. Were they having a gathering at the church for the needy? These people looked needy themselves. She watched as they crossed the road past the church and lay their goods on the footpath outside a sizeable hall building. What on earth are they doing?

Tessie paused on the corner to watch as a dozen others

made the same trip. In just the few minutes she stood there, they lay down eggs, pots of soup and even sacks of flour, before retreating the way they'd come. It wasn't a joyful giving. They hardly greeted or chatted to each other. It was solemn, their eyes on the road except for a glance behind them or up a side alley. They were watchful, Tessie thought, and the name of Paddy Mac again hummed on her lips. Were they too on the lookout for him? Had he something to do with this strange parade?

Tessie looked to her left where a sea of headstones rose over a hill. Out there somewhere was Faye, and the sight of it caught in her throat. She yearned to head towards them, yet the scene before her held her still.

A young boy in front of her deposited something in a sack and turned to run back past her.

"Hey," she called out to him. "What's going on..." She pointed across at the hall. "What's the deal with all the food, then?"

"Yer can't take it. It's not for yer." The boy bounced a small ball he plucked from his pocket.

"I'm not going to take it. What's it for?"

"Dues."

"Dues?"

"To Eamon Paddy Mac. Don't yer know?" He chased his ball to stop it getting away from him.

"Why?" she called after him.

"We have to. And if yer haven't paid yer ones yer should get away from here, miss. Everyone has to pay. They know if yer don't. Yer get in trouble."

They have to? Tessie scrunched up her nose. She had plenty more questions and tried to keep step with him, though his ball drew them closer to the hall in question.

"Hurry then, miss. Go on."

Tessie watched him continue but didn't follow. So Paddy

Mac was real. At least Siobhan had not completely led her astray. Tessie knew what she was watching now — they were paying their weekly protection. The injustice of it riled up in her. In the middle of the famine, this Paddy Mac had folks paying their dues in goods and baked cakes, smoked hams and probably their very last coins. Siobhan had made him sound like a punk who was trying to be bigger than he was. How bad could he be?

Tessie looked along the building, now far closer than she wished to be. Eggs and milk, fresh-baked bread and even utensils of tin and copper. She was tempted to crouch down and inspect them but kept her chin up and eyes forward, her apprehension growing in waves. She knew better than to linger now, but as she pushed herself forward and around the corner, a strong hand gripped her wrist.

"Did yer pay your dues, love?" A man with dimples and curly hair grinned widely. He pushed her towards another man who gripped her by the shoulders.

"I don't think yer did. I ain't seen yer pretty face before."

"Cut that out," Tessie shot, struggling to get her balance.

"Cut it out? Yer the one whose come through empty-handed. Terribly impolite of yer."

"I'm not from here. I didn't know." She gritted her teeth. "Look," she said going for her pocket, "I have a shilling for yer."

"A whole shilling?" he mocked. "Well, lookie here. We gotta rich girl."

"Well, how much, then? How much do you need?" She looked back and forth at them.

"It's not what we need, love. It's what yer have got to offer. The best of what you got. That's all Eamon Paddy Mac asks."

"That's it there. It's the best of it because it's *all* of it."

"It don't need to just be cash, love. Show your respect with more than money."

The dimpled one moved in closer and looked her up and down. She was in for a struggle and she felt the adrenaline prickle up on her skin, stiffening her arms. "Yer best back off me."

He tilted his head to the side in consideration, but it stilled him for just a moment. The second man moved behind her so that she was sandwiched between them. *Think.* She had to think. His hands moved to her waist but as soon as they did, she dropped to her knees and took them both by surprise. Scrambling for the knife in her boot, Tessie had just enough time before the two men scooped her back upright. She slashed the weapon wildly in front of her, cutting the dimpled one across the chest.

"Sweet Jesus, if we ain't got a fighter."

He laughed, but Tessie didn't stop. Reeling her head back, she struck the one behind her in the nose. He loosened his grip just enough for her to slash again at the one in front. This time she caught his shoulder and anger flared in his eyes. He punched her, striking her chin and toppling her backwards away from them. Pain shot through her face, but it didn't matter. She was just out of reach now. Tessie scrambled to her feet and ran, tripping on her skirts, but still a few steps ahead of them. It was just enough.

A family on the corner watched on.

"Help me." Tessie rushed towards them. "They attacked me. They've attacked me."

"Get back here, yer bitch!"

The men called after her as Tessie looked into the eyes of the man and woman who had seen her attacked. There was terror in their eyes; they wanted to help, she could see the shame, but they didn't move. Instead, they glanced back at the men fast approaching and backed out of the way.

Tessie's eyes widened. "Damn yer!" But she didn't turn around. She ran.

essie burst into Aileen's kitchen expecting to see Sam or Siobhan, but it was Finn who leapt from the table at the sight of her.

"What on earth has happened to yer?" Dropping his playing cards, he rushed towards her as Mickey and Madochée watched in surprise.

Her jaw still aching from the blow, Tessie fell back against the counter to catch her breath. "What are yer doing here?"

"Are yer alright? Who did this?"

"Lady Tess!" Madochée stood on her chair next to Mickey. "Yer face is red."

"I'm fine. I'm fine," Tessie assured them, still clutching her knife in one hand. "Did yer not wait at the hotel?"

"Never mind that. Who are yer running from?"

Siobhan appeared in the hall. Tessie gestured with her knife at the fresh bruise forming on her face. "Is this what yer wanted? Is it?"

Siobhan didn't answer but stayed half hidden by the door, innocent shock in her eyes. Tessie couldn't tell if it was genuine or just pretence.

"What's she done now?" Aileen called down the stairs. As she entered the kitchen, she saw the state of Tessie and directed her accusation at her instead. "Christ Almighty. Should have known. What have <u>yer</u> done?"

"Eamon Paddy Mac," Tessie said, squaring her shoulders.

Aileen's face turned to stone, and she swiped at Siobhan. "What have yer told her? What?"

"Nothing!" Siobhan threw up her arms.

"This ain't yer business, girl." Aileen pointed at Tessie.

"I saw what's going on up there. I saw the control he has. He's pushing yer out, ain't he?"

"I told yer to stay away from there. Yer look like a wild cailín with knife still in hand. If you've gone up there and stirred up the bleedin' hornets' nest—" Aileen's fury creased her brow.

"The Angel will back him, won't he? He'll back Eamon Paddy Mac. He's coming, Aileen. Yer need to get out now before it's too late."

"I told yer. If he wants me gone, he can face me himself."

"All our lives are on the line. Yer and yer." Tessie pointed at Siobhan and Sam. "Ours too, damn yer. If I can't convince yer to step aside, then Finn and I are in just as much danger. This is about all of us."

"Ooh, he's got yer running scared ain't he, love? Where's yer stones when it counts, girl?"

"I want us to get out of this alive. Is that so hard for yer to believe? Yer are my mother, dammit."

"From yer own mouth yer decried being stuck with me and we both know that to be the truth."

Tessie held her mother's gaze. "Tell me. How could he get a foothold so quickly? Paddy Mac. Eamon. Whatever he calls himself."

"Aye. That's the real question, ain't it, Tessie-muck? What happened not so long ago that blew it all open? Think girl!"

Aileen jabbed her in the shoulder with two fingers, shoving her back.

"Hey!" Finn leapt to her defence, edging to get between them.

"Get back, boy. Think!"

"I were here."

"And what? What else?"

The realisation plunged through her, and she slumped against the wall. "Faye."

"What about her?"

"I got her killed."

"There it is." Aileen stood back, letting the gravity of the statement hang in the air between them. "Yer got our Faye killed. Everyone knew she were my girl. She were *my* girl. That used to mean something around here. It kept them safe. After that ain't nobody feel safe. So if you're worried about the state of this place, then take a good look at yerself, girlie. Because when they got to Faye, that was the start of it." Aileen drew back hard on the cigarette barely lit in between her two fingers. "I sent them all away. All my girls. I had to. All of them. They had no trust no more. That's what yer took from them. That's what's underneath all this. Understand that. Understand *that*."

Tessie's chest sunk. That's what Sam had meant. *Everything had changed.* If they could get that close to Aileen, who couldn't they get to?

"That girl stood by me every day of her life. Faye never hurt a damn fly. She looked after the girls in here. She were soft-hearted, not head-strong like yer are. And yer led her out there like a lamb to the slaughter. To have her throat cut in the street. She ain't deserve that. She ain't deserve it."

Tears stung in Tessie's eyes but she blinked them back.

"Don't yer dare stand in here and cry, girl. Bad things

happen when people don't obey my orders. How many times do I have to say it before yer listen?"

Tessie turned away, sucking in deep breaths, trying to loosen the tightness in her chest. In and out, she breathed. It was anger, and grief, the whole bloody mess of it. She forced herself to turn back and hold her mother's gaze.

"Yer made me leave. Yer ran me out of here."

"The damage was done. It were already done. Getting yer out of here kept us safer."

"That's not what yer said at the time—"

"It kept us safe, girl."

Tessie looked at the knife in her hand, the events of that night with Faye flickering through her. It all made sense now. She'd run out of here and they'd been left with the consequences. Consequences that stretched far deeper than she could have imagined. She wasn't welcome here, and for good reason. There was nothing she could do to change what had happened, nor its ripple effect. And what could she do now? She couldn't leave, and she couldn't stay. She couldn't force her mother to step aside, and she couldn't fail the Angel. There was nowhere to go.

Aileen stormed up the stairs having said her piece. Siobhan and Sam quietly followed. She was a marked woman. She felt ashamed to have been so oblivious and there was nothing she could do to hide her guilt. She looked up at the staring faces of Finn, Madochée and Mickey.

It was Madochée who broke the silence and launched forward, wrapping her arms around her skirt. "Don't be sad, lady Tessie, miss. We are here."

She patted her on the back and hugged her close, though her eyes held to Finn's. What were they to do now?

"This Eamon, is he the same? Your brother-in-law?" Finn asked of Mickey.

"I don't know. Eamon Paddy Mac. It could be what he calls himself now. I'd have no idea."

"What are yer talking about?" Tessie asked.

"It's why we left the hotel. Mickey's brother-in-law had us followed. It's not safe there."

Tessie's head spun. She looked down at Madochée's ever-hopeful face. "It's too much. Too much for yer, Mado. Yer hold close to us wherever we go, yer hear me. Yer stick close."

"I will."

"Yer should take her and go, Finn. I can't leave, but yer can try."

"I'm not leaving yer here. I told yer. And where would we go? To Kyran's? He sure enough has him watched too. They'll see us or they'll find us."

"To Boston. Go to Boston. I can meet yer there later. This was my deal. If they're watching, it's me they want."

"Yer know as well as I do he'll use whatever means he can to get what he wants. That means me or Mado too. Yer want him to get his hands on Mado?"

"I'll escape, mister. Escape big." Madochée held out her arms to show just how adamant she was.

"She is safer here, kept out of sight. We all are. Together."

Tessie moved to the table, squeezing her eyes closed as she thought it all through. Pressing her thumb into the small gap in her front teeth, she looked to Finn. "Then what do we do here? What can we do?"

Finn shrugged, his shoulders heavy and slumped before placing his hands on his hips. He had no answer. Tessie felt a pull deep in her stomach. She pushed back a wave of urgency and stood up. "If we can't leave and we can't fail, there is only one thing we can do."

CHAPTER 15

She looked out from the rooftop at the sea of smokestacks prodding the ashy horizon. The coldest of January winds blew harsh and unforgiving as her mother stood with her back to her, overseeing the city. Her city. Tessie cleared her throat, signalling her approach.

"Yer needn't come say goodbye." Aileen's voice was low and croaky.

Tessie folded her arms against the chilling wind. "Shamed as I am, I'm not leaving."

Aileen dropped her gaze and roughly rubbed out her cigarette on the brick wall. She didn't flinch at the icy air that whipped at her bare neck. "Yer a stubborn little bitch. Go on and leave me be. I'm tired. Tired of all of this."

"If yer so tired, come with us. Leave all this behind."

"That's not how this works, love." A wry smile crossed Aileen's lips, but she jutted her jaw and shook her head at the absurdity of it. "I don't know what world yer live in, darlin', but there is no retiring from this life."

"Don't yer be so stubborn it kills yer."

"I'm the Black Bonnet. Being stubborn is the only thing what's kept me alive. I won't be changing that."

"Then maybe I'm just as stubborn as yer are. I can't let this go. I might have been sent here on an errand from him, but I'll not see any of yer hurt."

"For Christ's sake. Do I need to wallop yer? I'll hurt yer myself if it'll get yer out of here."

"If things are this bad because of me. Because of Faye. Then yer have to give me a chance to put it right."

Aileen closed her eyes and exhaled, her shoulders shifting under the weight of decision and pressure. "What are yer going to do?"

"Whatever yer need me to. Within reason. Just let me help. Give me a chance."

"I will not let that man snuff me out like I never been what I am to this city. Aileen Fisher won't be fading out to a whimper. And the Black Bonnet definitely won't cower to the likes of Eamon fucking Mac. That's twisting the knife that is. Replace me with a sniffly, snot-nosed gutter rat, will he? I ain't think so."

Tessie leaned over the wall. The shadowed alleys wove through the city and the dotted gas lanterns appeared like a murky constellation through the fog. She knew her mother had fought her way to the top and held onto it with the bare grit of her fingernails. Her mother's eyes, restless as always, surveyed the landscape. She couldn't imagine what it would mean to leave such a place. To abandon her post. Tessie's jaw ached with the blow from Eamon's men. She felt only a splinter of her mother's rage, but these too had been her streets. Her city, once.

"The Angel can't replace yer with Eamon if you've already beaten him."

"Beaten him? That boy don't have the bollocks to face me

himself. He hides behind that pistol but yer pry that from his hands and he'll fold like a worthless pissant."

"I don't understand how he's become a contender."

"It's the cargo, love. The goods. Whoever holds that holds the money. This city. The networks. All of it. Without it, yer have nothing. Not a fucking thing."

"He has the cargo?"

"He had it. I told yer when Faye died, they all lost faith. I had a turncoat in my midst. The weak bastard gave it up for a bottle of whiskey and a side of bacon. He told them when and where it were coming in. They took us by surprise, right there on the dock."

"What can yer do?"

"That were last month. This month we'll be ready. He likely knows when but he don't know exactly where except it'll be at the docks. He'll be watching and he'll be coming for it. But we'll be ready for him this time."

"Let me fight with yer," Tessie said. "Let us help."

Aileen gritted her teeth, her wary eyes darting at Tessie and back out to the murky cityscape. Tessie could see she was considering it at least. She needed numbers on her side, surely, even a pesky daughter she couldn't get rid of. Tessie could be another set of eyes. Another resource. She had to let her in.

"Who'd yer cut with that knife of yours?" Aileen asked, rolling another cigarette. Tessie looked down at her hands. "One of them with curly hair and dimples. But just enough to get away. He's alright."

"Shame." Aileen nodded as if she knew him. "Next time aim here." She pointed straight at her windpipe. "Or cut those bleedin' dimples clean off his face." She breathed out smoke, holding the cigarette between her teeth and leaning forward on her palms against the brick. "And what about yer precious Angel then?"

Tessie joined her mother's gaze across the city one last time. "He'll be here in four days. Let's make sure Eamon Paddy Mac is no longer an option."

~

TESSIE AND FINN turned onto Lower Ormond overlooking the Anna Liffey as the Ha'penny Bridge beckoned in front of them. Their backs to the icy wind, Finn ripped open the paper parcel he carried and held it out for Tessie to take a piece of fish.

"What about the Angel?" Finn asked. "What on earth will we tell him? He's not going to accept—"

"I don't know. I just know this is the only way to help her."

"Aye. Her. But what about us? He sent yer here to get her out the way, not reinstate her."

"I know," Tessie snapped. She caught herself. He was right. She reached out to squeeze his forearm. "She won't budge. We will be failing him either way. At least this way I can try to help her."

"Can we send word to stall him? Something to throw him off?"

"He won't be stalled. I'm sure he's got someone watching us anyway, if it's not Castor himself. It won't be long before he's informed." Tessie felt a glum knot form in her throat. They hadn't come to Dublin to fight. Tessie wasn't even sure what that meant, but she had to rally if they were going to get through this.

"Bloody hell." Finn rubbed his hands roughly through his hair. "We aren't gangstas, Tess. I'm a dock worker and yer bake cakes. We're a long way from home."

"We've both killed men..." she offered, though it felt lame to say it out loud.

"And that's where this is heading. More of that. I didn't

like it. I didn't like the feeling of it in my gut. I don't want to be that man. I don't want to be like them."

"We aren't like them." Tessie pinched the leather band he had given her at her wrist. She still wore it every day. "But we're no better than them neither. I know that he sent me here, but if I'd known how bad it was, I would have wanted to come. Even if I knew it was useless and she'd never listen to me." She took a deep breath and bit down on her lip.

"What is it?"

"The Angel. Arthur. I saw the way he looked at Kyran. I saw it in his eyes. For all his power and the want of it, he compromised for Kyran. For his son. Only for him." She swallowed. "And my mother... I don't know..."

"Yer wanted her to do the same?"

Tessie looked out over the river, not sure what she wanted. Aileen had always held her at a distance, no matter how often Tessie had reached back towards her.

"Yer can't change who she is, Tess."

"How can she not feel it?" She pressed her hand to her chest, the ache rising to the surface. "I want to save her. For her to be alright. If she asked me, I'd do whatever I could to have her be alright. But she..."

"Yer can't change her."

Tessie looked down at the fish in her hand, unable to stomach another bite. Finn licked the grease from his fingers and reached for her shoulder.

"We can't change for her neither. We can't lose what we want and who we are."

"I know. This all came from us telling the Angel there could be another way. Without all the killing. I have to hold to that."

Finn turned to lean against the railing overlooking the river. "She is something else. I'll give her that."

"Aye. Yer've seen both halves of me now. That should be enough to scare anyone off."

"Fortunately for yer, my love, I've never scared easy. Yer a sight in that dress, mind yer." He gestured to the bright stripes on her skirt and gave her cheeky wink.

Tessie leaned in and smacked a greasy kiss on his lips before turning back to the river. "I think pink is my colour, no?"

The surrounding gulls were loud and angry over the water, swooping low at the ready for any scraps they might leave behind. Finn tossed out a hunk of fried fish and they watched the comical frenzy erupt and die down as one lucky gull gobbled it down.

"Do yer have any pleasant memories of this place?" she asked.

"Some." Finn looked across at the uniform brick buildings stretching along the riverfront, the bright shopfront doors and awnings their only variation. "Tadhg and I spent much of our time around here." He nodded up the river towards Eden Quay. "That's where the shoe shiner took a wallop outta my bleedin' skull." He reached for the faded purple scar cutting across his left eyebrow. She saw the light dull in his eyes as the memory sunk in.

"Yer had no way of knowing anything were about to happen, mo chara. Yer did what yer had to, just like we all do. And yer were just a boy."

"I tell myself that. Somehow it don't make me feel any better."

Tessie took his hand and they turned back to Capel Street. This man had stood by her through it all, pushing through his own angst at returning to this city. Her chest flooded with warmth for him. She couldn't quantify the strength he gave her, for all the things they'd had to face, and for all that remained ahead.

CHAPTER 16

The house had been full of whispers since returning from their walk. Aileen hadn't surfaced from her room and Siobhan and Sam spoke in hushed tones in the front room, keeping to themselves. Tessie knew they would still be suspicious of her, makeshift allies or not. She had not yet proved herself.

She sat with Finn at the table, as Madochée practised shuffling a worn pack of cards and Mickey paced the length of the room over and over and over. His eyes were bloodshot and he had not yet slept, but right now, they could do little to help him. Her knees bounced with tension and it took all her energy not to join him pacing.

Finn reached for the bottle of whiskey high on the shelf above them and quickly filled a glass for the three of them.

"That's Aileen's," Madochée said.

"I know." He looked to Tessie. "She owes us one, don't yer think?"

She put her hand on his shoulder and didn't stop him. She quickly downed the drink and closed her eyes as it fizzed hot in her belly. All the silence and waiting were unbearable.

What had she gotten them in to? What promises had she made she could not keep?

"When this is over, I'll help yer get yer boy, Mickey." Finn held a glass out for Mickey. "I promise yer. Yer just got to hang in there."

"I know, brother. I know." Mickey took his whiskey.

"And if this Eamon is one and the same as yer brother-in-law, then let's hope we can bring him down a peg or two. That can only help yer."

"Yer are right. I know. I'm here for it."

A clatter on the stairs drew their attention as Aileen strode into the kitchen. She shot a look at Sam and Siobhan in the front room and they immediately followed her, a hush rolling over the room as it filled.

Aileen eyed the whiskey glass in Finn's hand. She stood over him at the table, her eyes hard as she reached for the glass and swigged the last of it down. "Pour another. We have business to discuss."

Finn obliged as the others gathered in the chairs around him — all except Mickey who kept pacing, hardly seeming to notice what was going on.

"Alright." Aileen took the floor as Sam set a lamp at the centre of the table. She paused, taking the time to roll a cigarette. Tessie's chest tightened with each inhale of breath.

"Mado," Finn whispered and nodded his head towards the stairs.

"Do I have to go?" She squirmed.

"Aye. I told yer. Go on."

Tessie hated for her to be out of sight, but they'd not have her in the middle of this. Madochée begrudgingly slunk up the stairs and Finn watched to make sure she went.

"Alright," Aileen repeated as Sam lit her cigarette on the lantern and passed it back. "We have the Broker Boys in place. And the Penny Brothers?"

"We're covered." Sam leaned back with his arms folded. Siobhan sat beside him, mirroring his posture.

"Is that enough men?" Tessie bit her thumb. Her tone was quick and sharp, nearly panicked. They were in this now, and she felt her throat dry as she sipped down on her whiskey.

"That's thirty right there. I've sent word to a few more who should be here in time if they answer my call and the blighters bloody should, I tell yer that much."

"Alright."

"How many men does Eamon have?" Finn asked.

"Upward of sixty."

"Bloody hell," he said and shot Tessie a look.

A ball knotted in her stomach, but she rested her elbows on the table and breathed deep. The situation wasn't lost on any of them. This was not an easy task before them, and she had asked to be a part of it. So here she was. She wouldn't shirk at it now.

"But he's not expecting us to put up a fight. It's not likely even twenty of them will come for the goods."

"Not likely?" Finn challenged.

"What's the plan?" Tessie sat up straight, casting an uneasy smile back at Finn. It wasn't going to help any of them to focus on how outnumbered they were. "What can we do?"

Behind them, the sound of Mickey's dragging feet intruded, and Aileen rubbed her forehead. "I can't think for Christ's sake." She turned, expecting him to stop, but he barely registered he'd been spoken to. Aileen looked to Finn.

"Will yer join us, Mick?" Finn stood up.

"What?" Mickey's eyes shot back at the group in confusion. "Oh. Right. Sorry. Yer can fill me in later, brother. I have to…go…" He trailed off and they waited as he closed the door behind him.

"Right." Aileen rolled her eyes. "For God's sake. Alright.

The shipment is due tomorrow." She leaned forward, getting down to business.

"The shipment?" Finn frowned.

"The goods, son. The wine and tea and whatever else they've crammed in there this time. They'll be coming for it. No doubt about that. If they take possession we'll be good as done."

"Alright." Tessie sat back in thought. Aileen gestured at Finn to pour another drink. "We have to protect the shipment. We can't fail. If they have that, there is nothing left to fight for."

"Are there traitors in the group yer have sent for?" Finn asked. "Tessie mentioned yer'd been sold out. Will any of these men tell Eamon Paddy Mac what we're planning?"

"No. The ones coming into town are separate to all of this. They're extra. And what's here with us, are with us."

Sam shifted in his seat. "They're loyal to 'Leens, but one or two who don't know to keep their mouth shut. They work with whispers to Eamon's men for a side cut, not a rallied mutiny. That's something else entirely. And if I but see a whisper of it in their eyes, they won't make it to the docks."

"Alright, alright!" Tessie broke in. "So the shipment comes tomorrow night. We want the shipment. So does he. Assuming he knows the time and place, how do we stop him taking it besides an outright fight when we don't have the numbers?"

The table fell silent, each waiting for a light to dawn on another's face.

"A diversion," Tessie said finally. "To keep them from making it to the harbour. Or at least having to divide their manpower. Is this just about buying us time to get it out?"

Aileen nodded, pressing her thumb to her temple as she thought it over. "Aye. We could draw them in somewhere, into something they can't get out of too easy."

"How much time do yer need? To collect the stuff, I mean?" Finn looked to Aileen and Sam both.

"We gotta pull them barrels up," Aileen said. "Need at least an hour to do that quietly and transport them somewhere safe."

"And where is somewhere safe?"

"My warehouse behind the main harbour."

"There are men there?"

"There will be. Enough to keep anyone away. Not even Eamon will try that. Sam has that covered, don't yer?"

"Sure do. Locked down tight as a—" And he smiled as if he was about to say something lewd but thought better of it.

"Well alright then," Aileen clapped her hands together. "What's the diversion?"

"A fire. A fight...a..." Finn trailed away.

"A fire where?"

"This is yer city. Yer tell me..."

Aileen kept her sharp eyes on him. "They'll be heading towards the harbour."

"What time?"

"Midnight. They'll be heading that way..."

"Do we know what route they'll take?" Tessie asked.

"I do. We do. What's likely anyway..." Aileen still held his eyes.

Sam cleared his throat. "They'll skirt around through Circular Road. At least hitting North Strand before heading toward the Vinegar Works."

"Yes." Aileen pointed at Sam. "That's what they'll do. Try to flank us so we don't see them until they're right on us."

"Can we control the route?" Tessie asked. "I mean if we block off any side streets or control the route we can be sure of the road they'll take and funnel them exactly where we want them."

Aileen was nodding fast now, as if the pieces were falling

into place. "Aye. That'll do it. We're brimming on a riot at the best of times in this bleedin' city. Sam, let's see if we can set one off right where we need it. That'll do it." She stood up as if the conversation was triumphantly drawing to an end. "Sam, yer with me?" She pulled on her cloak. "We've got less than twenty four hours to pull this together. Let's walk the route. We need to let a mob loose in the city."

"Got it." Sam followed, closing the kitchen door behind him and leaving Tessie, Finn and Siobhan alone at the table.

"That's it?" Tessie asked.

Siobhan held her eyes. "That's all they need. They know what to do."

It was meant to be another slight, but Tessie didn't shy from it. Her mind had already wandered to the starving rush of people they'd seen at the harbour, imagining a timely stampede of malnourished bodies flooding the alleys. She remembered how it had felt to be in that surge of people and looked with concern to Finn. "I'm sure it can work. But a mob unleashed can be dangerous—"

"Ain't that the point?" Siobhan quipped.

"—especially a hungry one."

Finn emptied the last of the whisky into the glasses on the table and slid one to Siobhan. "No. The point is to get the cargo and get us all out alive."

"Well, they know what they're doing. Sam is smart. Yer listen to him. It's him what's in charge."

"We're on the same side now," Tessie said, holding her own glass up to clink against hers. "How abouts we remember that."

ry as he might, Mickey felt on the outside of it all. They'd been in Dublin only two days and yet the hours since he'd held Connor had passed in a blur of quick-worded conversations, badly hand-drawn maps and the stir of adrenaline burning in their chests. The Angel would be here in four days, and they were making their plans. Mickey could feel it building as he watched from the outskirts. Something dangerous and anxious. They wanted to win, and Mickey hoped they would, though his heart was hopelessly elsewhere.

Finn had told him the plan. They would be stationed at the North Strand crossroads, blending in with the rioting hungry to block off any alternative route. If Eamon's men went a different way, it risked the entire plan going awry. Eamon. That name seethed in Mickey's belly now and it took all his might not to charge back to his in-law's house and take Connor in the dead of night. But he knew Eamon would have the house watched now, and he'd not risk Connor by having thugs wrestle him from his arms.

On the afternoon of the cargo's arrival, they all had their

jobs to do. Mickey slunk to the side. He couldn't muster the enthusiasm of the others. He would be there and he would help, but he had not the brainpower to add to the mix. Winking at Madochée, who too had drifted to the periphery, he gestured her to follow him and they slipped quietly out the side door.

"All a bit serious in there, isn't it? We'll get back before they need us." He nudged her shoulder, and she skipped ahead of him enjoying the chilly fresh air outside.

Near the street sellers by the Anna Liffey, Mickey stood with his hands on his hips searching the line of vendors. He was sure he'd caught a whiff of sweet apple tart on a previous morning, though now looking up and down the line, there were none to be found.

"When yer want apples and have to make do with cabbage," he mumbled under his breath. "This is the life, ain't it, Madochée?"

She squinted up at him and he ordered two scoops of cabbage with ham hock and brown bread.

"I ate already," Madochée said.

"Well, don't go braggin'," he quipped. He passed her a filled tin cup, but as they moved to the river's edge, Madochée slung her cup of cabbage to the ground and darted through the crowd.

"Maddy!" Mickey shouted after her. "Christ." He gave chase, spilling cabbage down his front and gripping his cup and spoon. He saw her small head charging between the surrounding adults. "Maddy, stop!"

As he caught up to her, she lunged forward, tugging on a woman's arm and forcing her to whirl around. She was young with skin as dark as Madochée's, a parcel balancing in her other hand.

"My dear!" the strange woman gasped, looking down at her.

Madochée stood frozen, her arms hanging at her side and her mouth open.

"I'm sorry," Mickey apologised to the woman. Madochée crouched down, burying her head in her arms.

The woman walked away as Mickey kneeled beside Madochée in the street.

"I thought it was her," she said, her voice muffled into her dress. "I thought it was my mama."

Mickey's heart sunk. "Oh, Mado." He fell back to sit properly now, wrapping an arm around her. "I wish it were her. I wish it were."

"It is never her. Never. Ever."

Mickey couldn't think of anything to say. He sat quietly beside her as the street moved around them.

"Never. Ever. Ever."

"I wish I could make her appear for yer."

"Where did she go?"

"I don't know, darlin'. I don't know where anyone goes. But if I had a thousand pounds, we'd sail all over the world to look for her. So we would. And we'd never stop until we found her."

"We would?"

"Aye. We would."

"Why am I invisible?"

"Girl." Mickey nudged her chin with his thumb so that she looked at him. "Yer've never been invisible. If they can't see yer it's because they're blind. And a whole lotta people are blind and don't even know it."

"How do they not know?"

"Because if yer can't see something, yer don't even know yer missing it."

She huffed her small chest and lifted her face, her wide eyes peering out at the legs rushing by her. Mickey's heart broke for this young girl who would do anything to find her mother, while his own son lay in a crib not two miles away.

Just then a figure loomed over them. "Hey, Mickey." As he looked up a fist came down hard on his jaw. "Yer made a mistake coming back here."

Mickey tried to pull away as the figure grabbed his collar. He was too dizzy to focus. "Run, Mado," he tried to say, though it came out garbled and messy as they dragged him away from her. "Run!"

He heard her small voice cry after him. "They taking him! Mister stop!"

"Run, Mado. Run!"

MADOCHÉE'S CHEST heaved with panic. Run. She did run, but not back to Aileen's. They were taking him. Her little hands balled into fists and her boots pelted against the street. They would hurt him. Bad men. She knew they would. She needed to help him. She needed to tell Finn and lady Tess. But first she had to know where they were taking him.

Her breath rose fast and sharp as she darted through the crowd. *No, mister Mick. I stay with you.*

Staying back just far enough, she held her eyes on Mickey's kicking legs. She knew how to be small and quiet. She knew how to move fast. She could be invisible.

They were too strong for him. He could not get away. They were taking him far. Far to the river. Back to the docks where they had been before.

Mickey's struggling slowed as they reached an old building. When they stopped, she stopped too, peeking through the slats to see inside. Her chest ached from running so fast and she crouched low into a ball, covering her mouth to keep her breath quiet.

Night had swallowed up this corner of the city. She thought they might see her, the slivers of light on her black skin, but they weren't looking for her. They only wanted Mickey. Squinting hard, she pressed her forehead to the splintery wood as the stink of animals wafted over her. Big hooks hung from the ceiling, and hay covered the mud floor. Her heart pounded. Why had they taken him to a stable? What were they going to do to him?

"Get him up. Sit him up," one man said, and the other kicked Mickey hard in the back to make him move.

"Young Rafferty Walsh? Is that yer? And Brec? Not yer Brec? Working for bleedin' Eamon?" Mickey said.

"I ain't so young now." The man he called Rafferty stood, gripping the top of Mickey's hair and forcing him to look up. "What did yer think would happen? Eamon weren't gonna let yer come back in here."

"Brec? Talk to me, Brec."

But the man called Brec wouldn't look at him. Before he could speak again Rafferty punched him in the stomach. Mickey doubled over, coughing and spitting and falling to his knees. Madochée gasped and covered her mouth tighter. *No!*

"Go get him," Brec said to Rafferty. "Go now."

"Get who?" Mickey managed, holding his stomach.

"Who do yer think?" And with that Rafferty strode back out into the greying light.

"Yer shouldn't have come back, Mick. Yer really shouldn't." Brec turned his back to Mickey and stood watch at the door.

Madochée took a slow breath and backed away. She had to get help before that other man returned. Now. She had to go now.

CHAPTER 18

The church bells tolled over the city and the household gathered with solemn faces and bright eyes. The countdown had started. Tessie could hardly breathe for the anxiety sparking in her belly. They moved around each other with hushed voices for no other reason than the gravity of the moment demanded it.

"Layer yer clothes," Aileen had told them as she and Sam tended to last-minute errands. "Extra jackets, coats, whatever. That's two dresses or more for yer, yer hear."

"She ain't fighting," Finn corrected.

"I don't care if she's singing them a song. Layers." She pointed. "There's a crate of coats in the front room. If yer can fit them, get them on yer. Many as yer can wear and still move."

It was a simple instruction, but they knew what it meant. They would be harder to stab with a blade, more difficult to wind with a punch. So, they obeyed, and with Siobhan in tow, they rifled through the box of clothes before making their way back to the kitchen sweating under the extra layers.

Tessie hadn't seen Madochée since that morning and ran up the stairs to check she hadn't snuck in unnoticed. "Where could she be?" She opened the back door and peered out. Madochée was more than used to getting about by herself, but this was a strange city and she knew they needed her here and safe. Tonight of all nights.

"She went with Mickey. He isn't back either." Finn's expression was serious, but Tessie didn't want to dwell on his meaning.

"Perhaps they've run off," Siobhan offered with a shrug.

Finn was pacing now. "Neither of them would do that. They know we'd be worried. And now I am bleedin' worried."

"Where did they go? Why?" Tessie reluctantly pulled the back door closed again and returned to the table.

"I don't know. I just seen them leave. I assumed they were getting some air. Or some food."

"Well, there is still time. There is plenty of time," she said, though even she heard the doubt in her voice.

"I hope so. I need him, if not only to have a friendly face down there. And Mado needs to be safe or we'll all be distracted."

Siobhan tugged uncomfortably at her neckline. "We've dressed too early. I can't breathe like this."

"We'll find it harder to breathe with a knife in our guts." Tessie spoke to no one in particular. Her thoughts were still focussed on Madochée and a rush of adrenaline suddenly hit as she contemplated everything they were about to do.

It all felt surreal. Tessie had joined this battle of her own free will, and yet she had never experienced an orchestrated confrontation on a scale such as this. It was dangerous. They would be at risk every minute. It was too late to back out. Too late to change the plan. She squeezed Finn's hand. He would be the most vulnerable. She was to be on the roof watching, ready to give the signal, while he would be in the thick of the fray, and he was doing it for her. At least Siobhan had her own skin in this game, even if she was no more use in this kind of fight than Tessie.

"Are yer sure yer want to stay?" Tessie asked of Siobhan. She dipped her eyes when Siobhan shot her a look. "I heard Aileen say yer could go is all. And wait for us tomorrow."

"If yer staying, then I'm staying. I'll not leave Sam." Siobhan twisted in her seat, turning her back on the table. "He don't want me here neither but I'll not be left out there on my own wondering and waiting for what's coming. Yer will not leave him, will yer?" Siobhan pointed at Finn.

"No. I won't."

"Aye. Well then. I'll be on that roof with yer, so yer can just get used to it."

Tessie just nodded, tugging at her stuffy double-lined sleeve. "I could do with a friendly face too, don't yer worry."

Something flickered in Siobhan's eyes and Tessie realised her vitriol was mostly for show. She was nervous underneath it all, buzzing with adrenaline just like Tessie. She cared for Sam; that was real for anyone to see.

"We'll be able to watch the whole thing from up there," Siobhan lamented.

"Just don't forget to give the bleedin' signal," Finn scoffed.

"I ain't daft. We ain't daft," she said, but she smiled. She was teasing now.

Just then the door opened, and Aileen looked at each of them, her eyes shrewd and intense. She was dressed in a dark green dress and a heavy grey coat. Tessie noted the lower buttons remained open, probably so she had easy access to her hatchet and whatever other weapons she had tucked inside. "It's time," Aileen said and pointed at Finn. "Yer need to go now. And yer two." She indicated to Tessie and

Siobhan. "Sam'll be here in an hour so yer can head up to yer positions now too."

So soon? All three stood to attention, their chairs scraping on the floorboards. Tessie's mouth went dry. Finn moved first toward the door, and Aileen left quickly without another word. She'd given her orders. The time was now.

"But Mado..." Tessie felt a chill. Finn darted his eyes into the dark and Tessie prayed the little girl would show herself. "We can't go without her. We can't..."

"I'll go," Siobhan said, quickly. "I'll go ahead. Yer can wait for her."

Tessie agreed, giving Siobhan an appreciative smile as she rushed out into the night and Finn looked on. "I have to go too. I'll miss my cue if I don't."

"Yes, yer go. Go now. I'll wait as long as I can."

Then there she came, barrelling out of the darkness, her small figure ploughing straight into Finn and wrapping her arms around him. She looked up at him with flushed cheeks and breaths so heavy she couldn't speak.

"There yer are!" he gasped. "Go on now, go to Tess. Thank God." Finn ushered her towards Tessie.

"Mister..."

"Come now, Mado. Come now." Tessie took her hand and started her towards the stairs.

"Have yer seen Mickey?" Finn asked quickly.

"Yes. Yes. Mister Mick...he gone..." Madochée swallowed. She pointed out the door.

"Alright." Finn squeezed her hand. "Take her up. Hurry and I'll walk with yer."

Tessie tugged her towards the stairs. "Come Mado, come with me. We need to go. Time to get up to yer hiding spot. Do yer hear?"

"They took Mickey. They got him."

"Who? What do yer mean?" Tessie raced her up the stairs. There was no time to stop. "Yer were with him, no?"

"Yes. I seen him. They got him. He's gone there."

Tessie didn't understand and she barely had time to question her. She had to get to the Vinegar Works. She just had time to get Madochée safe and run.

"I'm sorry, Mado. We have to go. They need me in position. Mickey will be fine. We'll deal with it afterwards, yer hear me? He will be alright."

Tessie opened the door to the tenement's rooftop and ushered Madochée through to the open air. "Now listen. If we don't come back here, or if someone else shows up. Listen to see it's us, and if it's anyone — *anyone* else, yer are to scoot across the rooftops like I showed yer, and across to the church on the other side of the canal to Father John. Yer remember the one?"

Madochée's worried face nodded quickly. "But Mickey—"

"He'll be fine, love. Fine. He can take care of himself. I know he can. Now I've put a blanket here for yer, and something to eat, and Sam has lent yer his cards. Mind yer see to them."

Madochée's eyes darted back and forth and Tessie could see she wanted to argue further. Tessie squeezed her shoulders and smacked a kiss on her forehead before nudging her further beyond the door. "Lock it behind me, Mado. I need to go now."

MADOCHÉE STARED at the closed staircase door, the night sky beyond the tenement's roof stretching out behind her. She moved her numb fingers over the lock and bolted it closed as Tessie's footsteps descended the stairs below. She gulped hard. Her heart still raced from running so far and her face stung from the freezing night air.

A blanket had been folded neatly beneath a make-shift shelter and, as promised, some brown bread with a teaspoon of sour orange jam had been laid out for her supper.

Out across the rooftops, the church spire she was to run to if things went awry stood out. She could see the buildings stretching towards the river where Finn and Aileen were at that moment preparing. She crouched down on her haunches. They were all out there and there was no one to help. No one at all to help Mickey.

Stuffing the brown bread in her mouth with the whole spoon of sour orange jam, she made up her mind.

She wrapped the blanket around her, shuddering against the cold. She would hide in the shadow. Yes. She would hide. Just as she knew how.

As she leapt over the rooftop, Madochée's heart beat faster still, and she scuttled down the other side just as Tessie had shown her. "I'm coming, mister. I'm coming."

CHAPTER 19

A bitter wind cut past Tessie and Finn as they rushed in the darkness, avoiding the better lit main streets. Tessie could smell the tension. It ate her up with each breath of icy air; the unknown laying out before them. Whatever was about to happen, she felt it pulsing through her. Please, let them make it. Please, let them get the cargo up and let them survive.

Tessie thought of Madochée and wondered if she should add to Finn's stress. "She said they'd taken him."

"What?"

"Mickey. That's what she said. She said they've taken him."

Finn grimaced and stopped in the street, his breath fogging out into the cold. "Christ." He buried his face in his hands. "Surely not. Not now."

Tessie pulled his hands away. "There's nothing we can do. We have to get through this first."

"Shite bastards." But Finn nodded. "Bloody Eamon. They'll hurt him, Tess. I could see it in his eyes. I don't know if he's one and the same, but he were mad as could be."

"Alright." Tessie held the calm in her voice even though

she didn't feel it. "At least they didn't take Mado. She is safe. We have to get through this and then we can help him."

Finn nodded, and they looked towards the crossroads. It was time for them to part.

"If I see Sam I'll tell him yer down here on yer own. But watch yer back, mo chara," she said. "Please be careful."

"I'll be fine. Shite." Finn shook his head. "Yer watch yours. Stay up there on that roof. Stay close to your ma. Or far away from her. I don't know which is better."

Tessie stood on her tippy toes and Finn kissed her firmly on the mouth, wrapping his hands around her waist and squeezing her to him. They would make it through this. It was a strong plan. It was a good plan.

"See yer after," she smiled and pulled away, watching as Finn turned to the dark street beside him and walked into the shadow.

FINN CROUCHED beside a wagon in the dark, his chest pounding and his head full. Stationed in a narrow, dead-end alley just before the crossroads, he waited on his own. Where was Mickey? What were they doing to him? Had Tessie made it safely to the rooftop? He hated not to be beside her through this, but he had to focus. She was depending on him.

Up ahead, he heard the hum of the gathering crowd. Sam had handsomely paid some vocal paupers to stir up a rabble and lead them toward the river warehouses to raid the food stores; that was the plan. But Finn knew as well as anyone that once a mob dispersed, it would follow the path of least resistance. That was his job. He was the resistance. He was to block the side streets with the wagons now waiting beside him, packed to the brim with combustible materials and fodder. It had to look like part of the chaos, part of the riot, lest Eamon Paddy Mac's men be watching and be tipped off. Eamon's men too would relish the cover of a riot, and if Finn couldn't block the crossroads, they could easily skirt around and flank Aileen.

It was a two-person job and Mickey was supposed to help him. How could he block both side streets on his own, with four wagons to move? He didn't even know if he could blend in with the riot. He didn't feel unleashed and riotous, but heavy with worry. He would rather be anywhere else. In any other city. Anywhere with Tessie. But he was here. He squeezed his shoulders and tilted his head from side to side. A bolt of icy air gripped the back of his neck and sent a wave of anxiety down his spine. *The mob was coming. Dear God, they were coming.*

The low rumble grew into thunder. Voices and yelling. Footsteps and rolling carts. The beat rose in his chest. Drumming louder and louder.

He saw their bright torches first, emerging from the darkness as they rounded the corner towards him. Starved faces and angry eyes flashed in the flickering light, their enraged fists raised in the air. It was a stampede of desperation. And while Aileen's men had struck the match this time, the city had been ready to erupt.

Finn's heart surged, and he ran first to one wagon, then back to another, unsure which to move first. Without Mickey he couldn't block both sides of the street at the same time.

He ran back to the first wagon, and breathing into his hands, rubbed them together. His fingers were so cold he could barely make them work as he waited with his small bottle of paraffin oil and match strip at the ready. The crowd engulfed the crossroads, the light of their torches gleaming over their famished faces. He'd have to be fast. The noise filled his ears and his hand shook as he struck his first match.

Holding it to the wagon, he held his breath, waiting for its contents to ignite. The flames erupted in a small burst flashing over the alley walls. Thank God! Thank you!

Throwing his fist in the air, Finn thrust the wagon forward into the crowd and marched across the thoroughfare. He locked it in place across the side street and hurried back to the alley.

Without pausing, he rushed to the next wagon and lit it up as the cries of his countrymen filled the alley. The rhythmic marching reverberated like a drum, urging him on until all four wagons burned as bright beacons across the intersection funnelling the crowd towards Aileen's waiting operation.

Finn held to the side as they passed him, knowing that Eamon's men moved among them. He had no way of recognising them, but his eyes scanned the faces just the same, suspicious and alert. As the rabble continued on to the food stores, he watched with interest to see who, if anyone, would file off the crowd towards the Vinegar Works. That's how he would know them.

After a moment, there they were, single file at first, but gathering in a growing cluster and walking with purpose towards the cargo site. Towards Tessie. Finn's heart raced. There were more of them than Aileen had said. Ten. Twenty. He lost count. There were more breaking away. Why so many? It was too many! Finn's eyes struggled to count them as they headed toward Aileen's alley. His feet instinctively followed. Would their plan still work with so many men?

For now they were moving in the right direction, exactly where Aileen needed them. But it would only take one of those wagons slipping out of place for some for them to split off and attack Aileen from the other side. The wagon blocking the alley had to be secure. Had he done it correctly?

Would it be enough? It was still burning, ferocious and hot, but something held his eyes to it. Something wasn't right.

Then he saw the slope and it hit him with a blow of panic — the alley sloped away from the crossroads, ever so slightly, but it was enough. It was sliding off-kilter even as it burned and crackled and popped. It was clearing the path to Aileen. It was clearing the path to Tessie!

Finn leapt to his feet, unsure which direction to run, but he needed another wagon to reinforce it, and he needed it now.

$\mathcal{A}$ dirty sky stretched over the tenement rooftops as Tessie stood beside her mother. She stomped her boots trying to shake the chill in her bones though it did little but agitate her anxiety. Overseeing the alley entrance behind the Vinegar Works, they watched all the pieces of their plan moving into place. Sounds of the riot approached slowly at first, but rose quickly in a loud and angry rumbling. Sam might have orchestrated the when and where this time, but the city was ravenous and the desperation was real. The curdling angry cries raised goosebumps on her arms.

Tessie held her breath, trying to distinguish Finn's frame among them, but there was no way to see him. He had to be there on the corner of Sheriff Street and a burst of pride and relief flooded through her as she saw the wagons alight, first one, then another. Yes! He'd done it! She almost wanted to jump for joy, though the mission was far from over.

While the mob moved toward the food stores on the docks, Eamon's men were likely down there this very moment forced to walk past the Vinegar Works, exactly as they had planned. Tessie glanced at her fellow onlookers, serious and methodical. They had to stand watch. They had to be careful. There was so much left to do.

Behind them at the river, Aileen's men frantically moved in the dark, pulling their precious cargo from the river in water-laden barrels. A chain of men hurried them into wagons, and Tessie imagined them being whisked down the North Wall and onto a barge. They were working fast. She could see their dark figures darting back and forth along the gangways and running nimble and quick with heavy wheelbarrows. *Hurry. Please hurry.*

"Are they almost done?" Tessie urged. "How much more time do they need?" Perhaps they would get out of here without Eamon Paddy Mac's men even reaching them. Oh, what a break that would be!

Aileen's eyes were calmly surveying the scene, looking back and forth from the Vinegar Works to the dark stretch of water below. It held everything she needed to secure her position - the Black Bonnet of Dublin, so she was. Her expression gave away nothing. No inkling of triumph for Tessie to hold on to. They weren't out of it yet.

Aileen bit her lip and flicked back her hair as the wind tossed it forward. Her hand hadn't moved from the hatchet in her waistband, and even though there was no one within earshot or movement, she was at the ready.

Tessie squinted to see a group of men emerge from the mass, walking calmly, almost in formation. Aileen too lurched forward, clutching her hands to the roof's brick wall. Nerves danced along Tessie's spine. That had to be them. Eamon's men were here. She counted them. Two. Then five. Ten and more. My God. There were more!

She darted eyes at her mother who crouched now, assessing.

"There are more of them..." Tessie heard the panic in her voice and swallowed the rest of her sentence.

"It doesn't matter."

"There are too many..."

"It doesn't matter." Aileen was calculating their pace. She raised one arm, getting ready to signal Sam who waited on the opposite roof. It was about to go down. Tessie sucked in a breath. Oh God.

One of Eamon's men let out a yelp. Then a holler. It was a war cry, and it pierced Tessie's lungs so that she couldn't inhale.

"That's for us. They know we're here!"

"No. They think they're coming for us. But we are coming for *them*." Aileen's arm waved up and down, striking it back against her side. Tessie lurched forward as the chain reaction activated. The timing had to be perfect, and all the pressure was on Sam. He had to time it just right.

"Come on, Sarge." Siobhan stood beside her, her hands pressed to her mouth in prayer. "Come on."

Tessie glanced at Eamon's men below, then back in Sam's direction, seeing a small light fizz across the rooftop. He'd lit the fuse. A faint rumble echoed towards them as a barrel rolled. And rolled. And another. One by one. Then a momentary silence as they dropped off the roof.

Exploding on the ground, the barrels shattered to pieces, flames rippling across the cobblestones as Eamon's men scattered.

"They know we're here now!" Aileen's mouth curled into a smile as she ducked down to watch them run. Another barrel rolled off the roof and *BANG*! It exploded again, like firecrackers, one after the other.

Eamon's men were yelling now. Two men lay splayed out injured, while the others screamed in anger. They were scattering, looking for an enemy to fight.

"It's time," Aileen hollered. Yanking the hatchet from her belt, she ripped open the rooftop door and led her men down the stairs. As they rushed away and left Tessie and Siobhan alone at their station, the hot, smoky air swirled in a vacuum around them.

Tessie gripped the stone ledge in front of her, her eyes instinctively scanning for Finn even though the plan placed him on the other side away from the battle.

Aileen's men rushed out from the building, flooding the side of the Vinegar Works and forcing Eamon's men into the barricaded alley. They were boxed in, even if they outnumbered Aileen. They just had to hold the men long enough to get the cargo away. They were almost there.

Sam darted through the crowd with nothing but his fists. She could barely keep up with his twists and turns as she watched on. The noise was thunderous, with blood pounding in her ears and breath choking in her lungs. Grunts of exertion and the thumping of body-on-body rose up from the street. Broken teeth and punctured mouths, bloody noses, the sound of glass smashing on the ground.

"Are we holding them?" Tessie cried out, desperate for it all to end.

"I don't know." Siobhan leaned further over the edge, and Tessie knew she was looking for Sam.

"He's over there." Tessie pointed, and Siobhan's eyes darted.

"Get 'em Sarge! Kill em!" She shrieked so loud Tessie covered her ears. How much more of this could she take?

Aileen was there in the midst of it, powering through the crowd, even at almost twice the age of the young men around her. She twirled in her skirt, her strong shoulders heaving and jerking as she raised her hatchet again and again. Tessie could see they stayed away from her. One blow and they could lose their hands, their fingers, a large chunk of their legs. She had them on the run, a spinning turbine, her wild hair churning. Tessie understood how she'd made a name for herself. She was fearless, her face a grimace of unstoppable grit.

Tessie checked the cargo crew at the river, and saw they were almost through. They just had to hold on a few more moments and they'd all be on the barges and pushed away into the darkness on the river. Then she could give the signal, and they would pull back. It would all be over.

She saw Aileen throw her head back. She was looking up at the rooftop for the sign that the cargo was safe.

"Are they through?" Tessie gripped Siobhan's shoulder.

"They're through." Siobhan beside her was just as urgent.

Tessie frantically waved the orange scarf back and forth so Aileen could see it through the smoke, and the triumph rushed through her as Aileen gave out the call.

"It's through. Pull back. Pull back!"

Tessie and Siobhan looked at each other, their joint relief thrusting them together in an overwhelmed embrace. They had done it. Hallelujah. She squeezed Siobhan's hand as they both turned to survey the damage below.

Tessie moved on her tiptoes, butterflies rising in her stomach as she looked down. She was still searching for Finn. The riot had moved on to the food stores and Eamon's men would clear out, surely, but the fighting was not stopping. Eamon's men were not leaving. The clashing parties could not pull themselves apart and Eamon's men were pushing back through the small gap in the barricaded alley. No. They were coming around the side.

"They are coming around," Tessie called down to Aileen.

"What?" she screamed up at her.

Tessie pointed to the alley, her eyes scanning the dark outlines along the periphery, and there she saw him. Finn. Her stomach dropped hard and sick.

His lone frame was hunched over, backing into the alley with a second wagon in tow. He was trying to block the path

— it would work if he could just get it alight. Except now he was on the wrong side of the barricade, surrounded by Eamon's men.

"Finn!" She screamed till her voice was hoarse. "Finn! He's trapped." Tessie's heart thudded as she saw several of Eamon's men appear behind him. "They're going to get him."

"What?" Siobhan craned to see.

"They have him cornered."

"Who?"

Tessie couldn't answer. She reeled forward, and then without a thought turned for the stairs. He couldn't even see them coming; she had to get to him first.

Down on the street, Tessie's breath caught and choked in the lingering smoke. Aileen whirled, still with her hatchet as she barked orders, letting her men know the cargo was safe. Tessie knelt to grab her knife from her boot, just as a young man darted at her, punching her jaw. She hollered and drove the knife into his ribs beneath his arm. He toppled her over. She had to do better than this, she thought, as the man struggled to the side of her and she pushed him off. She couldn't end up on the ground at every confrontation. Instead, she started running and slashing. A run-by slash at this man. A jab at the next. She couldn't be cornered; she had to get to Finn.

"What are yer doing out here — are yer mad?" Aileen screamed at her.

"Finn. They're going to get Finn."

"They're retreating, girl."

"He's blocked the path but he's cornered." Tessie ran away through the crowd and Aileen reluctantly followed, knocking back anyone who tried to halt her path.

"Where? Where is he?"

"There." Tessie pointed to the back corner. "Help him!"

Aileen set herself to move as a man stepped out in front

of them. Tessie recognised his dimples, though a large cap covered his curls.

"Aileen, yer mad bitch." He spat on the ground in front of her.

"Turn and run, boy. Yer are leaving here empty-handed tonight." Aileen gritted her teeth. "Tell yer Eamon fuck he ain't got nothing."

He waved his hand in the air in a circular motion, giving a signal. "Push back! We're leaving." He smiled, showing little acknowledgement of defeat, then he caught Tessie's eye. "Well look here, I remember yer." He pulled his shirt aside at the neck, exposing the knife cut across his chest. "If yer wanted to see me again yer needn't have gone to so much trouble."

But Tessie had no time for him, her focus entirely on Finn as he tried to fight his way out. But there were too many.

"Finn!" Tessie called rushing towards him.

The man saw her and the object of her attention. He ran towards Finn himself.

"Lads, scoop that one up! Take him!" At the bark of his orders, two men who were already engaged with Finn twisted his arms behind his back. Finn wrestled and fought as two more joined the pile-on and slogged him with blows to the face and belly, dragging him away with their retreating crowd.

"No!" Tessie ran, scrambling to get through.

"Not so empty-handed now," the man shot back at Aileen, who watched thin-lipped and staunch.

"Let him go! Let him go!" Tessie rushed at him, and he punched her hard in the mouth, knocking her back.

"Good day to yer, ladies." With that, he saluted, and turned and ran.

Struggling to her feet, Tessie watched in horror as the rival men vanished into the dark with Finn in their grasp.

"Stop them!" Tessie yelled at Aileen. "Stop them!"

Aileen let her hatchet fall to her side but she didn't move. Her shoulders slumped in the aftermath of adrenaline, breath heaving, as the lingering bodies writhed around her, and her men triumphantly slapped each other on the back.

Tessie couldn't just stand there. She ran.

"Wait, girl. Come back!" Aileen barked.

"We have to stop them!"

Aileen leapt forward and held her back, wrapping her arms around Tessie's waist as she tried to run. "Stop girl. If yer run after him, yer will get caught yerself."

The wagon Finn had pulled into place had caught alight and Tessie had no choice but to turn riverside around the building. Frantic, she ran through the remaining stragglers of Eamon's crew as a blow flew at her shoulder. It flung her backwards towards the water, dark and all-consuming. The piercing cold sucked the breath from her body and swallowed her screams. Her skirts grew heavy with water, dragging her deeper and deeper. She floundered, kicking and thrashing and getting tangled in her clothes. It was too much, her lungs screaming for air.

A strong hand gripped her by the collar and dragged her upward.

It was Sam, pulling her onto the dock where she collapsed on her knees. The distance between her and Finn stretched out and the smoke obscured the path.

"Yer stupid, girl," Aileen cursed as Tessie coughed and spluttered.

"Yer know what they'll do. Yer know," she managed. "We have to get him back."

CHAPTER 21

Sam struggled to light the gas lantern on the table, then moved to stoke the dying flames in the stove. Tessie huddled beside him, hardly able to breathe for her shivering. Her skin ached with icy tingles and she gulped back glasses of whiskey as Aileen thrust them into her trembling hands.

"Get these layers off before yer freeze to death." Aileen yanked hard on her top coat, ripping off two of the buttons as she pulled. She began peeling back the sodden layers of clothing, dropping them on the floor.

"They're gonna kill him," Tessie said, her teeth chattering.

The cold sank ruthlessly deeper to her bones. Siobhan wrapped a blanket around her shoulders and shoved her closer to the stove.

"They'll kill him."

Aileen turned to speak only to Sam, her voice lowered and her hands on her hips. They were trying to make a plan and Tessie skirted back around the table, trying to break into their stream of conversation.

"We'll move Tiny to the side street. Tell him to watch."

"Alright." Sam was readying to leave again, though his breath had not yet calmed and his face still flushed with exertion and the frosty air.

"Hey!" Tessie waved her hand in front of them.

"Then back here and we'll take a look at—"

"Hey! Hey!" There weren't listening. In desperation Tessie pulled the knife from her boot and flung it at the wall beside her mother. "Please. Tell me what we're going to do."

The room went quiet. Aileen let out a deep breath before plucking the knife from the wall and turning it in her hand. She passed it back to Tessie.

"How do we get him back? How?"

Aileen glared at her. She wouldn't be hurried. Shaking out her hair, she too stripped back her layers of clothing. Her sleeves had been nearly shredded through and torn from combat, though her arms beneath held barely a scratch. Her face had caught a few grazes, though she had fared better than Tessie, whose bloody lip was cut open and swollen. "We wait him out."

"Wait him out?" Tessie was distraught, her wet petticoat clinging to her legs. "God knows what they're doing to him right now. We got the cargo secured. That was all action and fight, and now to get Finn back we sit and wait? No. I won't wait. We can't wait."

"That's the only way."

"Wait him out for what? Come on!" Tessie stomped her foot. Standing now in the kitchen, they all seemed so small. Only hours ago they had felt bloated with adrenaline and the triumph of soon prevailing. They had achieved their goal; the goods were safe. But now she felt deflated. A stabbing pain hit her chest and she remembered Madochée.

She turned to Sam. "Can yer let Madochée down?" To Aileen, she demanded: "How can I tell her we're just going to sit and wait?"

"Yer knew the risks," Aileen said. "He did too. We all did."

Tessie stood with her hand on her hip, trying to calm the tremble in her lips. "That's not good enough."

"Walking into that part of town right now is a death trap. It can't be done. Not tonight. I won't sacrifice what little men I have left to save just one. Even if he's yer man. It's a nasty business, love."

"It must be tonight. He might not survive till morning, yer know that."

"What then? Yer tell me what special skills yer got that won't get more of my men killed?"

Tessie turned to the fire, staring at the low burning flame and feeling no heat at all. What could she do? What skills did she have? She was a nobody. Aileen poured them both another drink. Tessie gulped it back and stared at it, the leftover trickle of whiskey gathering at the bottom of the glass.

"I make bleedin' cakes. That's what I do."

"Ha."

"I make ginger cakes."

Aileen frowned and shook her head in exasperation, but Tessie was gathering momentum.

"I'll make some for Eamon."

Aileen stared down at her drink, and Tessie could see she was still numb from the fight, sifting through the clutter of it all.

"Can yer get yer hands on something...something that'll make them sick or sleepy?"

"Are yer serious?" Aileen wasn't catching on.

"Medicine, poison, anything that'll put them all to sleep. Knock them out. Anything so we can walk in and get Finn."

Aileen narrowed her eyes and Tessie could see her calculating. Was she on to something? Would Aileen listen?

Sam peeked his head back in the doorway. "She's not opening up."

"She must be asleep," Tessie said, rubbing her eyes wearily. "Please keep banging. She'll want to know we're back."

He left again, this time Siobhan followed him, as Aileen surfaced from her thoughts. "We'll put them all to sleep, yer say."

Tessie held her eyes. "Eamon likes an offering. I can bake him one."

"Aye. Girl. That's what we'll do. Weaken his men enough that we can take them." Aileen raised her chin, gazing almost proudly at Tessie. "We just need your man to last that long. Can he?"

Tessie knew he would have to wait until morning when Eamon's men surfaced hungry to collect their offerings.

"What'll they do with him?" she said, glumly taking a seat. "I mean...why did they take him? Just to kill him? Or will they...?"

"Sully took him because he saw he meant something. He hasn't thought it through anymore than that. But Eamon..."

"He wasn't down there?"

"Facing hand-to-hand battle?" Aileen almost laughed. "No, he weren't. But yer man will meet him. I have no doubt in that."

Tessie hung her head and rubbed her eyes. "He's already been through so much. I don't know how much he can take."

"He'll have to take it, won't he? He ain't got a choice. Now what do yer need?"

Tessie looked about the kitchen. Yes. Focus.

"I'll arrange yer supplies. Yer tell Sam what yer need and he'll send word to Ms Ellis down the way for whatever we don't have here. Yer'll just need to pick it up." Aileen tossed some money on the table. "I'll speak to my people. Whatever happens with yer man, we need that cargo moved outta

Dublin tonight. And then we need them to rally back here with us at first light if this is all to go down smoothly."

Tessie took a deep breath. She was starting to think nothing would ever be under control as Sam tumbled down the stairs again, leaping the last few steps and landing with a thud. Siobhan traipsed beside him. "I don't think she's there."

"Why wouldn't she be there?" Tessie frowned, confused. "We are back in plenty of time. She was only supposed to go to the church if we didn't come back."

"What about Mickey?" Siobhan asked. "Did he ever show?"

Tessie's chest tightened as she remembered Madochée's pleas. She almost couldn't say the words out loud. "She said they took him. Oh God. She said they took him."

"Who took him? What are yer talking about?"

She didn't know how to answer. It could have been Eamon. It could have been anybody. "The church. We need to check the church first."

"I'll go. Stay here."

Tessie buried her face in her hands, knowing Madochée wouldn't be there. The sick feeling in her belly spoke it loud and clear: Wherever Mickey was, Madochée had gone after him.

CHAPTER 22

The freezing night air had stiffened his bones and Mickey kicked his legs out, uncurling them from beneath him. Rafferty would be back with Eamon any moment, and he had to think fast. Eamon meant him harm — he knew that much. Why else had they brought him here? He looked at the man guarding the door. He had known that man. He had known Brec and Brec had known him, perhaps in another life, an earlier one before things became complicated. But he had known him just the same.

"Yer are really taking orders from Eamon now?" Mickey's voice was croaky as he tried to keep his tone conversational. "Yer used to pull his hair as he walked by. Yer can't take him seriously."

Brec stood with his back to Mickey, keeping watch outside the entrance. "He takes himself seriously these days, Mick. Or haven't yer noticed? It's not the Dublin it was a decade ago. Or even six months ago."

"It's all a joke, if yer ask me."

"He shot Dean McWillie dead in the face not four months ago. That weren't no joke. He fell like a dog in the canal and no one dared fished him out till Eamon left. Saw it with my own two eyes. He's crazy." Brec lowered his voice as if afraid someone might hear him.

"So take that pistol from him and then he ain't shite. Why yer are afraid of him, I'll never understand."

"He's not right in the head. He don't think straight. Yer can't reason with that kind of man."

"Even more reason to get rid of him."

"Yer ain't been here these past months, Mick. Madmen attract madmen don't they. It's not just him. Any crazy man with a fist is drawn to him. Any excuse to flex their muscle. That's how this all began."

"What's yer excuse?"

"He pays me. And I'll not have Nance out on the street. Not now or ever."

"So yer put up with this shite and his threats. Christ! He ain't the only man with a gun in all of Dublin—"

"I'll put up with whatever I need to, is what." Brec's voice was tense. "Maybe yer haven't noticed but folks is starving around here. Laying down in the gutters like skeletons."

"Well then, perhaps yer understand why I've come back for my son. I don't care if yer threaten me, or what yer do to me. I'll not back off this time."

"Tell it to Eamon, Mick. It's family troubles this is. It's between yer."

"Yer knew Ciara. Yer think she wants her son around him? Yer know she ain't want this. Not like this. And yer just said yerself he can't see reason. Let me go before he gets here. Or better yet, let's face him together and end this madness. Because that's what it is, brother. Madness."

Brec squinted out into the darkness surrounding them. For a moment Mickey felt a trickle of hope that he'd found an ally, but Brec didn't turn around. He didn't move. Mickey's heart sunk. No. He was alone in this.

Movement stirred across the entrance, and Eamon stood there, squaring his shoulders with a grin of satisfaction. His glassy eyes caught the moonlight, a mad sheen in his expression.

"Yer let me out of here now, Eamon," Mickey growled, the desperation deepening his voice despite his effort to sound fierce.

"That won't be necessary, brother. Yer'll be out of here soon enough." Eamon's light-blue eyes swirled around the room, barely resting to focus.

Mickey shrugged. "I'm his father. Did yer expect me just to forget that?"

"Yer should have forgotten if yer knew what was good for yer and for him."

"What then? What are yer going to do?"

"I'll tell yer what I wanted to do." Eamon pressed his face close to Mickey's. "I wanted to gut yer like a fat pig to feast on and throw yer body in the canal."

Mickey cleared his throat, holding Eamon's eyes. "But what?"

"But Ma wouldn't have it, would she?" Eamon rolled his jaw and lowered his eyes as if the disappointment still lingered. "So instead, I'm taking yer to the docks and seeing yer on a ship out of here. And if some ill should befall yer on that trip...well it's no fault of mine is it?" His eyes lit up as he outstretched his arms, as if feeling himself mighty clever. "I put him on the boat, Ma." He shrugged, enacted an imaginary conversation. "I saw him on the boat, so I did. Cross my bleedin' heart. He was breathing when I last seen him."

Mickey shook his head, feeling the threat growing. "He is my boy, Eamon. Mine and Ciara's. He's my boy! Don't do this!"

Eamon raised his fist high and swung it with all his might

into Mickey's chest, rolling him backwards off the pail. Mickey spluttered for breath.

"It's done, Mick. It's done." Eamon's large frame leaned over, gripping his hand around Mickey's jaw. Mickey twisted desperately to free himself, but it was futile. "Now yer boat leaves soon enough. So I suggest yer savour this sweet air of Dublin for the last time."

THERE IN THE DARK. Ever so quiet. Ever so small. Madochée crouched so very still. Invisible even.

Through the city she had run, the blanket wrapped around her, shielding her warm breath from fogging in the cold air. She watched the man stand over Mickey. She watched him hurt him, and she waited.

Do not worry, mister. I see you. I am here.

CHAPTER 23

Finn cursed himself. The wagons meant to block Eamon's men had also blocked him — the utter frustration of it seethed in him. He had heard Tessie screaming for him across the crowd and knew immediately how terrible his mistake had been. He'd drawn her into harm's way after trying so hard to keep her out of it.

Eamon's men had dragged him to a large hall where the walls were pasted with old church notices about food rations and soup lines. Long pews and tables had been clustered together for whiskey-fuelled banter, and some pews were half hacked to pieces for firewood.

After binding his wrists and legs, the men had seemed to forget about him. Left alone, Finn focussed on the layout of the room and who was in the crowd. He would be ready to run for the door with the clearest path if the opportunity presented itself. Or ready to fight. Whichever would get him out of here.

Discretely scanning the room, Finn found the dimpled one who'd directed his capture, called Sully. Though he was half a shoulder taller than most of the men in that room,

Sully seemed little more than a loud-mouthed agitator, strutting back and forth with loud declarations. "We should have been ready. Yer louts will get it now. Yer will get it now."

It was only a dark-haired man in the corner who dared to challenge his endless ramblings. "We shouldn't have taken it for granted that she wouldn't fight back." He spoke with authority, though he didn't stand to take centre stage. His hair flopped over his brow, and something in his manner caught Finn's attention. He was someone the men respected. He saw them nodding in agreement and gather around him as if seeking his attention or protection.

"We didn't take it for granted. Eamon said she had nothing left. She's a withering old bitch and dammit! This shouldn't have happened."

"We should have split into two groups, and we should have a group already out at the docks twenty-four hours before. Feck it, forty-eight hours before so we were there and ready no matter what she pulled together."

Sully glared. "Why didn't yer speak up then, if yer so bleedin' smart?"

"This is Eamon's show. If he's got his trust in yer, who am I to argue? Me and my men are just here for support."

"Fat lot of good yer all did for us tonight. Ain't that right?"

"A bad plan is a bad plan, don't matter what kind of support yer give it."

"I dare yer to say that to Eamon."

"I will. If he asks." The dark-haired man leaned back casually against the post. "But it'll only make yer look bad." He flashed a winning grin and some of the men chuckled.

Sully let out a frustrated growl and threw the bottle he was drinking in Finn's direction. Finn braced for impact as it shattered in pieces at his feet, showering him with ale and glass. He couldn't tell if it was blood or alcohol that trickled down the side of his face, but he sucked in his breath determined not to make a sound or draw more unneeded attention. It didn't matter. Sully rushed toward him. Finn twisted his body away, though his bindings held him in position. Sully gripped his chin and forced him to look at him.

"That pretty thing belongs to yer does she?" Finn tried to turn away but Sully gripped him harder still. "Well, she ain't that smart if she's shacked up with the likes of Aileen. Yer better tell me something if yer want me to let her alone."

"Yer even look at her—" Finn started.

"Leave him be," the other man called from across the room.

"I need something to tell Eamon, dammit. Something... " He flexed his fist at Finn. "And he's gonna tell us something, so he is." Sully glared into Finn's eyes. "I want to know what's breathed life into old Aileen. She were as good as dead last week, ripe for finishing, and now she's called her men back. Why? Tell me why!"

Stay quiet. Finn closed his eyes. *Wait it out. Just wait.*

But Sully's grip tightened. "I'm going to get her. Aileen and that bitch of yers."

Finn felt the anger rile up and he gritted his teeth. He spat into Sully's face. It was an ugly spit, and Finn heard the other man sigh, burying his face in his hands. Sure enough, Sully punched him and unable to fight back, his body twisted and fell back against the floorboards. Sully punched again. And again. Finn's head bounced off the floor.

"That's enough!"

"Yer…will…tell…me…something." Sully punctuated each word with a strike. "She will pay. She will." And finally standing, he hooked his boots into Finn's side.

"Enough!" The other man rushed at Sully and pulled him back. "He's gotta be able to talk if he's gonna be any use at all."

Sully let out an exasperated scream, clenching his arms

and jerking himself away to pace the room. The dark-haired man looked down at Finn. "Don't spit at him. Are yer daft?" He pulled Finn into a sitting position then walked away, the room a chatter with the outburst.

The front door burst open, and it all went quiet.

It had to be Eamon. Finn struggled to see him through his swelling eyes, but sure enough, Mickey's brother-in-law stood cane in hand, his frock coat open to display the pistol on his hip, his eyes flashing with wild fury. Sully scampered to Eamon's side and Finn expected the dark-haired man to follow, but instead, he propped his foot up on a pew, watching from the sidelines.

"What happened?" Eamon struck his cane down hard on the floorboards, his voice ringing with a shrill edge of panic. "What happened? How could this happen?"

"She attacked us. Her men. They've come back—" Sully spoke in quick bursts. "We didn't get it. We lost it."

Eamon struck his cane again. "They are laughing at us!" He pressed his lips together in a thin grotesque line, glaring at Sully who could only hang his head in shame. "She is laughing at me. At me!" Eamon screamed his words, doubling over in anguish with clenched fists. "I have made promises, damn yer all. If she is laughing what do yer think the Angel will do? He'll think me a bleedin' fool." Eamon outstretched his arm, scanning his finger over the onlookers. "And God curse any one of yer who makes me look a fool." Silence rang out as his finger continued to scan, then without warning, he whipped his cane across the face of the man standing closest. He moved to strike again, but before he could, the dark-haired man stepped in to block his arm.

"He is one of mine," he said, his voice strong with warning.

Eamon didn't move, his arm suspended in mid-air, his eyes darting over the dark-haired man.

Finn held his breath. Just who was in charge here?

The moment stretched out, Eamon's eyes flickering madly over his challenger's unchanged expression. For a moment, Finn thought he might strike, but instead, the rage in his eyes vanished as quickly as it had flared. He embraced the dark-haired man's shoulder, patting it awkwardly as if for reassurance.

Eamon spun around on his heel, noticing Finn curled into the corner. Finn couldn't help the bolt of panic shooting down his legs.

"Who is that?"

Sully rushed forward, straightening his shoulders as if he finally had something worthy to offer. "We took him. He's one of hers."

"What for?"

"There's a girl...with Aileen. Ah." Then he shook his head as if that were too complicated to explain. "He might be able to tell us something to, yer know, get the cargo back."

"Why didn't yer say so?" Eamon shoved the man he'd struck out of the way and moved towards Finn, scrunching up his nose in consideration. With his cane, he forced Finn's chin upward.

Oh God. Finn knew he'd recognise him as Mickey's friend for sure. Finn kept his eyes low, hoping his swollen face was enough to hide his appearance.

Eamon considered him closely, a hush coming over him. "I know yer." Eamon spoke quietly, just to Finn. "Yer were in my ma's house." His voice was a terrifying, husky whisper. "How perfect. How fucking perfect."

Finn reluctantly swung his eyes towards him, as Eamon suddenly pushed off him with his cane and stood again, a triumphant giggle escaping his lips. "Well, well, well. A friend of Michael Bell. Something to smile about after all. Now. The question is what can he tell us? Does he know where the cargo is?"

Sully cleared his throat. "We don't know yet."

"Yer haven't asked him?" Eamon's face flushed red, and he smoothed the lapel on his coat. "Well, string him up for God's sake."

A cheer went up around the room and fear surged through Finn. His breath caught in his chest. String him up? What did that mean?

The men rushed at him as he struggled against his ropes. What were they doing? What was about to happen? A flood of hands reached for him, tugging and pulling as Finn struggled to raise his voice. "Get off me. Let go!" They were growing louder, and the panic shuddered through him.

"Good luck to yer," one man whispered into his ear before surrendering him to the crowd.

They tugged at him, securing ropes around his feet. Unbinding his hands, they wrapped each wrist separately, stretching his arms out in the crucifix position. He was powerless to stop them as another rope tightened around his chest. Then he was being heaved up, the ropes tugging against his armpits and neck, suspending him from the ceiling. It was excruciating, stretching his bruised body so it felt it might pull apart.

Finn looked out over the crowd of eager eyes. They quietened in anticipation. Eamon was in the back corner, eating now, and seemed almost to have forgotten about him. But the crowd was waiting. Waiting for what?

Eamon swallowed his cheese and bread and lifted his eyes to Finn once more. "Alright, lads." He stood, raising his arms as if introducing a circus act. "The first one to get him in the head gets a bonus. And the one to break him..." Eamon rubbed his chin as if slyly choosing the most appropriate prize. "Will get a crew of his own. Target practice is open!"

The crowd cheered and Finn felt a surge of energy in the room as they flung objects from all corners.

"Tell us where the cargo is! Tell us!"

They spoke with one voice, jeering and poking at him as terror seized through him. Even if he'd been of mind to tell them, he didn't know. He was not involved in that part of the plan.

Most of the projectiles missed him, striking the walls around him, exploding in a thunderous racket. Some things did hit him — in the legs, the groin, the stomach, the shoulders and face. Food, plates, cutlery, bowls. Finn hollered for them to stop, that he didn't even know the answer, but they could not hear him over the crowd. His voice caught in his throat and he pulled against the ropes. In the momentum he was swaying back and forth, the ropes burning his skin raw as they grated back at forth under his arms.

He had to wait it out. That's what he told himself. *Wait it out. Survive this. Just survive.*

CHAPTER 24

The outside chill clung to her skin as Tessie moved through the deserted streets. Sam had advised her where to collect her supplies and she couldn't bear to linger by the fire a moment longer. Siobhan had found her a spare dress and coat to wear, and even though her hair still hung wet down her back and the cold still thawed from her bones, she pushed on through the night.

There was a time she had walked these familiar alleys with confidence, but now as a soft rain drizzled down, she wasn't sure what else they might steal from her. Anxious butterflies surged round and round in her belly. Digging in her pockets for the small pendant of St Brigid, Tessie realised she must have left it in the dress she had given to Siobhan. Her spirits dropped, and she barely had the energy to recite the words. Still, the prayer formed inside her. *Brigid of the Mantle, encompass us...Your hands upon ours, Our hands within yours...*

Finn needed to survive the night, just a matter of hours. Please. They were going to get him. Mickey and Madochée, wherever they were, let them be safe. And how long until the

Angel's wrath descended on this already horrible mess? It was too much for her to hold, and she pushed it to the sky. *Lady of the Lambs, protect us...Keeper of the Hearth, kindle us...*

She reached the tenement building on the corner. Tessie entered and walked up the staircase to the door on the upper landing as instructed. The stairs creaked in the late hour and Tessie braced before knocking in short, crisp knocks. The door opened quickly, and Tessie's eyes took a moment to adjust to the dim gas lamp burning on the table. A woman not much older than herself stood before her, a faint smile on her lips. Without a word she held out a sack and Tessie heard the light clang of its contents as it banged against the doorframe.

"Check it," she said. "Make sure it is enough."

Tessie saw the humble kitchen behind her — not unlike the one she and Finn had in the Old Nichol. She recognised the single stovetop and ingredients at the ready on the table. Opening the sack, she saw it was full of baking tins and two large mixing bowls.

"Do yer have enough left for yerself?" Tessie frowned into the kitchen behind her.

"I'll be fine, miss."

"Are yer sure?"

The woman nodded and moved to close the door.

"Thank yer." Tessie spoke through the narrowing crack in the door, though it closed without the woman's reply. Tessie knew she had taken all her tins. The ones she would have used the next morning to make what money she could. The guilt stirred in Tessie's belly as she turned away. Must every gain be another's loss?

"I'm sorry," she said into the empty hallway, then turned and ran from the building.

Outside, the darkness again closed in around her and this time she ran. She had to get back. She would be up all night baking. For Finn. For the hope she could free him before it was too late.

Flying down Capel Street and rounding the last alley towards Aileen's place, a strong arm gripped her fast around the waist and pulled her beneath an overhanging doorway. Choking back a scream, she lashed into the darkness, kicking and punching at the air.

"Tessie! Stop. It's me!"

She heard the familiar voice, and her body instinctively relaxed. But it couldn't be him, could it? Only the outline of his blonde hair and the cut of his suit caught the light, but it was enough.

"Kyran!" She fell towards him, relief flooding through her with such force she gripped him tight. "How happy I am to see yer here, yer have no idea!"

He smiled warmly back at her, holding her out to see her better in the dim light. "Are yer alright? Tell me, are yer hurt?"

"No, I'm fine. I'm alright." But she was sure her eyes disguised little.

"What are you doing out here alone? You'll catch your death in this cold. What is happening?"

Tessie swallowed back the words, unable to speak out loud what a horrible turn things had taken. "But why are yer here? I don't understand. Where is Ruby?"

Kyran's expression shifted; she could see there was something wrong.

"Oh dear, brother, what is it? Is it Ruby? What's happened?"

"No. No." He reached out and held her hands still. "The Angel. Arthur. I've come to warn yer—"

"He's here?" Tessie's heart stilled.

"He's coming. I've only a day's grace ahead of him, if that—"

"What? Why? No. Not yet. We still have time."

"He is coming, Tessie. He is coming now." Kyran's face was grave and Tessie felt a rush of blood drain away as if a wound had sprung up out of nowhere.

"No." She heard the panic and hopelessness in her voice. "Finn has been taken... Aileen is still fighting...I can't find Madochée...and Mickey...I need to get Finn out." Tessie gestured wildly as the words flooded out. "I need more time. Yer have to hold him off. Please. Madochée is gone. Finn has been taken by Eamon's men. I need time to fix it. One more day."

Kyran's eyes darted back and forth, trying to take it all in. "Yer need to listen to me, Tess." He held her shoulders firm. "He was never going to wait. He was never sending you here to save your mother."

Tessie's mouth fell open. "But he did. That's why we're here. I don't understand."

"Listen. He's come to take you both. You and Aileen. He wants you both. He wanted you here together. He wanted you away from me so he could...so he could end you. That's it. There is no deal. There is no anything."

Tessie collapsed against the brick wall. The cake tins in her sack fell to the ground and the clatter echoed through the alley. "All of this was for nothing?"

Kyran's face was filled with worry. "I heard him speak the truth of it to Castor. That's how I know. He couldn't get to you while we were together. He needed to separate us and to make it look like an accident, or like you'd gotten caught up in the way. But I heard him."

"And his word to you? And Ruby? Is she safe?"

"I've had her moved and she is for now, but we leave for Boston the moment I return. My father might own London but Boston is still open. I came only to warn you. I couldn't have lived with myself if I'd not let you know. He is coming, Tessie. If he is not here already, he will be here tomorrow."

Tessie looked at Kyran feeling the fear and anger and panic well up inside her - the muddy mess of it all.

How could they ever get out of this when so much was against them? The task before them was bigger now than ever. Save Finn, defeat Eamon, and the Angel, find Mickey and Madochée. How could she do all of that before tomorrow?

Kyran's eyes were earnest as ever and she loved him for coming to warn her. "Yer go, brother. Go to Ruby. She needs yer."

"What can I do? What can I do to help?"

"This is my fight now. Mine and my mother's."

"Tess—"

"Go. If we can, we will find yer in Boston. We will find yer."

Kyran's eyes shone with unshed tears. "I didn't come to leave you in such a state."

"Ruby needs yer, yer know she does. And our fate is in our own hands now. Please. Go."

Kyran didn't want to — she could see the torment ripple his brow. It wasn't in his nature to turn his back, but she'd spoken the truth. This was her fight now. He squeezed her hand and they embraced. It filled her with so much hope it almost lifted her feet off the ground.

"I'll see yer in Boston, brother. Go."

CHAPTER 25

It could have been a matter of minutes, or a matter of hours, when Finn woke next. The rage in the men must have died down, though he still hung from the beams. He was a dead weight on the ropes, covered in a smattering of blood, sour vegetables and many other things. He couldn't feel his arms or his legs. His fingers moved as he commanded them too, but there was no strength. He was nought but a rag doll.

As he raised his head in the quiet room, Finn saw the stray scattering of the men who had pummelled him. They were less intimidating figures in the faint morning light, grey and old with liquor, sprawled in all the ways of a party that had fizzled out.

Finn swallowed, trying to clear his throat. It was clogged with hours of coarse hollering and nothing to quench his thirst. He thought of Tessie, and how fraught with worry she would be. How could he escape this? He had no voice to bargain with them. No strength to fight them. He felt the ominous fate of it all hanging in this dimly lit cavern.

From the corner below him, a sound stirred. A lone figure

approached and pressed a wet sponge to his face. Finn jerked back at the sudden cold touch, though bit down on the sponge, squeezing cool water into his mouth.

"Don't struggle," the voice said, and after replenishing the sponge, he let Finn drink again. "I'm going to cut yer down. Be quiet about it."

Finn had no response and no recourse but to let the man smooth the sponge over his head and shoulders. He poured water over him and it washed away some of the blood and food, showing the naked bruising on his skin. "They've done a number on yer that's for sure."

It was the dark-haired man.

Finn cleared his throat and felt his teeth were still intact. His lips stung as he moved his jaw and dried blood cracked in the corners of his mouth.

"Yer passed out after a couple of knocks to the head. Yer didn't say anything of consequence if yer were wondering. But that's how this game always ends so..." The man shrugged.

"They do this a lot?" Finn's voice scratched.

"They do it enough. It's a consolation prize. A way to vent when things don't go their way." The man held up a knife to the ropes and stepped forward to hold up Finn's body.

"Their way?" Finn asked. "Aren't yer one of them?"

"One bound man against a rabid crowd ain't my style. That's for Eamon and his men. Brace yourself."

He sliced the ropes at Finn's wrist and his arm fell to his side. Slumping forward, he leaned heavily on the man as he cut his other arm free and helped Finn to sit back against the wall.

"Here. Drink some more." He passed him a cup and helped Finn wrap his fingers around it before sitting at the table a few feet away, letting Finn gather his thoughts.

The man was younger than Finn, with a lean athletic frame and a calm demeanour.

"Can yer eat?" He passed him some bread too, ripping it into small pieces for him but Finn snatched it away.

"I can do it."

The man took no offence and leaned back at his table, taking in the sight of him. "It really is yer, isn't it?"

Finn looked up at him wearily. "Me what?"

The man didn't answer. Silence lingered between them. Finn held his gaze. Did he know him? Had he seen this man before? The words tumbled through Finn, searching for something to grab onto. Had he? His dark eyes, not so different from his own. It was squeezing him now, the familiarity pressing down on him, heavy and sharp. The crop of the man's hair. His shoulders. His stance. It dug in like a gouging blade to his heart.

"Tadhg?" The name cracked in Finn's throat, the word slipping out before his brain could fathom its meaning.

The man let out a long breath, stretching his legs out in front and crossing them over. "Ah. There yer go."

Finn felt the room crash in around him, taking his breath. How could it be? The walls tumbled, spinning with years, with memories, with loss. How? How could he be looking at the brother he was sure he'd lost? But he was. It was him. It was Tadhg.

"Tadhg?" He raised his voice, finding the strength to edge forward on his knees. "How can it be yer?"

The man looked down at him, a slight mocking smile. "I saw it was yer the minute they dragged yer in here."

"What are yer doing here?"

The man raised his arms in defence. "This is Dublin. I'm here, right where yer left me." Bitterness twisted Tadhg's lopsided grin as he swigged back a large gulp of whiskey.

"I didn't leave yer."

Tadhg shrugged. "What would yer call it, brother? Yer didn't take me with yer."

"I couldn't find yer. I tried. I tried to find yer."

"Did yer? Dublin ain't that big, is it, brother?"

"I looked for yer."

"Don't yer know what happened to me? Didn't yer wonder?"

"Every day." Finn still couldn't believe his eyes. Was this some kind of trick? He couldn't make sense of it. Tadhg simply looked down at him, unhurried and calm.

"And what did yer wonder every day then?"

Finn's breath came in short sharp bursts as he tried to keep up. "Everything. I wondered everything. How can yer not believe that? Yer were my brother. Yer are. I looked everywhere."

"Ah. Not everywhere, though. Not everywhere." Tadhg waggled his finger.

Finn held his hands out. He was begging. Pleading. Yet no words came. Was this really happening? The blood in his head rushed so fast, spinning and surging with his breath, his heart racing. Tadhg's eyes drank him in, pinning him down as if seeing right through him. What could he possibly say?

"They let me watch yer," Tadhg said finally. His voice was quiet and thoughtful, as if in each breath, he too tumbled back in time.

"Who did?"

"The ones what took me." Tadhg looked away. Finn saw the flicker of hurt underneath. "Every evening they let me watch yer."

Finn shook his head in disbelief. "Why didn't yer call out? I was out looking for yer. Didn't yer see me looking for yer?"

Tadhg paused, the sharpness in his gaze cutting Finn deep. "They only needed me for one job. That's what they said, anyway, because I was small, see. I could fit where they couldn't. Just one job and I could go. And then one evening they took me to the docks, and I stood on the tallest building and I watched yer boarding that ship. I seen yer sail away from here and never look back."

Finn took in his brother's expression, almost masterfully composed, giving away little. "Why didn't yer stop me, Tadhg? Why?"

Tadhg's eyes were cold.

Finn dropped his head to the floor, overcome by it all. "I thought yer were lost to me. I couldn't bear it. I couldn't bear being in this city without yer. Tadhg. That's the truth."

Tadhg just raised his eyebrows, holding up his drink. "Slainté, my brother."

"I can't believe it. I can't believe I've found yer."

"Yer didn't find me. We found yer, brother." Tadhg stood up. "And when we're done with yer, we'll kill yer."

essie's heart beat so fast she thought it might explode. If she told Aileen the Angel was here in Dublin, she risked her abandoning the plan to save Finn. She couldn't afford that. No. She would keep it to herself, even if with every movement in the periphery, or creak of the floorboards, she expected the Angel's men to attack. Saving Finn was the first and only thing she could do right now. She had to save him first.

Racing into the empty kitchen, she dumped her sack on the table and looked around. "Madochée? Mickey?" She'd hoped they'd returned in her absence, but her heart quickly sunk as the silence rolled back at her. "Sam? Anyone here?"

Siobhan's head poked over the railing. "I'm here."

"Are yer not resting?"

"I can't." Siobhan thumped heavily down the staircase. "Tonight keeps replaying in my head and I can't stop the racing in my chest. Not while Sam is still out there."

Tessie knew exactly how she felt — her nerves still fluttering and fighting to keep the worst of her thoughts at bay. "Yer can help me bake if yer like."

Siobhan settled at the table and picked at her nails, half watching, half returning to her thoughts. Tessie moved into a well-practised routine, her mind whirring as her hands moved over the ingredients and arranged the cake tins. As she madly whisked the batter, images of Finn being hurt and of Madochée lost in the dark city outside clouded her thoughts. Her chest ached. She had let that little girl down. Madochée had warned her about Mickey and if only she'd listened enough to make another plan or to reassure her. Madochée had spent many more nights alone in big cities than in safe confinement, but she prayed her street-smarts would guide her well, wherever she might be.

Tessie poured them both a glass of whiskey, needing its warmth and its distraction. She slid one over to Siobhan, who took it without response, then drank it down, aloof and solemn.

"Yer and Sam," Tessie started. "How long have yer two...?"

Siobhan gave a wry smile. "Been together? I don't know if we are together. Quite." She shrugged as if it didn't matter.

"Yer care for him. And he for yer."

"Does he? It's always me. He's never even..." Siobhan flashed her eyes. "Yer know."

"Well." Tessie smiled. "Not all men are so...forward."

"Every man I been about sure is and Susie Mira tried to get him to... well...I punched her in the nose—" Siobhan cut herself off as if remembering who she was talking to. "But I think he don't...because...yer know...because of...because of...what I am."

Tessie saw the earnestness in Siobhan and felt a wave of warmth for her. "He knows who yer are and he cares for yer. I can see that."

Siobhan abruptly stood as if the depth of the conversation was all too much. "If the Angel don't kill us all, maybe we can go to Boston with yer." Siobhan seemed to speak the words by accident. She immediately bit down on her tongue and quickly filled her glass.

"Would yer really like to?"

"Where there is no Eamon? No Angel? None of this? Aye. And I wouldn't have to feel sick with fear every time Sam left the house. We've spoke of it once or twice."

Tessie wondered at the irony that Siobhan could understand that which yet eluded her mother.

The table around her lay covered in cake tins waiting for the beaten batter. Her adrenaline urgent with every whisk and scoop and grease of the pan, she finally stood back and surveyed the mess. Flour dust and the scent of ginger hung in the air. There was nothing left to do but add the poison.

The back door opened and Aileen and Sam moved into the light, dusting the light rain from their shoulders.

"Did yer get it?" Tessie asked.

"Aye." Sam reached into his pocket, retrieving a small blue glass bottle.

"What is it?"

"Something what'll do the trick." Aileen took off her cloak and surveyed the mess filling the kitchen. "Jaysus, girl. Yer've made enough for an army."

"That's what we need, isn't it?" She took the bottle from Sam and held the innocent-looking vessel in her hand. "How much do I need?"

Aileen seemed to have an inaudible conversation with Sam before she stepped forward and snatched the bottle back from Tessie.

"What is it?" Tessie repeated.

Again Aileen didn't answer. Instead, she moved to the mixing bowl and pulled the stopper out of the bottle. She drained it clean into the thick brown batter.

"There yer go. It's done."

Tessie leaned in close to inspect the foreign liquid. "It has no smell."

"No taste neither."

"And it'll make them ill enough for us to go in and get Finn?"

"It'll do that alright. Now do what yer need to do. We head out at dawn."

"No sign of Mado?" Tessie looked hopefully towards Sam.

He shook his head and lowered his eyes as Siobhan wrapped herself about his arm like a sleepy pet. He patted her hand.

"I searched the dock and along the river. But if someone took Mickey, and she's followed them, there's no telling where she'd end up."

"She knows where we are. She'll come back to us when she's good and ready." Aileen spoke it as fact as she ascended the stairs. "Now finish up. Get some rest if yer can."

Sam looked around at the kitchen. "Do yer need any help?" he asked Tessie.

"No. Yer two go along. I'll be right up."

She watched as Sam and Siobhan left together but didn't allow herself time to linger further. She quickly lashed at the batter with her spoon, stirring in the clear liquid until the batter looked innocent again. Spooning the contents into each tin, she lined them up as she had done so many times before, ready to slide over the stove at first light.

She imagined the faces of all the men who would devour the cakes — the perfect comforting breakfast after a night of defeat and drunken consolation. Irresistible.

And then she would get Finn back.

CHAPTER 27

The men were mostly a sleepy lot. Only the leftovers simmered by the fire, lost in the endless bleak hours before dawn. Finn's arms and legs were still bound in front of him. A rope joined his wrist bindings to his feet, though he could still move more comfortable than before. He forced himself to focus on trying to escape, but he could scarcely stop himself looking for Tadhg. He wanted to get back to Tessie, but he felt anchored to that room. Memories of his brother rose from all corners and the shame of it stung his skin. He relived getting on that boat all those years ago and wished he'd somehow known to lift his eyes to the very spot where Tadhg had watched. How could he ever make up for such a thing?

He wanted so badly to speak to his brother, a cry in his chest burning all the words that might express everything he had felt for all those years. But Tadhg was now a man, hardened with life. He was all broad shoulders and rough hands, and far from the wiry frame he had as a boy. Finn wanted to read his eyes again, for him to spill all the secrets of those ten lost years so he could finally know exactly how he'd lost him. Who had taken him and put him to work and parted them forever? But the blame in Tadhg's words stung deep. Perhaps there was nothing he could ever say to repair the damage done. And he had to get back to Tessie. He had to make his break for it.

Across the room, Tadhg perched on a stool by the fire. Now and then his brown eyes darted in Finn's direction. There was a hall entrance to the right which Finn assumed held the stairs, and windows lined the room to either side of him, with the large front door furthest away. His best chance was a window, though how to do that quietly he had no inkling. If only he'd had his head about him while the men were still rowdy and distracted. With his hands bound, it was going to be nearly impossible to create a distraction of his own, at least one that was big enough to allow him to cross the room and somehow scramble through a window. It seemed useless, but he had to try. Tadhg had said they would kill him, and Finn had to believe him.

He made up his mind to move at the next burst of laughter from the opposite corner where Tadhg sat with his men. One of them was in the midst of a story only they could understand, and he listened intently. His joints ached from being wrenched in all positions, but he had to find the will to push through the agony and pull at least one arm free. A roar of laughter hit and, gritting his teeth, Finn yanked his right wrist against the ropes. Biting down a scream, he felt it pull loose, hot and bloody as the laughter too died down. His left wrist was still bound to his feet, but loose enough that he could stand and hunch over. That had to be enough. With one arm free he could push the window up and try to make his way over. He just needed to time it right.

It was a long story they were telling, often interrupted by a drunken comment or a side story by someone else. Finn crouched at the ready, keeping his head low so they may think him still asleep in the shadows. Then there was a clatter as someone threw a bottle at the fire. A small scuffle broke out. This chance was as good as any — Finn heaved himself to his feet, though his ropes only released him to a low crouch. Adrenaline surged through him as he hurried to the window. Hurry. Go!

His eyes fixed on the windowpane; he fell against it with a thud, urging his hands high enough to push it upward. It didn't budge. It wouldn't open at all. Finn's heart raged in panic and he thought to head-butt the glass and smash his way out. He had to get out! As he struggled to raise himself high enough, a stranger's hands were quick about his neck dragging him back in a stranglehold.

"Trying to leave me again, my brother?" It was Tadhg, his forearm strong against Finn's throat. "So quick to part us again, are yer?"

He dropped Finn to the ground where he gasped for breath, rolling onto his back. If it had been any other man, he might have fought back, tried to kick his legs out from beneath him and used his ropes to choke him. But it was Tadhg, and he could only look up at him.

"Let me go."

"Why? I'm broken-hearted already." He gave a quick wink and gestured to his men to pick him up. "Put him back over there. And tie the loose rope to his chair so he'll have to take it with him if he tries that again."

"Let me go!" Finn demanded. "I have somewhere to be. Hate me if yer like. Yer have every right to, but let me go back to her."

Tadhg ignored him, and Finn let himself to be dragged back to his place in the corner.

"I need to speak with yer," Finn called out to him.

"No, yer don't."

"I thought yer fell in in the river." Finn's words caught in his dry throat. "I thought yer fell in the canal. I turned around and yer were gone. Just gone. That's it. The only thing that made sense was that yer toppled in just trying to keep up with me."

Tadhg's jaw clenched as he considered the possibility. "It wasn't the canal that took me, brother." He turned away.

Finn calmed his breathing, heavy and aching in his chest. He gazed through the window at the budding morning. What would happen to them now?

CHAPTER 28

In the early hours, Tessie crawled into the bed, cold on both sides, and stared up at the mildew-spotted ceiling. Her heart had not stopped thudding since the fight at the docks. The Angel was here in this place already sticky with strife and chaos. She could feel its mess seeping into her clothes, her skin and bones beneath. If she let it, this city would get a hold on her so tight she'd never be free - its madness so engrained that one day she would barely notice it. It would just be there. This was not the fight she'd envisioned. Not the battle she'd wished to engage. And yet here she was, in the midst of a Dublin power struggle, with the Black Bonnet and Eamon Paddy Mac, and the Angel underpinning all of it.

When Aileen hammered on the door in the early hours, Tessie was sure her eyes were already open, staring endlessly at a particular constellation of black mottled mildew near the window.

"Time to go," Aileen called.

Tessie rolled, fully clothed off the bed and stood up.

Moving to the kitchen, she waited for Sam to finish with the pail of water and splashed her face. She let her auburn hair hang into the pail as the cold water flooded her eyes and ran down her neck. What was Finn doing at this very moment? Was he asleep? A blissful moment of ignorance at what had happened the night before? Perhaps they had let him be, had thrown him in a room to get on with their drinking. Perhaps he was dead already....and the thought hardened in her like a sinking stone.

Aileen waited at the kitchen door, pulling it open to let the earliest grey morning light hit the floor and a gust of icy air fill the room. She had changed her dress, her hair newly twisted up into a bun on her head, her hatchet nestled at her side where it so often stayed. She was crusty and tired too, and she meant business.

She cleared her throat, stepping forward to gather one of the four baskets Tessie had prepared. "Sunup won't be but an hour away. We have to move fast."

Tessie, speechless, nodded, and twisting her own messy hair into a knot, she followed her mother into the early morning cold. Sam, a silent shadow behind them, brought up the rear. His thick hair disappeared into the bleak darkness around them.

As they made their way north, they didn't speak, moving into a sombre line with Aileen leading the way.

"They smell good," Aileen offered as the aroma rose on the breeze.

"They're supposed to."

The landscape opened up as the cemetery that housed Faye appeared ahead of them. Tessie looked across at the alley where her encounter with Eamon Paddy Mac's men took place. The light was still low, though as they walked by the rows of houses they could hear movement and the quiet shuffling of people starting their day.

Quickening their pace, the group came to the large hall and theirs would be the first gift of the day. Her heart thudding, Tessie passed the baskets to Sam, who rushed forward and placed them squarely at the entrance. Whoever opened the door would have to step over them, or pick them up and take them inside.

Returning to their position at the corner, Sam readied to leave. "We'll be gathered behind the warehouse and ready to go when the time is right."

Tessie watched Sam disappear into the shadows as she turned to the cemetery behind them. From there she and Aileen would watch and wait for the taking of their bait.

They ambled up the grass, damp and slippery with early morning frost, towards the only oak tree in the field. A single headstone caught her eye. Aileen had no need to point it out. It was as if Faye's grave had been selected entirely for this one moment. It was still clean and shiny from a soft mist of rain, and the air grew heavy in Tessie's chest. Her letters were just good enough to make out Faye's name, though the small inscription was beyond her. She swallowed hard, pressing her palm to the cold stone. This was not the way she'd imagined standing before her fallen friend, not now, in this moment, with the chaos below them about to unfold.

"Here I am," was all she could speak before her words faded into the weight of grief uncurling in her chest. It was not the time, but it couldn't be helped.

Aileen watched, keeping a step back, her hands clasped in front of her and never quite letting her eyes rest on Faye's name. "She can't hear yer."

"Yer don't believe that."

"She's dead. Yer can't hear things when yer dead."

"Yer needn't be so cruel."

"I know what's real. Death is real. I'm sorry if that's cruel." She turned to sit behind a short bushy hedge as they faced

Eamon's hall, watching and waiting, as all of Dublin around them slowly surfaced from the foggy night.

Tessie squinted through the clearing mist to the hall's rooftop as the buildings emerged clear and dark in front of them. She imagined her mother's younger self menacing those streets, carving out a place for herself between the dark alleys and shadows, against anyone who crawled out of them.

Her mother's dark green dress blended with the damp grass around her. She was as much a part of the landscape as the vines weaving their way through the gravestones. Tessie imagined the vines themselves springing up and binding her mother to the earth. This was Aileen's home — this mess sprawled out in front of them. Her mother's chaos.

The understanding tumbled through Tessie like a low wave, deflated and yet somehow calming. If she was finding it hard enough to disentangle from this place, and all its tendrils of hopelessness and raw despair, how unfathomable it must be for Aileen, the idea of tearing herself away, like a stitch of fabric. Who was she if she wasn't the Black Bonnet? What was she without Dublin? What was Dublin without her? They were etched from the same earth. The same struggle. She wore that struggle on the back of her hands, the wrinkles around her eyes and scars on her skin, just as it was on the well-worn cobblestones and crumbling corners on the buildings. Asking her to leave this city was like asking her to stop breathing.

But the Angel was coming. Nothing could change that now.

"What happened between yer?" Tessie spoke into the quiet. "Between yer and Arthur? The Angel?"

Aileen looked at Tessie, her eyes fierce, then back at the hall door in front of them. "Same thing that always happens between a man and a woman. They try to take more than their share. More than what's owed to them."

"He betrayed yer?"

Aileen's mouth curled into a wry smile. "That's what I said. Take that as yer lesson. I should have done him like any other and come in high and fast to wipe that bleedin' smirk off his face. Would have saved us decades of trouble. All for a moment of weakness. That's what it'll get yer."

"What if yer went to him?" It was a challenge and Tessie watched Aileen's eyes dart back and forth.

"And do what?"

"Talk. Negotiate. Compromise."

"Next time I lay eyes on him it'll be to lay him open. Won't need much talking for that."

Tessie felt the breath catch in her chest. She swallowed, trying to gage the moment. It was still a risk. "He's here. He's here in Dublin."

"Here?" Aileen stood up as if to fight then and there, but ducked down again.

"Aye. Kyran came to warn me and..."

"Curse it to all hell." Aileen spat, hitting her boot. "Think's he's here to finish it, does he?" Her tone was sharp with accusation; the mother-daughter moment between them vanished in the fog. "He's here to damn well finish it." Aileen's eyes shifted, the calculations going on in her mind almost audible.

"Maybe not," Tessie uttered, but Aileen's eyes were glazed over in thought. "Maybe we can make a deal."

"Make a deal." Aileen spat the words out. "What he wants is a bleedin' slaughter in the streets and—" Aileen stopped mid-sentence. "Get down."

Tessie hunched forward on her knees in the damp grass. Sure enough, there was movement at the hall door. A figure appeared, staring down at the overflowing baskets of ginger cake. After leaning down and taking a quick look at their contents, he took the baskets inside and closed the door.

Aileen looked at Tessie, her eyes narrowed. "Get ready."

CHAPTER 29

Finn watched the new dawn breaking through the window. Men moved around in the rooms above him as they rose from sleep, coughing and spluttering from the night of revelry, spitting from the windows and into makeshift spittoons. One man opened the front door to hack up into the gutter, launching it over some baskets that sat side by side in front of the door before bringing them inside.

"Breakfast has been delivered," he called out to the room.

He grabbed what looked like small lumps of bready cake and shoved them into his mouth, leaving the baskets on the table where Tadhg and his friends had congregated.

Finn watched from the corner, still surrounded by the food scraps from last night, as the men took a share of cake from the baskets and returned to their seats. It didn't take long for the aroma to reach him. He recognised the warm spicy scent of that cake and it stirred an ache in his heart. It was so similar to the cakes Tessie had made — that scent had greeted him every morning in the Old Nichol as he roused from his warm bed.

Tessie would be mad with worry about him now,

probably wracking her brain with what to do to get him back and wondering if he had even lasted the night. He wished he could reassure her or somehow or get a sign to her that he was here.

As the crowd grew more fully awake, the low hum of morning conversation filled the hall. Each man ate his fill. Finn urged his senses to stay alert, though he was so incredibly weary. As he frowned into the crowd, searching for inspiration or hope of any kind, a shadow fell over him. He looked up. It was Tadhg. He crouched beside him with two pieces of cake, holding one out to Finn.

"Take it."

Finn couldn't bear it. The smell itself was enough to make him homesick. He just wanted to get back to her.

"Don't give him any!" An irritated voice called from the back of the hall.

"Sod off, Sully."

Finn looked at the cake in the palm of his hand, his throat so dry he wasn't sure he could even swallow it. "Are yer really going to let them kill me?"

"Give me a reason to stop them."

"Yer are my brother. Is that not reason enough?"

Tadhg stood and bit into his cake, dusting his hands and shrugging his shoulders.

"For God's sake, man." Finn railed against his ropes, as a man started coughing beside him. It escalated into violent retching and the surrounding men slapped him on the back. He lurched over the table and hurled the contents of his stomach into the bowl closest to him. Gripping him under the arms, the other men ushered him outside to the gutter, teasing him and cursing the smell.

Then another in the opposite corner also vomited. First with a slow gurgling sound that drained the colour from his face, though it quickly descended into a loud retching sound as he too grabbed the closest bowl.

"What is going on?" Tadhg rose to his feet and surveyed the room, searching for an explanation. Other men too clutched their stomachs, their eyes widening with horrified nausea.

Tadhg spat his cake to the floor. "It's the cake. It's the bleedin' cake!" He hocked it up from the back of his throat, bending over and trying to spit out as much as he could. Finn looked at the untouched piece of cake in his hand and sniffed it.

Quickly the room descended into a wave of moans and languid bodies draped over the tables, some vomiting, some half comatose, their faces a yellow shadow of sickly pale. Finn's chest thudded. Whatever was happening, now was his chance! Now! If he could get free he could walk out of the room and none of them would be able to stop him.

He wrestled with the ropes at his wrist, burning against his skin; he yanked as hard as he could, but they had secured them tighter this time. A hand gripped him by the back of the neck and forced him to the ground on his knees. It was Tadhg, his face clammy and his eyes bloodshot, but determined to hold him none the less.

"Let me go and I'll try to help yer." Finn tried to shake him off as Tadhg's fingers dug deeper into Finn's shoulder, but Finn saw the strength waning in his eyes. Sweet Christ. What was happening? Was his brother dying before his eyes?

adochée followed close as Mickey's companions led him from the building and into the early-morning hustle of the harbour. She'd crouched all night in the cold and her legs were numb and her throat dry. Her head had bobbed forward with sleep more than once, and now her eyes were sticky and heavy with exhaustion. It didn't matter - she wouldn't lose sight of him. "I will get you, mister Mick. I'm here."

Squeezed now between two large crates, hidden from view amongst the busying boarding docks, she could still see Mickey's bound hands behind his back and his coat draped across his shoulders. They'd reduced him to a prisoner, and none of the people hustling by paid him any attention. She didn't need them to. It was only a matter of time before the bad men moved him to the ship. She knew how to be invisible, and sneaking onto ships was something she had done plenty of before. She would wait for her moment.

MICKEY'S MIND was dizzy with exhaustion, his eyes blurry with the glare from the grey clouds bearing down above him. He had no idea how to get out of this. His pleas to Brec had been unheard, and no doubt Eamon would be back any moment to unleash whatever sick plan he had for him on the boat. Had Eamon paid off the crew to murder him once they embarked? Was he to be bound or drowned or suffocated or stabbed? Whatever it was, he should be fighting his way clear of it now. If they got him on the ship, it would be all the harder to get free. He felt the strain well up inside, bracing for the right moment. He could hardly breathe. He wasn't leaving Dublin this way. He wasn't leaving Connor.

Scanning the crowd, both Brec and Rafferty were looking for Eamon. Mickey let himself drift to the background, hoping to lull them into a sense of security that he had given up the fight. But he had no intention of going easy. He had no intention of going at all. There was a clatter as a large crate fell from a wagon and smashed on the ground beside them. Mickey took his chance.

Leaping to his feet and throwing off the coat around his shoulders, he bolted. It was nearly impossible to run with his arms tied at his back, but he kept his head low and tried to find the rhythm in his stride. Run. Run! He urged himself on though his legs were clumsy from inaction and heavy with adrenaline. He barely had time to check behind him when he felt Rafferty's large hand grip the back of his neck and bear down.

Toppling to the ground with no arms to break his fall, Mickey's face grated across the ground, the weight of Rafferty's large frame falling hard against his back. "Let me go, brother. Let me go!"

His struggling made no difference. Rafferty was too big, too strong.

"Can't do that, Mick." He yanked Mickey to his feet as Brec caught up to them.

"He's going to kill me, Brec. Yer know it and yer handing me over to him. Yer don't want to do this."

Brec shook his head and Mickey could see the torment and regret. "If I let yer go, it's my neck on the chopping block. And Nance. I can't do it to her. Not for yer. Or anyone. I'm sorry, Mickey. I am."

"Sorry for what?"

It was Eamon, and Brec's eyes lowered as he stepped aside. But Eamon wasn't waiting for an answer. He was only interested in Mickey.

"It's time, brother."

Gripping the front of Mickey's shirt with both his fists, he thrust him forward. Mickey pushed back against the hands in his back, but couldn't fight the momentum.

The ship in front of him grew in size as they rounded the gangplank.

"Up. Go," Eamon urged, the glee evident in his voice. Onboard, he steered Mickey below, going deeper into the belly of the ship. A few workers stood aside as others watched on. One stepped forward.

"Where?" Eamon barked at him, and Mickey understood they'd made some arrangement.

"In there." The man nodded at the door in front of them, and Eamon thrust Mickey through into a room stacked with barrels. "Where's the cash?"

"Where is it first?"

"Right there. In the corner," the man added, not without a hint of attitude.

Eamon swung Mickey around to see one empty barrel pushed to the side.

"That was hard work, that was. It takes time to scoop corn from a barrel into a sack."

"Well that's what the cash is for," Eamon quipped, digging in his pocket.

He thrust a handful of coins at the man who silently checked it and left the room. Rafferty closed the door behind him, and Mickey felt his fate looming fast.

"Get in." Eamon pushed him towards the barrel.

"What?"

"Get in the bleedin' barrel," Eamon hollered. He had lost his sense of humour and sounded impatient.

Mickey stared at the empty barrel but didn't move. Eamon nodded at Rafferty who thumped his big paws onto Mickey's shoulders and lifted him into the small space with barely a strain. Mickey's legs collapsed beneath him, his knees knocking against the sides; he folded into it, and Rafferty pushed down on him so he curled beneath its rim.

Mickey felt the air rushing out of him. He could see what was coming. It was closing in on him. What could he do? How could he fight this? Eamon couldn't win. He couldn't win.

"Don't look so terror-stricken," Eamon said, calm again. He licked his lips as if savouring the flavour of the moment. "This ship is bound for America. You'll arrive in yer beloved Boston in no time. Even if yer don't know it."

"Yer piece of filth. Yer scum."

"We'll look after yer boy, Mick. He's my nephew. My blood. He'll be just fine." And then he turned to Rafferty. "Fill it."

Mickey squirmed his shoulders back and forth as Brec stepped forward to hold him down but didn't look at him. Rafferty lifted the sack of corn onto his hip and started pouring into the barrel over Mickey's head.

"No!" Mickey shouted as the corn filled past his waist, to his shoulders and chest. Rafferty kept pouring, and with his other hand tilted Mickey's head to the side.

Terror rushed through Mickey, his breath surging into short, sharp heaves of panic.

"No!"

He puckered his mouth closed as the surface of corn rose past his chin, clenching his eyes, the hand pressed down hard on his head. He screamed with his mouth closed; the noise muffled in his ears as the barrel shifted. All he could hear was the pounding of the lid being hammered into place.

Then there was no sound. No light. No air. No anything.

It was Sam who flung open the hall door and Tessie watched as he and his men disappeared into the darkness inside. Plucking the knife from her boot, she followed as hollering, grunting and cursing emerged from within the building. Gritting her teeth, she braced herself for the scene inside.

Her eyes adjusted quickly to the dim light, squinting through the clusters of men, who were sure enough hunched over in distress and rancour. Some rallied to fight as Aileen's men circled the room. Tessie's eyes frantically scanned each face, searching only for Finn.

There, behind the chaos of men sprawled on the floor and lurching on the tables, Finn's tall frame crouched in the corner. She ran towards him, falling to her knees and scrambling to pull the last of the ropes from his ankles.

"My God!" Tessie pulled his bruised body towards her and held him close.

"I'm here, mo chara." His voice was raspy in her ear, but he was alive.

"Can yer walk? Can yer stand?"

"If yer help me up. Come on."

She buried herself briefly in his chest, running her hands over the cuts and bruises before the tussling bodies around them drew their attention. "We need to get out of here." Tessie focussed on helping him up as he staggered to his feet and leaned heavily on the wall.

"What's in the cake? What is it?"

"We poisoned it. To weaken them. There were too many otherwise."

"Poisoned?" He suddenly pulled away from her and lunged towards a body on the ground.

"What is it? What's wrong?"

"We have to get him out of here. We need to get him help."

"We can't!"

"This is Tadhg. This is my brother. He's my brother."

"What?" Tessie couldn't understand. "How can it be Tadhg?"

"It is! And he's dying. He ate it. He ate it."

Tessie heard the panic in his voice. "Oh, my God. No. He'll be alright, Finn. It'll just make him ill."

"They're not sick, Tess. Look around yer. They are dying."

Tessie didn't understand the tone in his voice and urgently looked around the room.

"Dying?" She frowned at the sea of waning men. Were they really? She leaned down to another man at her feet. She touched his forehead and looked into his face, his eyes vacant and his chest still. Her heart jolted. Had she put in too much? Was it more potent than they'd thought? What had Aileen given her?

"We have to get him out of here!" Finn struggled to drag Tadhg towards the front door.

"Put me down, damn yer." The man in Finn's arms struggled, but Finn ignored him.

"Eamon will be back with the others soon," Finn said to

Tessie. "And I have to get him help."

"Of course." The breath caught in Tessie's chest. "Wait. Eamon isn't here?"

"No. He left early this morning. They'll all be coming back. We need to hurry."

Tessie scanned the room, and it was true, this was not all of his men. "My God. Take him. Take him. Go!" She ushered Sam over to grab Tadhg's feet and urged them to the door. "Go. We'll be right behind yer."

Tessie saw her mother across the room, hatchet in hand as one of her men stabbed his knife into the body of a barely conscious man. They were slaughtering them. She felt the colour drain from her face and a surge of rage.

"No!" Tessie ran towards her. "This wasn't the plan. They are dying!"

Aileen rushed with the movement of her men through the room, finishing the job and spilling blood across the floor. The scene hit Tessie in the pit of her stomach and ruptured her with shame. Had this been Aileen's plan all along? Was this what she wanted?

"I said, make them sick. Not kill them!"

"What's the fucking difference? Take them all out now."

"What if Finn had eaten it? Did yer think of that? This isn't right to kill them like this. Not like this. Look at them!" Tessie held her hands to her head thinking of what might have happened if Finn had eaten the cake. Aileen shrugged off her protest.

"What did yer think would happen? Christ, girl. Yer said yerself the Angel is here. We don't have time to waste."

"Yer lied to me!"

Aileen shook her head in disgust. "Yer want to save this scum so they can come back for more next time? Move out the way, girl."

Tessie looked down at the men who were her enemies.

Men she had wished ill upon. Men she had rage in her heart for and had imagined running through with blades and knives and hatchets. Now they lay helpless as babies, powerless and fragile as Aileen plucked them off one by one.

"This isn't right," Tessie protested, though she knew it was weak coming from her now. It was wrong to kill them this way. It was not the right way to do it.

"Are yer out of yer mind, girl? Yer think they would think twice before running yer through in yer sleep. Get Finn and get out of here if yer can't stomach the reality. Leave this to the grown-ups."

Tessie looked at her mother's face, focussed and rigid. Her chest raged with anger. Just an hour ago she'd felt some semblance of understanding. But this, she would never understand this. "I can't make yer change. I can't make yer want something different from this."

It was chaos as heat swirled in Tessie's head. She'd been a party to killing these men. Would she have protested if she had known? Would she have knowingly killed them to get Finn back? She couldn't face the question right now. Eamon and the rest of his men were on the way back.

"We have to go!" she screamed back at Aileen, urging the other men back out onto the street.

"We're almost through." Aileen raised her head, sweaty, her face flushed.

Tessie looked around at the bodies that lay strewn in vomit, sweaty and pallid, now mixed with the draining blood. Panic stung her veins. "Eamon will be back with the others!"

Aileen heard the words and stood up on the table to survey the chaos. Not all of them were there. Tessie looked back to see Finn and Sam carrying Tadhg. They had made it clear and, glancing one last time at Aileen, she pushed through the door and ran after them.

$\mathcal{M}$adochée waited until all she could hear was her breath. She'd slipped aboard the ship like a shadow. Workers still loading cargo marched back and forth with crates below her, but she was not concerned. Even if they passed her hiding place, they would not even see her.

When the way was clear, she reached her small hand to the door handle and turned it. Slipping inside, she saw a multitude of barrels stacked from floor to ceiling. And no Mickey.

"Mickey?" she called to the quiet room.

Nothing. But she had not seen him come out! Scanning the dark edges of the barrels, she searched for any sign of him. Was there a pathway through them? Was there a secret door? She'd seen one of those before and started pressing on the panels. Nothing popped out and no door revealed itself.

Taking down the gas lantern by the door, she held it up to the dark crevices between the barrels and saw nothing suspicious and no trace of Mickey. On the floor was an empty sack, and she placed the lantern on top of the closest barrel to crouch and inspect it. It was nothing but an average hessian sack with some stray bits of corn. But as she tilted her head to look, the lantern's flame caught her eye. It flickered in a jerking motion as if the surface beneath it shook. Peering closer, she pressed her hands to the barrel's sides and held her ear against its timber. The barrel was rumbling.

Pressing her ear even harder against it, she heard it. A low muffled moan, drowned out and fading.

"Mister Mick!" she cried louder than she should have and knocked frantically on the outside. He was in there! There he was! He was there, inside the barrel!

Quickly, she moved the lantern to the floor and gripped the barrel's side. It was far too heavy for her small frame to move. She pushed at its lid with all her might, but it would not budge.

"I will get you out, mister. Out. I will!"

She turned, looking around the room and spotted a mallet left on the ground. She picked it up and struggling to lift it above her head, she brought it down hard on the wooden seal. It bounced off the rim with such force that she dropped it.

She couldn't give up! Climbing on top of the barrel, she inspected it from all angles, jumping heavily on the lid in utter frustration. How? How could she get it to move? She was running out of time!

Leaping down again, Madochée gripped her fingers around the rim of the seal, pulling back hard with all her strength, her fingers chaffing and straining as her knuckles shook. It rocked only slightly. She barely grabbed a hold of the rim before her fingers slid out of place, scraping them raw at the tips and breaking two fingernails. She wasn't strong enough. She wasn't heavy enough.

"Mickey! Mister Mickey! I am here!"

Crouching on her haunches and huffing deep breaths, she

inspected the nemesis of a barrel before her. How could she get in? Panic scraped at her throat. Her eyes stung. Mickey was going to die. He was in there, and he would die if she couldn't open it. And she couldn't.

Standing again, she took a deep breath. No. She would save him. She had to. She pressed her back hard against the wall. She lifted her feet to the barrel, pressing firmly so she could walk her weight to the top edge. She had to budge it. She pressed the small of her back into the wall where it stabbed and bruised her spine, but she pressed her thighs and gritted her teeth, crying out in strain.

The barrel started to tip. Her weight shifted to the very top of the barrel. She awkwardly swivelled around so she faced the floor and braced down with her arms. She squared her legs so she was completely horizontal pressing against the rim of the barrel. She had to find the sweet spot. The right angle to position her weight and leverage her strength. She walked her body higher up the wall and locked her boots into the rim and pushed — she bit down to stop herself screaming out.

The barrel went over in a sudden burst. It gave way quickly, and she crashed to the ground as it tipped away from her.

Landing on her belly, she scrambled to her feet. It still had not opened. Again grabbing the mallet, she swung it hard against the seal. And again.

"Open!" she commanded. "Stupid barrel open!"

It bounced off, but the edge was moving and loosening with each blow. Was it wide enough to wedge the handle in? Grappling with the handle, she jammed it into the small space and reeled back with all her might. With a thud, the lid burst open, and corn spilt over the floor.

Mickey's straining face appeared. He stumbled out on his knees, coughing and spluttering in the spilt corn. His face was blue and red as he gasped for air. Madochée pushed the barrel away and dusted the corn from his back. He was still alive!

"Alright? Alright? Mister?" She patted his head as he flopped over on his back. His eyes closed and for a moment she thought he was still dying, his breath heaving in slow and steady. His hands grabbed at his neck and chest, as she crouched beside him and waited for him to speak. "Don't die, mister. Don't die now."

"Yer saved me, girl. Yer saved me, Mado."

"I follow. I stayed. I know where you went to."

Mickey tried to sit up and reached his hand out to pat her on the shoulder. "Bless yer, cailín. Bless yer." He hung his head and rubbed his eyes, still reeling, but there was no time to waste.

"Come," Madochée tried to pull him to his feet. "Up. Need to get up, mister."

The door flew open. Madochée and Mickey simultaneously recoiled, slipping in the corn now all over the floor. But it was not Eamon, only the man from before — Brec, all on his own. His eyes quickly scanned the room, blocking the doorway with his body.

"Where did yer come from?" he asked of Madochée.

"I follow all of you. To here. Follow you here."

"Thank God she did," Mickey said. "Yer held me in there, yer rotten rat."

"Yer know I had to, Mick. But I'm here now." He gestured for them to follow. "Hurry. It's not long before they leave."

"Eamon has left?" Mickey asked, straining his throat as if parched.

Brec nodded. "Aye. Come now. If yer are going to get off, yer need to go now."

Madochée took Mickey's hand as he pulled himself to his feet, and they followed quickly after Brec.

The man in front of them moved slowly through the ship, checking each hallway was clear. He was going the wrong way. Madochée knew a better way and wondered if she should tell him, but she just followed. They passed many more men and corridors than on her way, but it wasn't long before they poked their heads back out into the daylight.

"Alright. Go, go." Brec urged them towards the gangplank and followed.

Madochée felt Mickey's hand on her shoulder as she expertly navigated the narrow plank — it was something she'd had learned to do quickly in the dark.

As the trio moved back to the safety of cover by the warehouses, Brec looked around them, still checking for prying eyes. "Now yer should go. Get back on a boat or anything. But don't let him see yer. There'll be no tricks or chances next time. He'll kill yer on sight, Mick. Yer have to know that."

"Thank yer." Mickey gripped his old friend's shoulder with sincerity and Madochée peered up at them. "But I told him I won't leave without Connor. And I meant it."

Brec nodded and patted Madochée on the head as he departed. "Be safe as yer may, then."

"And to yer, brother. And to yer."

MICKEY LED Madochée back through the city at a running pace. With her hand gripped in his, she struggled to keep up but he couldn't slow down.

"Stop, mister. I can't run anymore. Stop."

He could hear the panic in her voice and saw the faltering in her step. He tried to hold her weight up. Weaving below a bridge, Mickey finally paused in the shadow, sliding down the wall into a crouch and hunching over to catch his breath.

"I almost died in a fucking barrel of corn." He heaved. "I almost died in a barrel of corn."

Madochée too crouched down, but she peered out from under the bridge. "They did not follow us, mister. Did they Mickey?"

"No. Pieces of shite."

He spat angrily to the side of him and slid down the wall entirely, running his hands through his hair. Eamon thought he could just snuff him out as if he had never existed in his boy's life. The thought of Connor growing up with Eamon's voice and Eamon's stories in his ears made his stomach turn. Ciara would never have wanted him to have a hand in raising their child. He was spoiled to the core, twisted and rotten. Mickey had to take matters into his own hands — he could hear Ciara's voice scolding him for the mess he'd made of things. If he could have done it over, he would have sold the farm for whatever small price he could and taken Connor with him from the start. No gambling. No drink. No bowing down or cowering to the wishes of his in-laws. But now, after so many mistakes, he had to make things right. He had to fix it.

Mickey stood and started pacing, his heart still pounding from the run and his panic at what might come next. Clenching his fist, he peered back out from under the bridge. "Yer should go, Mado. Tell them I'm alright. Tell them I'm coming. Do yer know yer way back?"

Madochée shook her head. "I'm staying with you."

"No. I can't go back yet. I have to make things right."

"I help. I come too."

"It's dangerous, Mado. I can't have yer hurt or in trouble because of me." He wrapped his arm around her shoulder.

"I'll not hurt. No, mister. I help, mister. If they get you again I help. I must come."

Mickey looked down at her wide eyes staring back at

him. She was right. She had just snuck aboard a full-sized ship and single-handedly saved him from suffocation in a barrel of corn.

"Don't tell me to go. I will follow, mister. You go, I follow."

Mickey dropped his head. He knew that was true. She would follow him just as she had before. He didn't have time to take her back to the others. He had to act now.

"So. Where are we going?"

Mickey looked in the direction of the small terrace home south of the river. "We're going to get my boy."

CHAPTER 33

Finn carried his brother on his back. Tadhg's head sunk against the back of his neck, though he moaned in protest. "Get the door," Finn urged Sam as they approached Aileen's kitchen.

Tadhg's weight was slowly sliding down the back of Finn's legs. He couldn't hold him up much longer. Sam instead moved alongside him, offering to take his brother's weight, but Finn pushed him aside.

"Go!"

Sam ran ahead and opened the front door, rushing through to the lounge and pushing everything clear of the sofa. Finn stumbled behind him, lurching forward just in time to swing Tadhg's limp body onto the cushions.

"Where am I?" he mumbled.

"At the Bonnet."

"What? Like hell." Tadhg rolled over, struggling to kick his feet out to stand but couldn't.

"Stop it."

"Let me out of here."

"Yer need to rest, dammit. Lay back."

"Are yer kidding me? That bitch will run me through the moment I close my eyes just like she did the others."

"She won't. She won't touch yer. I won't let her."

Finn wiped Tadhg's brow and loosened his collar. Tadhg suddenly jerked forward and Finn grabbed a bucket beside him, placed to collect a water leak in the ceiling. Tadhg wretched hard, but nothing more than bile came out. He flung himself back against the sofa, exhausted.

"Damn yer. Damn all of yer."

"What does he need? Get him something!" Finn snapped at Sam.

Sam watched wide-eyed, holding out his arms. "There is nothing. It was arsenic, man. There's nothing."

"Get the doctor then. Get someone." Finn rushed to the kitchen. He ransacked the shelves for a cup, scooped it into the pail of water by the door and grabbed a stale oat cake. "He needs fluids in his stomach. Food. Something to throw up again. I don't know." In a rush, he ran back and slopped the water into Tadhg's mouth.

"We didn't know yer had a brother. We didn't know he was in there." It was a weak statement and Sam faded away.

"Yer knew I was in there! I almost ate it. Go. Find someone!" Finn couldn't look away from Tadhg's droopy frame, his arm draping onto the floor.

"There is no one to get," Sam said, his voice filled with regret. "That's why we used it. There's nothing to be done."

Finn knelt beside Tadhg, feeling as helpless now as he had for all these years past. His brother couldn't die, not now. Not now!

"Yer shouldn't have brought me here," Tadhg managed, his voice raspy as his eyes rolled back. "If I'm to die I want to be with my men, not here with her."

"If I'd have left yer there, Aileen might have sooner run yer through as yer lay there."

"And what's to stop her doing that when she sees me here, hey?"

Finn held up the water to his brother's lips. Tadhg struggled to take a small gulp.

"My men are back there. She's bloody slaughtered them! What's she doing to them?"

"Yer can't help them now."

"Damn all of yer." Tadhg's eyes rolled back in his head and Finn recognised his anguish brought by helplessness.

Behind him, Aileen burst back into the room, her breath heaving and her face flushed. She set down her hatchet on the table and guzzled messily from the pail of water. A gathering of her men pushed past her to the front room, slumping against the cupboards and walls.

Catching a glimpse of Tadhg, Aileen spat out her mouthful on the floor and rushed towards him with more gusto than Finn expected. He blocked her path.

"What the fuck is he doing here?" she cursed.

"He's with me."

"Get him out of my house now. Let him die in the street like the others before I crack his skull open."

"Fuck yer. I'll have yer throat for what yer have done..." Tadhg seethed back at her but didn't have the stamina to complete the attack.

"What *I've* done?" Aileen spat. "It's yer mate Eamon who's done all this and if yer'd had any sense yer would have run him through yerself and saved us all the damn trouble."

"He's my brother." Finn held his position.

"What?" Aileen met his challenge and stepped closer. "Yer have no idea who he is. He'll run us through in our bleedin' sleep. Don't be daft, boy. He's with them."

"I said he stays!" Finn turned to scan the room, looking for back-up. "Where is Tess? Where is she?"

Aileen wiped her brow with the back of her hand, still aggravated and waiting for Tessie to rouse.

"Where is she?" Finn asked when she didn't step forward.

"She's here."

"No, she ain't. She went back to warn yer Eamon's men weren't all there."

"And she did warn me. She gave me a damn earful and ran after yer."

Finn felt the blood drain from his face as he glared at Aileen. "She ain't here."

"Tess? Get out here, girl! Christ Almighty, get out here!"

No answer came, and only blank faces looked back at her.

"Damn all of yer!" Aileen tossed her hatchet across the floor and hunched over the table, her breath heaving. "If the Angel don't take me down himself, it'll be that bleedin' girl who does me in. What happened to her? Did yer see? Did any of yer all see her?" Aileen's men shook their heads and shuffled their feet. "Christ Al-fucking-mighty. Check the route." She turned to the men in the corner. "Go now, damn it. And look out for any hiding spots. If she got cornered, she might have gone to ground. Quick now. Don't come back without her. Go!"

"I'll go with them." Finn moved to run after them.

"Yer won't move. Yer won't do a damn thing." Genuine anguish drew beads of sweat on Aileen's brow and she turned away in disgust, beating her fist down on the table.

Finn was about to press her further when Tadhg lurched forward to vomit. Putrid foaming stomach bile gurgled from his throat and he spat into the bucket.

"God save us." Aileen leaned over him, jabbing her fist in his face. "If Eamon Paddy Mac has that girl, if he lays a finger on her, whatever arsenic is soaking in yer veins won't matter. I'll slit that throat of yours, yer hear me!"

Tadhg half-smiled through his weary gaze and

summoned his voice. "If he has her, yer only chance is to let me go."

Finn stepped forward to protest, but the reality of it sunk in. What would stop Eamon hurting Tess?

"It'll be the only thing to save her." Tadhg glanced back at Finn, satisfied.

Finn closed his eyes and let the truth of it settle on his shoulders.

"Get this bastard whatever he needs," she said to the room of men awaiting orders. Then turning to Finn: "But get him off that sofa before he damn well shits on it."

CHAPTER 34

*E*amon rushed Tessie through the hall door, thrusting her back into the sickening scene now spilling out into the street. The stench of sour vomit, sweat and excretion hit her in the face, and she flinched.

"Get a doctor here. Now."

Eamon's voice wavered, though he didn't lessen his grip. She could feel the frantic twitching in his arm as he pushed her forward. She dared to look back at him, taking him in for the very first time — his eyes were pools of unhinged madness. She felt their coldness as a shudder ran through her. What was he capable of? What was he going to do?

He forced Tessie to look at the unfolding chaos before her. It had all happened so quickly, Tessie could hardly believe the carnage herself. How had she been the author of this? Her mouth went dry and her chest turned to stone, though she felt the heat of Eamon's glare. Whether he knew it or not, she was responsible for all of this.

A body beside him flipped over onto his back, vomit smeared across his chin. Eamon turned away in repulsion.

"What is it? What's done this?" His voice took on a low

rumble as if he didn't want to breathe in the surrounding stench.

"It was the cake. We poisoned the cake." Tessie dared to look back at Eamon with whatever boldness she could summon. But she didn't feel bold now. She felt flat and empty to the pit of her stomach.

Eamon flashed his teeth as he gripped the back of her neck again. "Count them." He thrust her forward, bending her over the man at her feet and forcing her to look into his face.

"What?"

"Count them!"

Tessie took in the man's pained expression and told herself he was a bad man. He would have killed her! He was probably there when they hurt Finn overnight. But that didn't diminish the sickness and sympathy she felt. She turned to the man beside him and scanned the room towards the door.

"Nine. There are nine," she said. Her hands shook as she glanced around at the bodies.

"Nine! And there." Eamon pointed her to the ones still sick and moaning, sprawled and half comatose. "How many there?"

She whispered under her breath, getting the count. "Twelve."

"Twelve who might yet join this line! "What kind of sick whore murders men in such a way?"

"It wasn't meant to kill them." Her voice wavered as he came closer.

"What?"

"It were just to make them sick so we could get Finn. That was all."

Eamon struck Tessie across the face. "Who are yer?

Where have yer come from? Who are yer? Just a two-bit whore with...with...nothing!"

Tessie bit down, trying to summon a defence. She felt the gravity of those questions more than Eamon would ever know.

"Tadhg isn't here," a voice said behind them, interrupting Eamon's fury.

"What?" Eamon loosened his grip at the distraction.

"We've searched upstairs and in the alleys. But one of the boys saw Aileen's men dragging him away."

Eamon turned his attention back to Tessie, pushing his fingers into her collarbone. Her mind whirred with the man Finn had dragged out of here. His brother, he'd said. Tadhg. Dear God. Tessie could barely breathe.

"Perhaps he's hiding his face in shame. He let this happen on his watch. We don't need him." Eamon's nostrils flared and he licked his lips so fast she might have missed it.

"We have to find him, Mac."

"I said we don't need him."

The man behind him looked set to argue, but turned to his companions and gestured for them to follow him.

Eamon seemed oblivious, his eyes fixed solely on Tessie. "Does that bitch think she can scare me off? Does she think there is anything she can do to stop this? She won't stop me taking her place. She can't stop this. She won't stop me coming. And if she thinks I won't hit a woman..." He pulled the pistol from his hip. "She's wrong about that too."

CHAPTER 35

Finn waited until Aileen's footsteps faded before he rushed at the kitchen door. Two of her men stepped in to block his path.

"Yer heard what she said." One man shoved him back.

"I'm going after her." Finn pounded on the door, but the men pulled him back and tossed him across the kitchen.

"Get back, damn yer! Let them look for her. Just wait."

Wait? Finn gripped his hair in his fists. If Eamon had her, there was no telling what he could do before they got there.

"What'll he do?" he called across the room the Tadhg. "What'll he do to her?"

"Yer know what he'll do. Yer ain't daft."

Finn saw no sympathy in his brother's eyes and felt the ache of dread turn in his belly. Where the hell was Mickey? He needed a friend. He needed help. He needed to do something.

Moving back to the stairs, he looked up as Sam's frame appeared at the top. "I'm going up."

Sam shook his head. "She's gone to the rooftop. She don't want to be disturbed."

"Well, she's about to be." Finn pushed past him on the landing, grateful that Sam didn't block his way as he ran to the narrow staircase leading to the roof. Taking a minute to still his breath, he moved more slowly towards the door. Pushing it open he found her.

Aileen sat on a crate in the corner, her arms resting on the cold brick walls either side as if sitting on a throne, though she was in anything but a triumphant pose.

Finn wanted to yell at her, but the words fell away. It was quiet up there. A different view of the city. A different view of Aileen. Suddenly all of it felt futile. It didn't matter what words he yelled at her. They wouldn't change a thing.

"Yer look like yer been rolling around in pig slop." Aileen barely cut him a glance, and Finn ignored her.

Instead, he looked across at the small shelter they'd put together for Madochée. A bolt of anxiety hit his chest as he realised he hadn't seen her. "Madochée? Did she go for the church? Is she alright?"

"She went after yer friend. Mickey."

"After him, where?"

"Wherever she is now, I'd say."

Finn crouched down, the weight of everything feeling too much. All three of his companions were lost somewhere in this bleedin' city. "Perhaps the city is going to hell after all. It's falling apart. All of it. Whatever is left of it. Of this thing yer are holding on to."

"What do yer mean? The cargo is safe. Discounting yer two, the whole thing was a success. We had that done and finished and if we can get it where it needs to be we'll be home free for another month."

"No, yer won't. The Angel—" Finn began.

"Don't speak to me about him. Yer think this is the first time? Yer think this is the first time I've had my back against the wall and him coming for me? Because it's far from it and

I'm still here, ain't I? Christ, he has yer trained, don't he? Yer all bleedin' tremblin' at the mere mention of his name. Pathetic."

"I don't care if yer scatter that cargo up and down the Liffey. It's Tessie what matters. And yer sit there like a—"

"Like a what? Don't forget whose house yer standing in, boy." Aileen gritted her teeth. "It's my men who went in there to get yer. We had the cargo. We didn't need yer. But we went anyway, and it's my men who've come back here with fresh scars and bruises. No one invited neither one of yer into this, but here the fuck we are. So now we do it my way."

"How can yer not act?"

"I'll tell yer what I told her. Right now they're reeling from that mess. They're mad with fury. Mad fucking wild. They'll mow yer down before yer get a word out. And what good will that do our Tess? Nothing!"

"If that's what they'll do to me then what'll they do to her?" Finn knew the terror in his eyes pleaded shamelessly with Aileen, but he didn't care. What would they do to her? He wanted her to tell him something different than the worst in his mind. But she just looked back at him and drew hard on her cigarette before lowering her eyes.

"She talks like a tough one, our Tess. And if she ain't, she'll have to be now. She'll have to find some stones of it somewhere deep down in herself."

"Don't talk about her like she hasn't had it hard. We know struggle. We know what it is to fight. And to lose."

"And yet yer still come crying to me. I don't make the fucking rules."

"Damn it—"

"We don't even know if they have her yet."

"She'd be here. If she had any—"

"Alright." Aileen flung her lit cigarette at him. "Alright."

Finn dusted the embers from his shirt and clamped his

mouth shut. The anguish was eating him up. What were they going to do?

Aileen stood and breathed deep, looking to the sky. For the first time, he saw a hint of worry in her.

"What are we going to do?" he asked.

"The minute Eamon knows we've got Tadhg O'Shea, she'll have more value to him. He'll make a swap for her."

"What if he won't?"

"He'll have to."

"Why?"

"Because he needs him, that's why. Eamon Paddy Mac ain't shite without the backing of all them bleedin' factions. He didn't have the bollocks or the numbers to come at me all on his own. It took the whole damn lot of them banding together to even make a dent. He won't have a choice. Without Tadhg, it don't matter if he has the cargo or not."

"He cares that much about Tadhg?"

"I didn't say he cared about him. He *needs* him. Tadhg's a whole different breed. He can rally the men or turn the tide if he wants to. They'll listen. He's got value. Believe me."

Finn turned away.

"Hey." Aileen nudged him. "Don't be getting confused about who that is down there. It don't matter if he were yer brother once. He ain't yer brother now, so don't be thinking he has yer back. He'll slit my throat just as easy as yours if it comes down to it."

A shrill scream curled up from the alley below.

"Christ," Aileen hissed.

She dropped to her knees and moved to the ledge to peer over. The guttural noises of a struggle rose up towards them. Finn crouched beside Aileen, and she motioned at him to be quiet as the noises faded.

"What was that?" Finn asked. "Is it Eamon? Are they coming now?"

"Not Eamon. Look there." Following her gesture, Finn saw two bodies laid out on the ground and three men moving away up the alley. "Their wrists. Yer see?"

His heart seized. They each wore a black leather cuff. The Angel's men were here in Dublin!

"She said he was here," Aileen cursed. "I guess she were right."

"He's early. Why is he early?"

"Yer are a fool if yer believed his deal. He's here in his own time. His majesty, his fucking self."

Panic flooded Finn's chest. The Angel was here. Their time was up.

CHAPTER 36

Finn dashed down the stairs after Aileen as a man burst through the kitchen door. Bloodstained and limping, his eyes searched for her as the room gathered around him. "We were on our way back, and they came out of nowhere. They got Joyce and Masters. They're dead. The Angel is here. He's here."

"What of Tessie?" Finn pushed through the crowd to get to him. "Did yer see her?"

But the man was too distracted, pointing back down the alley from where he'd escaped the struggle. "They bid me to tell yer. To warn yer. The Angel. He's here. They're here. They're coming for us. They said to tell yer that he's here."

"Hush!" Aileen commanded, but the panic had seized him. She stepped forward, slapping him hard across the face. "I know it. I were watching from the roof. No reason to lose yer wits." Aileen directed more men to run after them. "Go now. Gather Joyce and Masters. Bring them in and the rest of yer cool yer straps."

"Did yer see Tessie? Did yer see her?" Finn repeated,

gripping the man by the shoulders, though he shrugged him off.

"They have her. I didn't see her but we grabbed one of the men and he confirmed it. She's there."

"Yer heard it," Finn said to Aileen. "We have to go."

"Quiet!" Aileen raised her voice above the crowd. "If I hear any voice but my own, that man'll feel the end of my boot, so he will." The room stilled and Aileen climbed up on a chair so all could see her. "Aye. The Angel's men are here. That there was nought but a scouting mission to feel us out. See how easy it was to get close. See how many strong we are. We knew the day would come, boys. But they've been for us before. So hold yer tongue and yer fear because it'll serve for nought. It's only yer courage and strength that'll mean anything now."

"My God. He can't be here." Siobhan was turning white in the corner, her shrill voice rising above the room. "He can't come. We have to get out of here!"

"Listen up." Aileen flashed Siobhan a look to simmer down. "Whoever yer have, whoever is left for yer to call upon, now is the time to call them in. Now. If yer need a favour. If any man owes yer but a penny, he ought to line up beside yer. Get them. Guard the alley entrances, dammit. It were too easy for them to take Joyce and Masters and we won't let it happen again. We need more of yer out there so they don't scamper on back any time they damn well please. We'll meet their fight when we're good and ready." She looked around, taking stock. "Take care of Joyce and Masters," she added in a quieter voice. "Get them to their families. That's all we can do for them now."

"We can't just barricade ourselves in." Finn's mind was rushing. "What if Tessie is trying to get through? What if—"

Aileen pointed at Finn indicating for him to come in closer as she spoke with Sam. "Listen in. Go now. Talk to

Eamon Paddy Mac and Mac only. Tell him we have Tadhg O'Shea in our hold and he best hold his fists off that girl and make a time to exchange them. Go. Now. Run."

Sam sprinted from the room and Siobhan moved after him, running to the door and watching as he disappeared into the street.

"And yer." Aileen turned to Finn. "Get yer brother ready to move."

Finn's heart was pounding. The Angel meant to obliterate them. All of them. Tessie's mission had failed and now it wouldn't matter if they all went down together, swept up in one great bloody battle. The Black Bonnet and the Angel. Aileen and Arthur. And Arthur had come to stand over the ashes.

Dublin was rising up to swallow them up into its endless tar pit. Finn had to find a way to make it right. To get Tessie back and get them out of there. Lifting his head, he watched his brother across the room. Tadhg's eyes darted around at the action. Whatever poison had been in his system hadn't been enough to kill him. That at least calmed Finn's heart.

He stared down at his shit-covered shirt. Beside him, Siobhan had backed herself into the corner, biting her nails.

"Can yer find me a fresh shirt?" he asked.

The question pulled her from her thoughts as he gently touched her arm.

"Take us to Boston with yer? Will yer?" She said it with a wild urgency in her eyes that gripped Finn's attention. He'd not seen her in such a state.

"When we get through this, yer two can go where yer like. Promise." He knew the words sounded empty but he held his expression firm, willing the conviction to rise from somewhere. Now was the time to quiet all doubt. To pull the strength from every crevice in his being. If this city wanted them, he would not go willingly. He would not give up on their future. Somewhere out there Tessie was fighting it too, and he would not give up on her.

"Are yer sure?" She lowered her eyes as if reticent to share any moment of understanding. "But I hope yer get Tessie back."

"We will." His voice sounded firmer, and he gripped her forearm, willing his belief to pass to her. "Can yer get me a clean shirt? If we're to fight and die today, I'd choose to do it not covered in shite."

Siobhan lifted her eyes, a small beam of cheekiness still in there yet. "Sam'll have one." She left for the stairs and Finn turned to Tadhg waiting on the sofa.

"Yer going to get yer wish after all." Finn crouched beside him. "Can yer move or walk?"

"I can do what I need to." Tadhg sat up and managed to swing his feet around to the floor. He looked pale but alert and ready.

"Here." Finn passed him some more water and waited as he drank slowly. "Yer mustn't have eaten as much as the others. Yer've perked up right enough."

"Ain't I the lucky one." Tadhg cut his eyes at Finn.

"Luck must lurk in yer shadow or somewhere close by if yer've lasted as long in this city ."

Finn looked down at his brother, all the conflicting feelings he held competing for space — the relief at finding him, the guilt for leaving him in the first place, the terror that he wouldn't reach Tessie in time, and the fear that the Angel would crash down on all of them before they'd time to make it right.

"Don't look so serious, brother. It's yer own neck yer should be worrying about just now." Tadhg wore a wry grin, though Finn didn't try to smile back. He had to focus on Tessie now. If Tadhg was alive and well in Dublin, that would have to be solace enough.

"I'd only hoped for more time. I'll not apologise for that."

"Time don't change the past, brother. Never has, never will."

"I know that." Finn gritted his teeth, taking a deep breath. "Yer follow Eamon. And I'm here with Aileen. It is what it is. Strange messed up world."

"Follow? I'm far from a follower of Eamon Paddy Mac." Tadhg spat the words out.

"What would yer call it then?"

"Sometimes yer let a loose cannon run its course and be there to pick up the pieces. That's what I'd call it."

"So that's yer plan? To let him do whatever damage he'll do to this city and—"

"Damage to the city? He ain't no different to Aileen. And Aileen ain't no different to me. That's the game, Finn. If yer don't know that yet I don't know what yer doing here."

"I just want us out of this alive and on a bleedin' boat out of here."

Tadhg smiled. "Haven't changed that much then, have yer brother?"

"Is it wrong to want something better? Don't yer want something else other than this?"

"There is nothing outside of this, brother. Guess wherever yer been yer haven't learned that yet."

"You're wrong. There is."

"We fight to get by and protect what is ours. That's what yer need to do to survive these streets. That's Dublin. That's *my* Dublin. The way I see it ain't nothing so wrong about that."

Siobhan came back down the stairs and threw Finn a clean shirt without warning. He caught it just before it hit him in the face.

"Yer want to know why I left? Why I didn't spend years more wandering in this cesspit?" Finn gritted his teeth as he ripped his old shirt over his head and slipped on the new. "It's because I could feel it even then. This place is nothing but death. It took Ma. It took yer. And I could feel it clawing at my heels if I didn't get out when I did. Yer were gone. And that was the worst pain I ever felt. I carried it with me all these years, don't doubt that, brother."

Tadhg's expression had calmed, though he looked up at Finn without speaking.

"So judge me if yer will. But yer my brother, the same one that was with me when we were kids, whether we're friends or enemies now. Time won't change that neither."

Finn tossed his dirty shirt on Tadhg's lap and walked away. He was ready.

CHAPTER 37

Tessie gathered her strength as Eamon lunged to take another swing. Blood filled her mouth and her lip stung but she held her eyes on his. She couldn't just stand there and take the beating. She reached for her knife, but he was too fast. Gripping her ankle, he plucked it from her boot and thrust her back against the wall. He triumphantly held up the knife and Tessie's stomach turned at the sight of it.

"They're going to come back for me."

"It doesn't matter what they do. It's just me and yer right now." Eamon squeezed the back of her neck. "I have yer all to myself. And I have the Angel backing me. Me. Life ain't half bad, darlin'."

"Not if—"

Eamon back-handed her, his face flashing with a lunatic's grin. "Close that mouth, girl."

Tessie swallowed it down. She was Aileen's daughter, dammit. She was the Angel's daughter. She wanted to spit it at him as the only weapon she had left. But she couldn't let him know that. Not for a second, even as it danced on the tip of her tongue.

"Do it then. Do what yer will. Yer a pathetic excuse for a man."

The rage at all of it of swelled up inside of her. Her mother's betrayal. This impossible city. And the Angel's evil design rippling through every step. She burned with it, willing it to spill over this wretched man before her - this one man standing in her way. She would not cower to him. Even as madness flickered in his eyes, his desperate fragility beaming back at her. He was dangerous, but right now, she felt nothing but the burning heat of fury in her chest.

"The Angel ain't care nothing for yer. Nor for Dublin. All this is just to hurt Aileen," she said.

"I'm the only who can do that."

"Looks like she's the one whose hurt yer. What about yer men?"

"They know it. They know who I am. They know I can lead them to—"

"Do they?" Tessie felt the flash in her belly. This man was standing in the way of her whole reason for coming to Dublin. He was dragging her mother down. He'd taken Finn, and now he held her fate. She had to swallow her rage and find a way out of here. "Let me walk out of here. That's my only warning to yer." She didn't know if it held true.

Eamon's face contorted as if summoning something deep inside himself. But before he could spill it, the door swung open and he lurched towards her with his arms out, protecting his prey from whoever was to enter.

"Mac," an urgent voice said. Tessie saw the curly-haired man with dimples. He'd clearly eaten some of her cake and stood pale-faced and clammy as he leaned against the doorframe.

"What is it, Sully? What?"

"Sam is here. Needs to speak to yer."

"Sam? Well, he's not a bleedin' guest — grab hold of him. Take him!"

Tessie saw Sam standing at the entrance and relief flooded through her. They knew she was here. They were coming to help her. Sam's eyes grew wide as Sully suddenly grabbed his arm. It was more of a symbolic hold than an aggressive one and Sam didn't pull away. He gave Tessie a brief nod as if to check she was all right and she reciprocated, flashing her eyes. She needed him to see it and tell Finn.

"Yer dare show yer face here?" Eamon rumbled.

"I have a message."

"No. *I* have a message!" Eamon spat back. "Tell that bitch I'll kill her. I'll kill her. The next time she lays eyes on me it'll be to draw her last breath. In fact. No. She won't see me coming. I'll get her. I'll—"

"We have Tadhg O'Shea," Sam interrupted.

Eamon stopped. The room went quiet as the men watching exchanged glances.

"Alive or dead?"

"Alive. We'll swap him for girl. Name the time and place."

Tessie's hope rose and the men around her seemed to be holding their breath. Eamon looked around at them as if reading their thoughts and backed protectively towards Tessie.

"I don't bend my knee for the whereabouts of Tadhg O'Shea. Was it Tadhg who approached the Angel of Bishopsgate? Was it Tadhg who brought us this far? It was me, damn all of yer." Eamon's face flushed red, spit flying from his lips. "The girl stays here." He grabbed Tessie by the top of her hair, pulling her towards him. "She lives here now. She's staying here with me. She's mine."

A murmur of protests swept the room. "Get Tadhg back.

Make the trade." One of the bolder men stepped forward and Eamon seemed shocked by the audacity. He pressed the knife into Tessie's neck.

"Listen to reason, Eamon. We need Tadhg. He would come for me or any of us and we'll do the same for him."

Eamon's boots skidded on the grainy floor as he dragged Tessie with him, lurching forward. "John Mason. Yer don't tell me what to do, John Mason. I make the decisions around here."

"Make the deal." A threatening tone rumbled in the man's throat. Tessie didn't understand what was happening? Did the men choose Tadhg over Eamon? Was Eamon not truly in charge after all?

Eamon's eyes grew wild and he flashed them at John, inhaling a sharp burst of air as he plucked the pistol from his coat and pointed it. "I said she stays with me."

Sam too stepped into the room, shaking Sully's loose hold. The whole room could sense it — a mutiny in the making. "Yer best not to hurt her, Eamon Mac." Where Sam's voice had been that of a meek messenger, now he took on an authoritative tone. "Make the trade."

Moving backwards, Eamon shoved Tessie, blocking the way and putting himself between her and the others. "Did yer wonder why this girl is so valuable? Did yer? Why would Aileen make that deal? Think about it, yer brainless scum!"

The room didn't answer, and Tessie cringed waiting for someone to identify her. If Eamon knew he had Aileen's daughter, he'd never make the deal.

Sam stepped further into the room. "This is yer last chance, Eamon. Think now. Yer already hurting. Yer men are down. Make the deal."

"Seize him!" Eamon screamed.

But the men didn't move. They stood to the spot, his words falling flat. What was happening here? Had Aileen's onslaught taken the fire from their bellies rather than igniting it? Tessie scanned the men, their eyes darting from Eamon to each other. Was it possible they wanted Tadhg back more than they wanted revenge?

"Eamon." Sam was stepping further into the room, his voice bold above the other men. They didn't stop him. "Just tell me where to meet yer."

"Come on, Eamon. We have to get Tadhg. We have to." The men were closing in.

"No! Damn yer all! No!" He was pacing again, but his men were edging forward, crowding him. Tessie saw the wildness reappear in his eyes. He had no plan. He had nothing. There was empty panic whizzing through his head.

Gripping the back of her neck, Eamon thrust Tessie forward, rushing her through a nearby doorway. He cast her aside, and slammed the door, quickly barricading it shut with a heavy desk. His men pounded on the other side. But it was too late. She was alone, just she and Eamon Paddy Mac.

She felt a rush of energy and fight, followed by the overwhelming urge for quiet. She wanted to go home. She wanted to see Finn and Madochée. She wanted them all to be safe and away from this damned place.

"Yer need to make the trade." She heard her voice crack but stilled herself to sound more confident than she felt. "Yer need to do it. It's the only way to keep yer men onside." She got up from where he'd flung her to the corner and moved closer as if she were his friend — his only friend now in the world.

"Shut yer mouth!" He jabbed the pistol at her. "Let me think. Just let me think dammit! These ungrateful maggots. Why does she want yer back? Why would Aileen trade yer for Tadhg O'Shea? She should have wiped him out the moment..."

Tessie swallowed. "That doesn't matter now!"

"Tell me."

"Because yer got something that's hers. She uses me for whatever serves her purpose. Simple as that. I'm a tool. But yer have to think of yourself now. Make the swap or yer will lose everything."

"Don't tell me what to think. I'm the leader. The author of all of this. It were me who planned to bring her down. I saw where she was weak. Me!" He pointed at his chest with the pistol before waving it back at her. Tessie's breath caught as she ducked out of the way. "I used to work for her, yer know. I lugged her bleedin' cargo. All night I worked. And she looked through me like I was guttersnipe. Well, who's the guttersnipe now?"

"Yer have done well."

Tessie held her hand out as if to touch his shoulder but pulled it back again. For a moment she thought he might cry. Instead, he let out a scream so loud his face shook. His eyes moved quickly so that she couldn't tell one moment from the next how best to play it. He could just as easily shoot her and it would all be over.

"Now they look at me with...fear. Fear." He pointed the pistol in the air, triumphantly, his brightly coloured frock coat flaring out behind him.

"I see it in their eyes," she agreed.

She moved closer again. It was just them. She and Eamon. Her voice soft and reassuring. She had to lull him into surrender.

"They see yer power now. They feel it. But don't lose yer grip. Don't give it up. They will take me with them if yer don't act. Make the trade yerself. Show them yer leadership. Lead them." She wondered how much fear he saw in her eyes; she felt it bubbling up inside her ready to spill.

Eamon pressed his temples with his knuckles, heaving his breath in quick tight huffs so that she thought he might explode. He crouched like a child, his face flushing red. "Take charge. Take charge." He whispered to himself. "If those maggots want Tadhg, I'll bleedin' give them Tadhg."

He grabbed at her, pulling her close and pressing the knife to her throat. A wordless prayer raced through her and she squeezed her eyes closed.

Kicking away the makeshift barricade, she braced as he booted the door open and held the pistol out at his men. He fired without warning straight at the man called John Mason. Tessie screamed as the bullet pierced his forehead. He fell in a heap without a word. The other men stood silent. He had their attention now. He had everyone's attention.

Eamon stepped over the body, keeping the knife tight at her throat and the pistol pointed. "If anyone is taking her, it's me. I'll make the trade. Me."

CHAPTER 38

$\mathcal{F}$inn searched for a weapon. He picked up a discarded mallet from the table as the other's readied for the trade. Sam had just told them Eamon had agreed, albeit with a knife to Tessie's throat. They had no time to waste.

Aileen's dark eyes darted back and forth as she spoke to her men. "We can't leave this place open for the Angel's taking. Sam, gather yer best fifteen to follow us and leave the rest here to stand their ground should the Angel's men storm the damn place."

"What about me?" Siobhan stepped forward. "I ain't staying here waiting on the Angel. I can't."

"Dammit, child. I told yer to get to the roof."

"I won't. I can't. I can't be up there trapped—"

"Yer will go to the church like the young one was supposed to."

"I won't."

"Hush!"

Siobhan looked around and grabbed a stray knife from the table, holding it up as if ready to join the fight.

"Jaysus, girl." Aileen rubbed her eyes.

Sam moved towards her. "Yer need to stay, Shiv. It's not safe."

"I won't stay back here, just waiting on yer. Waiting to hear if yer dead or not. Not again. I don't care what happens. I'm going. I'm telling yer—"

"Please!" Sam reached for her hand. "I can't do what I need to do if I'm worried about yer."

"I don't care."

"Shiv!"

"Dammit!" Aileen interrupted. "We don't have time to argue. Yer stay at the back, girl. At a distance. And yer run if yer must. Yer don't get involved and yer leave Sam to do his job."

"I will. I will." Siobhan clutched the knife awkwardly at her chest.

"Alright then," Finn urged. "Let's go."

He looked at the gathering of them, sleep weary, eyes red with exhaustion. It had been a brutal twenty-four hours for all of them. His body moved in lumbering strides, fighting against the bruises and aches still rising from deep in his bones. Would they be enough to get Tessie back?

Aileen led the way out into the street pushing against a wintery gale; the gang making their way north again towards Eamon's hall. The mallet was heavy in Finn's hand, but he gripped it as hard as he could, staying at the ready. Tadhg walked in front of him. He watched him closely, the way his shoulders moved and how he tilted his head. It was not unlike Finn's own way of walking, though it was obvious Tadhg still felt weak and poorly from the poison. He had a stubborn streak — that much was clear — and a head for leadership and strategy. Finn didn't know if he could trust him. His own brother. Was he planning a double-cross in all this? Was this a trap of their own making? Would he run to his men before they had Tessie back with them and secure? Tadhg hadn't wanted to be at Aileen's in the first place. She was his enemy. Eamon was his ally. Finn couldn't spread the pieces out enough to make sense of them, but the doubts started to ripple. No matter how he looked at it, he was stuck between his brother and Tessie.

As they came to the long narrow alley Eamon had named as the exchange point, Aileen snaked to the side, urging them to be quiet behind her. His eyes bore hard on the back of her head, her wild hair blowing in the wind. This woman who neither commanded nor bowed to the chaos in this city — he would have to trust her now.

She gestured the way was clear and ushered them around the corner. It wasn't just Eamon they had to be on the lookout for. The Angel's men were here in Dublin, and they had no idea how long before they would strike. The Angel could be following them now, watching them scurry the streets in a last-ditch attempt to save the shattered pieces of this mess.

The sour scent of the Vinegar Works swirled around them as they gathered in the alley behind it for the second time that day. Finn's head raced with images of Tessie. He thought he heard her screams, but the sound of her vanished on the wind so that he couldn't be sure if he heard anything at all.

Aileen ordered them into position behind a stray wagon at the far end of the alley. They expected Eamon would approach from the other side.

"He better not change his mind," she quipped.

"He won't," Tadhg assured.

"Rate yerself highly, don't we, friend."

"I know my men, is all."

"And I know Eamon. Fickle coward."

Tadhg sneered. "That much we do agree on."

Movement sounded at the other end of the alley, and all eyes fixed on the far corner, waiting for a figure to emerge from the shadows.

"Let's see where the axe falls this time. Hold steady." Aileen gritted her teeth at Tadhg and pulled her hatchet free. She turned to Finn. "Keep hold of him."

Finn could barely contain the rush of energy shooting up his legs. He needed to see Tessie come around that corner. He needed to see she was safe. But turning to Tadhg, he knew his brother was the key. He held his mallet out to Siobhan who was huddled at the back and indicated to swap it for her knife. She obliged and he quickly took position behind Tadhg, pressing it against his neck.

"Really, brother?" Tadhg shook his head.

"Brother or not, I'll not take the chance. I will get her back in one piece."

"I told yer, he'll make the trade. He has to."

"It's not Eamon I'm worried about."

Tadhg nodded his head slightly. "Ah. Now yer thinking, brother. Now yer thinking. But yer know what they say." He paused for effect. "Don't pull a weapon unless yer prepared to use it."

Finn gritted his teeth and pulled the knife firm against his brother's neck. "I won't want to. But I will do what I have to for her. Only for her."

Tadhg held his hands up in mock surrender. "Alright. Easy." He smiled.

Finn ushered him forward to stand beside Aileen, vying to see for himself as figures appeared at the far end.

"Yer cool yer wits, yer hear," Aileen warned him. "Let me feel it out first."

Finn was about to answer when there was Eamon,

marching Tessie out in front of him, a knife pressed to her throat and his eyes wild.

"Dear God."

"Yer wait!" Aileen cautioned.

But Finn couldn't wait. He flung himself out into the alley, dragging Tadhg with him.

CHAPTER 39

The pounding in Tessie's ears drowned out everything else as Eamon pressed the blade hard against her skin. He forced her into the alley, and she had to be careful not to move too hard or too fast lest she slit her own throat against the knife. Through the blur of movement, she saw Aileen coming into view at the far entrance and Finn beside her holding his brother out in front of him. The last time she'd seen them Finn had been cradling Tadhg, desperate to save him. Whatever Tadhg's position now, he'd survived. Thank God he'd survived.

She held her eyes on Finn as the distance between them grew smaller. His eyes were wide and solemn as they too searched for hers. It broke her heart. She knew the panic he held down with each breath, while beside him Aileen's composed expression gave little away. She was an impressive figure. Even now, she commanded this space just with the glare in her eyes.

Still, they were a bedraggled sight. Beaten up and weary. Kyran had been right. This was what the Angel had wanted. To rid himself of Aileen or not, he wanted to pull at the tattered hemline of all their connections. To see them haggard and scraping at their most basic instinct to survive. He would destroy them if they let him.

Tessie wondered if she'd have done anything differently even if she'd seen through his plan. Would she not have come at all? Might she have approached Aileen in a different way? She didn't have the answer and, in this moment, none of it mattered.

"Look what we have here," Aileen called out into the vacuous space, her voice loud enough to push through the cold gust of wind that encircled them. "If it ain't Eamon Paddy Mac himself. Where was yer this morning when we paid yer men a visit? That's what I'd like to know. Cowering in the shadows like a dog?"

"Yer wouldn't have fled so easily if I were there, I promise yer that."

"Aye, big words from the boy who has never had the bollocks to face me. Yer always play shy with me, boy."

Eamon pushed Tessie forward, shaking her for emphasis. "Are yer blind, bitch? Don't think I won't gut her right here and now. I'm here for Tadhg. Hand him over."

Tessie searched the scene for something more. Were they just to make the trade and go back to their war? Neither party any further advanced or inclined to back down? Tessie looked to her mother — her face serious and solemn, though her eyes barely caught on hers. She'd made her play. She had the cargo, yes, but her men were wounded and tired, and their numbers dwindling. Aileen's play with the poison had been a despicable scene but it had barely made a dent in Eamon's numbers. And then, the Angel was coming and this would all soon be over. They had already lost. Aileen just didn't know it yet. Tessie swallowed, the sinking feeling rising quickly. What could she possibly do with a blade to her throat? She just wanted this over!

"Do it," Tessie urged Eamon through closed teeth. "Do it now!"

He was thrown. She could hear the hesitation in his voice and she nudged her elbow back to prod him. "Make the trade and get out of here."

Eamon cleared his throat and stepped forward. "Bring him up. Tadhg. Let him come forward."

"Alright." Aileen gritted her teeth and motioned for Finn to let Tadhg move. Tessie felt Eamon loosen his grip as he too edged her forward, ready to release her.

She wanted to sprint across that gap to Finn. She wanted to go home. But bracing to run she felt a prickle of hesitation hold her feet still.

She watched her mother, the proud tension in that woman's jaw. Staunch as ever. Never outplayed. Never relenting. She'd come to save Tessie, hadn't she? Wasn't that enough?

An ache of loss singed Tessie's edges. No. It wasn't enough. Exchanging Tadhg might save Tessie, but it did nothing for her mother. She would die here, Tessie thought. She'd die here in this city that no longer wanted her. The gravity of it plunged through her. The turmoil of indecision churned her stomach. Only one thing would save her mother. Only one thing Tessie knew to use, though it would cut Aileen to her core. One lifeline that Aileen could very well toss back at her.

She had only seconds to choose. Her mouth went dry. She tried to quiet the thumping in her chest, but it was building up inside her now. Was she brave enough to do it? Was she bold enough to stare down her mother? All it once the moment rushed through her like a wave.

"Wait!" she shouted.

Tessie planted her feet firmly on the ground and forced Eamon to stop. Her voice was lost on the wind and Finn's eyes widened with confusion. Tessie flashed her eyes back and forth, her breath quickening as the words came.

"No."

"Move, girl." Eamon shoved her harder and she pushed back.

"No. Wait." She twisted around to face him, trying to speak over the pounding in her head. "Make her give yer the cargo." The words caught in her throat. She could hardly believe them herself.

"What?" Eamon frowned at her.

"Come on, girl!" Aileen commanded. "Get over here."

"Wait!" Eamon put his hand up. She had his attention.

"Make her give yer the cargo. Demand the cargo." She said it loud enough for Aileen and Finn to hear this time, though it almost choked in her throat. "I'm her daughter. Use me to end this. End it now. Make her swap me for the cargo and yer will have it all."

Eamon turned back to Aileen, his eyes alight with impending victory. "Your daughter? She's yer fucking daughter?" He let out a hideous laugh. "Yer heard her."

Tadhg struggled against Finn who was holding him up. "Sod this." He lurched forward. "Let's get this over with. Get me outta here."

"Stop. Hold on." Finn held him back, but Tessie could see he had no idea what was happening or how to respond.

"Wait!" Eamon commanded, holding his hand up to stop Tadhg moving toward him.

Aileen gritted her teeth, her gaze locked on Tessie. This was the moment. Her daughter or the cargo. Betrayal raged through Aileen's eyes, drawing in Tessie's like a whirlpool. She'd be handing over Dublin for Tessie. Everything she'd worked for. Tessie felt the treachery swirl in the pit of her stomach.

"Yer wretched girl!" Aileen flared.

Tessie thought she might charge through and kill her herself. But the question held in Tessie's eyes. Even as she asked it, she knew it wasn't fair. She could feel the burn in Aileen's glare, her eyes stinging up and shiny as they wrestled with the answer. It choked in her throat, and in that moment Tessie wanted to hug that horrid battle-weary woman.

"The cargo or she dies. Now! Now, Aileen!" Eamon cared not for the significance of the moment.

"Yer have to do it!" Finn screamed at Aileen. "Do it! Tell him where it is."

Tessie looked only in her mother's eyes — hardened and bright. The panic in them was ripe and raw, neither of them looked away. *How could yer do it?* Aileen's expression implored. Her arms dropped to her side, the colour draining from her face.

"Sam."

Aileen's voice was low and raspy and she did not look away from Tessie. She was about to speak the words. She was going to give the order. Sam and Siobhan behind her looked bewildered and frozen to the spot. Eamon's eyes danced with glee, he bounced on his toes behind Tessie. Aileen was going to do it. She was going to surrender the cargo. Tessie felt the words float out before she spoke them, their slow ebbs, a warm wash flooding through her chest.

Then, before Aileen uttered a sound, a rush of adrenaline thrust Tessie into action. Reeling back hard at Eamon's distracted pose, she slid her hand into his coat. All at once, she plucked the pistol from his belt and leaned back to kick him high and hard to the chest. He fell, the knife barely nicking her skin as she stood firm above him, pointing the pistol at his head. She heaved her breath, trying to still herself through the rushing in her veins.

"I'll blow yer away. I'll do it." Her voice was gruff and firm. "Drop the knife."

Eamon stared up at her, puzzled. He let the knife topple from his hand.

"She'll not give the cargo for her daughter. Not for anyone. This'll always be her Dublin."

Tessie felt the moment crash down upon her, her hands quivering. It was not the first time she'd held a pistol. It was not the first time she'd aimed one at an enemy. She wanted to let it out. To vent everything she felt with a single twitch of her finger. It would be so easy. She looked down at Eamon at her feet. It was all slipping away from him and she recognised the terror in his eyes. She could end it for him in that very moment. She could end the war for Aileen. She looked to her mother staring back at her, eyes bright with shock.

Then she heard Finn's voice. "Tessie! Tess!"

The thrashing sound in her ears faded as she raised her eyes.

A flurry of shadows moved over the alley and everyone looked up. Men lined the rooftops on either side of the alley.

"What in the hell are yer playing at?" Aileen thundered, stepping forward.

Tessie saw in Eamon's face that he too was faltering. The sound of boots on the cobblestones rumbled towards them. Men spilt into the alley, blocking the exits.

Oh my God. Tessie felt fear tremble up inside her. They were the Angel's men. He was here.

CHAPTER 40

$\mathcal{A}$s the Angel's men rushed into the alley, those around Tessie scattered. A loud call thundered from above and Tessie saw Castor leaning out from a roof corner like the figurehead on a ship. He'd given a signal, and Tessie's eyes scanned for Arthur. Was he up there too, eager to watch a massacre? Had he come to squeeze the life out of her just as he'd promised?

At her feet, Eamon scrambled and tried to run. Tessie pointed the pistol after him but he was quickly caught in a scuffle. The Angel's men weren't just after Aileen, they were taking down everyone. The chaos crowded around her, forcing her to the wall. Her eyes searched for Finn, and Eamon's men were upon him. He was blocking blows as they tried to drag Tadhg away with them. Tessie screamed and ran as he was taken to the ground, boots jabbing and kicking his already battered body.

A hand gripped her arm and held her back. It was Aileen.

"Quickly, girl. We need to get out of here."

"Finn. We have to help him!"

She heard him holler as Sam ran to join the fight, but it was Tadhg's voice that rose high above the noise.

"Leave him. Leave him. He's my brother. I said, that's my brother."

The men heard the command and fell back. Tessie watched as he leaned down to Finn. They didn't speak, though their eyes locked and Tadhg helped him to his feet. As they stood opposite one another, Tessie saw their likeness — a mirrored profile with Finn only slightly taller. This was indeed the brother he had lost and grieved. The moment held as mayhem swirled around them, but Tadhg was being called elsewhere. He slapped Finn's shoulder with gruff warmth, and disappeared into the fray.

Breaking free of Aileen, Tessie ran and threw herself at Finn, but there was no time to linger. "We have to get out. How do we get out?"

"Follow me," Aileen commanded.

She yanked Siobhan up from behind a crate where she'd been crouched and hiding. Sam flanked her on the other side as Tessie and Finn followed suit. The rumble of battle was deafening and Aileen's men fell back with Eamon's. The Angel's men were making no distinction between them now. They were cleaning house, clearing Dublin of their enemies.

Aileen threaded their group like a needle along the edges of the fray, back towards the alley entrance. Tessie squeezed Finn's hand and clasped Eamon's precious pistol in her other.

As they neared the exit, the Angel's men descended from the side, lashing out with fists and knives. Tessie felt the air around her move as she twisted away, but the men came in a rush of fury against her body. Finn grabbed her up, yanking her just out of reach. Aileen twisted to block the blow, stepping between her daughter and danger. The knife meant for Tessie sliced Aileen deep beneath her right arm and she faltered only briefly before raising her hatchet high and striking back. Where that man fell, another took Finn to the ground. Tessie looked up to see Sam and Siobhan encircled in front of her. They weren't going to get out.

Strange arms gripped Tessie from behind, lifting her off her feet and carrying her away from the group. Struggling and kicking, she threw her head back to strike the unknown man in the face. She made contact, but his grip did not loosen. Clutching the pistol in her hand, she squeezed. The bang was sharp and loud and the man let go. Tessie dropped to the ground. She turned to see him stagger behind her, holding his leg as she struggled for breath.

Rushing past her, Aileen took her by the arm and urged her forward. "Go. Go. Go. Move yer arse. Get out of here."

Finn ran, gathering her up as Sam and Siobhan emerged frantically from the crowd. Siobhan had deep scratches across her face. Aileen's voice rang out behind them as she rushed them onward, holding her right arm tight to her body. Tessie saw the blood soaking through her mother's dress, but there was no time to stop.

CHAPTER 41

*A*ileen's stride changed as they drew closer to the house. Their faces ached in the freezing air but they did not have time to slow down. Her expression held steadfastly and focussed as they hastened through the northern streets. Tessie couldn't help but wonder how many times that woman's will alone had kept her standing when her body might have easily given out.

Tessie had no idea what time it was, though daylight was quickly fading and the evening chill had settled in. The five of them kept close together. The sound of their pattering feet on the cobblestones echoed as they whirled past onlookers. Their eyes searched only for danger — expecting the Angel's men or Eamon's, to careen around the corner at any moment.

Aileen's men were nowhere to be seen. They had scattered or been left behind at the battle, and those remaining at the Black Bonnet would no doubt soon desert them. Word of what transpired would travel fast, and even if it didn't, one look at the bedraggled group pulling themselves back to safety would be enough to tell the story.

As they finally reached the house and burst into the kitchen, Aileen held herself up just long enough to make it to the table. She collapsed onto a chair, breathlessly holding her side.

"Sam, have them watch the street," she said. "They'll be coming. We need to get ready."

"Have who watch the street?" Siobhan interrupted. The shrillness in her voice filled the room. "They're all gone. Can't yer see! They've left us."

"Damn it, girl."

"We're all alone. He's coming. Oh, my God, he's coming." Her panic was revving up, spilling out the feelings they were all trying so hard to keep bridled. "Oh God."

"Get yer things and head up to the roof," Aileen barked.

"It's not safe up there. We're trapped. We're trapped here."

"Up to the roof!"

Siobhan turned to Sam for back up, but he only looked confused and solemn - torn between loyalty to Aileen and his affection for Siobhan. He didn't know what to do.

Tessie moved to Aileen. "Yer hurt. Let me see it."

"Get off me." Aileen pushed her back. "It's a nick, girl. I've had plenty before and they haven't brought me down." Aileen's gaze dropped to the floor, her breathing heavy and laboured.

It was bad, no matter what she said. Tessie could see that.

"Siobhan's right. We need to get out of here." Tessie spoke to everyone now. "He's coming here to finish us. It never mattered if Aileen stepped aside or not."

"What do yer mean it never mattered?" Finn asked.

"Kyran came to warn me. To warn us. It was all a lie to get us here in one place and away from Kyran. The Angel's here to kill us. That's all he wants."

"Oh, yer've got to be kidding me." Aileen hunched

forward with her hand on her knee. Even wounded she managed a wry cut-down.

"It might have been wrong to trust him at his word, but if I'd know things were so bad I'd still have come. I'd still have tried."

"Well, God save us all from yer trying, girl."

"We still have time to get out of here."

"Go then. All of yer go. I'll not run from that man. Not now. Not ever."

"Yer can't stay here—"

The door flew open and they all ducked for cover, reaching for weapons.

Madochée and Mickey barrelled into the room.

"Oh, thank you, God!" Tessie rushed forward as Madochée made for Finn and wrapped her arms around him. Behind her, Mickey lingered in the doorway holding something large in his arms. "Whatever happened to yer?" Tessie took Madochée's face in her hands and checked her over. She was rosy-cheeked from the cold air outside but all together unharmed.

Mickey moved into the room, shifting his feet and agitated. "We need to leave. Now."

At least he was in agreement, Tessie thought, the relief surging through her. They were all here. They were all safe. They might still get out of this yet.

"What's happened?" Finn asked of his grave expression, but before he could answer a baby's cry filled the small kitchen.

"Is that a bleedin' baby?" Aileen looked wilder by the second.

Mickey lowered his arms and unfurled the blanket to reveal a robust baby peering out at them. His large brown eyes flickered around the room before releasing another forlorn cry.

"What have yer done, Mick?" Finn urged. "Is that Connor?"

"Of course it's Connor. Who else would it be? I told yer I'd get my boy, Finn. He belongs with his da but they'll be on my trail. We need to get out of here."

"Yer didn't—"

"They would never have given him up. I told yer. Now we need to go. We don't have time to lollygag."

"Aye. Nor do we." Tessie ushered Madochée forward. "We must go. All of us." She turned to Siobhan who looked hesitantly at Sam. "If yer coming, get yer things. Now. "

Aileen held to her chair, still clutching her side. "Aye. Go. All of yer." Aileen was starting to sound drunk. Her words were slurring and slow as she flung her arm at them in dismissal.

"Yer coming with us. Yer don't have enough people to fight him or hold him off. We all need to leave now."

Tessie felt the burn of impatience strangle in her chest. Even now Aileen couldn't let go. She wouldn't give up. She would die here in this place. She would choose death over anything else. She would go down with this city, whether it wanted her here or not. The tragedy of it overcame her. She'd come all this way to look her mother's fate in the eye. She couldn't turn away from her now.

"Yer should go," she said to Finn. "Go with Mickey and take Madochée. Find us the first ship out of here and we'll meet yer at the docks. I'll follow with Sam and Siobhan."

Finn wanted to argue, but Madochée tugged at his arm. Mickey was already walking out the door.

"Listen." Tessie drew her voice to a whisper. "Mado can't be here if the Angel's men come, and Mickey has his hands full. He needs yer with him." She reached out and touched Finn's cheek. They'd barely had time to reconnect in the midst of all of this. "We'll be right behind yer," she reassured him. She just needed a moment more to fight Aileen's resolve. One last effort to convince her mother to leave before it was too late. "I'll wait for Sam and Siobhan and we'll be right behind yer."

Sam stood up and gave Finn the nod. He'd stay with her. He'd make sure they made it. She wouldn't be alone.

Finn squeezed her hand and lowered his voice as she walked him to the door. "Don't go down with her, Tess. If she won't leave, promise me yer'll walk away. Promise me. We'll be waiting for yer."

Tessie nodded, pressing her hand to his chest as the yearning in his eyes filled her heart. They were so close to getting away, and yet still so deep beneath the Angel's shadow. If she could get everyone to the docks, they could get away. They would finally be free. They would have thwarted the Angel's plans once and for all. Finn took one last look at her.

"Hurry, lady Tess. Hurry to us." Madochée beckoned her with wide eyes.

Finn closed the kitchen door behind them. Sam lifted the heavy wooden beam from beside it to lock down the door's brackets.

Tessie longed to run after them and felt the pang in her heart, but there was no time to waste. She turned to Siobhan and Sam who stood waiting for instruction.

"Hurry," Tessie said. "We have only minutes. Take only what yer can carry."

They rushed up the stairs as Aileen sat slumped forward, her head in her hands and her wild dark hair fanned out over her back. Tessie opened the stove door and stoked the dwindling flame, stirring the coal lit embers to warm her mother's hunched-over shoulders.

With every passing moment, Tessie tried to conjure up the right words to say to Aileen but they did not form. What words could possibly hold enough meaning to make her mother leave this place? Should she drag her kicking and screaming from her home, just the way she had dragged her to the workhouse all those years earlier? It was to save her, after all.

Tessie stepped behind her mother and touched the collar of her coat. "Let me see it."

Aileen winced but moved so Tessie could slide the coat down her arms. The blood was dark and thick on her dress and Tessie swallowed back any sound of shock or concern, though it rose sharply in her throat. There was so much of it — brown and murky blood on the dark green fabric.

"I'm no doctor. I don't know—"

"Get me a sheet to bind it," Aileen croaked. "There's one in the pantry."

Tessie hurried, scrambling in the dark through a basket of linen. She returned with a ragged-edged bed sheet and started on the buttons at the back of her mother's dress. Aileen let out a heavy groan and stood up.

"Forget that."

"Shouldn't we strip yer down?"

"Just do it now. We haven't the time."

Aileen struggled to raise her arms but held steady as Tessie looped the fabric around her torso and fastened it tight and firm. As she bound each layer, the blood soaked through, though Tessie didn't comment. She finished the binding and Aileen dropped back down on the chair, pulling out her tobacco pouch. She rolled a cigarette with shaky hands and passed it to Tessie to light on the stove.

Handing it back, Aileen inhaled deeply, her skin pale and shiny. Tessie felt a wave of sorrow. Was she watching her mother die? Aileen Fisher, the Black Bonnet, paling and fading in her small, quiet kitchen. No fanfare. No noise. After all this woman had carried, had it all come to this?

There was nothing Tessie could do. The feelings choked up in her throat and stung her eyes. Was this the end?

The silence dissipated as Sam and Siobhan ran back down the stairs. Tessie blinked back a tear and cleared her throat. "It's time," she said to Aileen, her voice low and pointed.

Aileen tilted her head to the side. "For yer. For all of yer."

Tessie looked to Sam and Siobhan, but they seemed equally helpless and lost. They didn't know how to budge her either. Tessie crouched down before her mother. How could she leave her here in this state? How could she abandon her?

Aileen drew in hard on her cigarette. "What is it yer want from me, girl? What?" Her voice cracked, though her eyes remained sharp and unrelenting.

Tessie stared at her hand on Aileen's knee. She didn't know. She had no idea, except something pulled at her to stay. She couldn't leave her.

"Whatever it is, I don't have it. Go, girl. Go."

Tessie stood but her feet didn't move.

"Go!" Aileen slammed her fist on the table. "I said go!"

Tessie couldn't. She didn't know how to.

Just then a thundering bang sounded. Siobhan let out a terrified gasp and Tessie's heart jumped. All eyes turned to the door as the person on the other side hammered again, ominous and booming through the small room.

"Aileen!" a commanding voice called from the other side.

"It's too late," Siobhan said, backing into the front room. "He's here."

She scrambled up the stairs and back down again, crashing into Tessie as she pushed through, panicking. She was rushing in circles. Sam stepped in, gripping her shoulders and holding her tight. He flashed his concerned eyes at Tessie. What were they to do?

Tessie thought of Finn. He was waiting for her. All she

had to do was leave. They still had time. They could get through the front door and slip into the night. They still had time to escape. But looking to her mother, Tessie knew she was not leaving. Whatever was about to transpire in this room, Aileen would stand to face it. She would see it to the end. The strength of it, her powerlessness to stop it, burned in Tessie's chest. She didn't know what to do.

"Open it," Aileen said.

"What?"

"No." Siobhan squeezed her hands to her chin, shrinking against Sam.

"Open it." Aileen leaned forward, her skin pale and clammy, and her hair clinging to her cheeks. She pulled herself to her feet. "We end this. We end this now."

The room was silent as the door thundered again. They were breaking it down. Tessie looked to Sam. It was written on each of their faces. Their fate was tied to Aileen's now. Whatever waited on the other side of that door for her, waited for them all.

Sam took one last look at Aileen, her eyes wild and her shoulders square as she gripped the hatchet at her belt. Then, he opened the door.

It was Castor, mid-stomp, who greeted them. Bringing his boot down hard on the floorboards, a gleeful smirk traced his lips, and he regained his balance.

Tessie held her breath, her eyes fixed on the darkness behind him as, sure enough, the Angel emerged. Arthur's robust outline stepped into the light. The sight sent waves of terror down her legs. Behind him, his men gathered deep into the shadow, numbering more than enough to overrun them. Those at the front stood rabid as the look in their leader's pale blue eyes. But he wasn't looking at Tessie. He was looking at Aileen.

All movement slowed. Not a sound escaped their lips as he stepped into the room, his face brimming with an energy that trembled through her — he was a wolf and he had found his prey.

With barely a flinch, Aileen launched her hatchet across the room, thwacking it hard into the exposed beam above Arthur's head. The whooshing sound cut through the silence, but Arthur did not recoil. As he bared his front teeth in a triumphant gnash, the room seemed to shrink around him, suffocating and still. Aileen and Arthur locked eyes.

"Yer finally have the bollocks to face me." Aileen's voice was low and harsh. Tessie wondered if the Angel saw the yellow pallor at her brow and the blood staining her dress. Would he notice she gripped the table to stand?

He reached his strong forearm up to the hatchet and plucked it from the wood, tossing it at the table, unconcerned. He scratched at his sideburns, savouring every moment. "I should have finished this a long time ago."

"Aye, but yer didn't have the stones. Couldn't bring yerself to do it, could yer?"

"No. If you understood any of it, we wouldn't even be here."

"I have the cargo. I still have it."

"I don't give a toss what you have. You think there isn't more? You think I can't get more?"

Arthur's voice was a low rumble as he took a step closer, almost within arm's reach of Tessie. His eyes remained locked on Aileen. Whatever was between them, none of them would get in its way. It would run its course. Tessie felt the helplessness well up inside her. She glanced at Sam and Siobhan, banished to the background as Castor guarded the kitchen door.

"Yer can get all yer like, it don't change the fact this is my city. Always will be."

"This city will answer to me and me alone. It all stops here today. It stops here. I've played games long enough."

Aileen took a step towards him, releasing her hold on the table for the first time. Could Arthur see she was injured? Could he see she was weakened?

Arthur's arm shot out at Tessie and he gripped her by the hair, yanking her towards him. "This girl of yours..." He spat at Aileen. "The canary who won't die and won't shut up."

Then he whispered directly into Tessie's ear, though his eyes never left Aileen. "Take my son from me, will you? Send him to Boston, will you? You were never getting out of this alive." He smacked a kiss on her temple.

Tessie struggled and kicked, though he did not seem to feel it.

"Yer want to end this?" Aileen said. "Then it's yer and me, Arthur. Angel. Big man. If yer can bring yerself to it. It's yer and me."

Arthur's nostrils flared. He flung Tessie across the room as if she was nothing. "That's why I'm here." He took a step closer.

"No." Tessie urged her mother as she gathered herself off the floor. "Yer can't." How could she fight him alone, injured as she was, weakened and fading?

"Quiet, girl. This ain't to do with yer now."

Tessie scrambled to her feet. "Please. Not this way." She'd never survive it. Tessie felt the grief already heavy in her chest. She'd not watch her father murder her mother. This was not why she had come to Dublin. She glanced back at Arthur, no mercy in his expression, his pale blue eyes wells of heat and rage.

"Get back," Aileen called. "It's been a while since the Angel here grazed his knuckles in a real fight. Ain't it, Arthur darlin'? Been leaving the fighting to yer boys. Still hold yer own, do yer, when yer opponent ain't shaking in her boots?" Aileen's eyes lit up. "Cause I ain't shaking, love. Not even close."

The Angel unbuttoned his coat and tossed it at Castor before rolling up his sleeves. "It hasn't been that long."

"We'll see."

"Don't interfere," Arthur barked at Castor, before pointing his finger at the rest of his men. "Any of you. I will have my vengeance." He moved into a crouching position as Aileen skirted around the table.

"Vengeance?" she scoffed. "Yer lies might fool them, but I see yer for what yer are. What yer have always been. That's what this is really about. Yer couldn't let it be." Favouring her right side, she turned towards him with her left, energy and grit raging in her eyes. "So let's call this what it is, shall we? Yer burying the last of it. The last remnants of who yer are so they'll never know what I know. What I saw."

Arthur lunged first, overturning the table and tossing it aside so it banged against the wall.

Aileen grimaced a deep look of disgust, but wasn't deterred. "It's taken yer this long to have the courage to look me in the eyes. Well, tell me what yer see, Artie. What do yer see?" She threw herself at him, wrapping her arms around his head and digging her thumbs into his eyes. Lifting her off her feet, he flung her away.

"I see nothing. You were always nothing. Nothing but the grit between my toes. A shit stain in my drawers."

"Come now, boy. We were more intimate than that." Aileen winked at him.

Tessie couldn't believe what she was watching. She gathered by Sam and Siobhan, her breath catching in her throat, trying to piece together Aileen's accusations. What had she seen of the Angel? What did she know? Whatever it was, the animosity echoed through them all as her parents stood before each other for the first time in almost two decades. Their energy twisted and curled like a naked flame. It could not be dulled. It would not be contained.

They circled again, clashing in the centre of the room. Aileen slashed his face with her nails. He punched hard at her side. Grunting at the stab of pain, Aileen clasped both hands together, slicing them sharply across his face.

"You are injured," he said with a light smile.

"Not enough for yer."

Tessie could only watch as the two exhausted themselves, tussling back and forth, grunting and twisting from each other's grasp. Heaving and spitting through gnashed teeth. It was not a pretty fight, but a personal waging of retribution.

Aileen tried to guard her right side, but now Arthur knew where to aim his blows. She let out a piercing scream as he threw himself on top of her. She writhed beneath his hefty frame. He was too heavy. Tessie lurched forward as he delivered another blow to her wounded side and Aileen recoiled in agony.

Castor gripped Tessie's arm and held her back. Tessie slapped him away. Aileen worked her arms free and, gripping his head, she bit viciously into his ear. Arthur roared — he shook her loose and staggered to get up.

Blood streamed down Aileen's chin as she spat a chunk of Arthur's flesh to his feet. "If I have to take yer one bloody piece at a time, that's what I'll do."

From his knees, Arthur roared and cupped his ear. Standing quickly, he swung his fist like a bear claw, catching her heavy across the side of her head and sending her reeling sideways.

"We have to stop them," Tessie said, but neither Sam nor Siobhan responded.

Tessie looked to Castor who held his post, but she could see his eyes too filled with unease. Was this to be the end of the Angel? The end of Aileen? Were they to just stand and watch as they destroyed each other?

A shrill war cry sung out from Aileen as she ran at Arthur. Producing a knife from her skirts, she slashed it at the air. He was nimble, though his thick neck shone with sweat, and the vein at his forehead pulsated. He twisted her wrist, forcing her to let go, and wrapped his arms around her in a suffocating hold. They were locked so tightly it was almost an intimate embrace, their faces mashed at the cheek, sweaty and flushed. They were tiring.

The knife fell to the floor, and finally breaking free, Arthur thrust her away, dishevelled and heaving. His waistcoat torn, blood streamed from his ear, trickling down the crisp white of his shirt. Aileen backed away, flicking her damp hair back from her face and smearing the blood from her chin with the back of her hand.

They were coming undone - their bitter feud laid bare for all to see in a scrappy and disorganised brawl. They would not stop. They would go until they had drained the last of their energy, their limbs heavy and weary until one strangled the life from the other.

Tessie saw the madness in their eyes. Desperate to end it, she edged closer to Sam as Aileen and Arthur momentarily caught their breath.

"We have to stop them," Tessie hissed.

"How?"

Tessie didn't know. She scanned the room, but there was nothing she could do. Castor blocked the kitchen exit, and behind him, a multitude of the Angel's men waited for an order to destroy them. Her eyes moved to the front room.

"We need an exit," she whispered, keeping her eyes forward to avoid Castor's suspicion. "Can yer clear the boards from the front door?"

Sam discretely surveyed the room and calculated for himself. "They're nailed in but not too secure. I should be able to." He moved into the shadow as Aileen and Arthur erupted again and thundered past them. Tessie took the opportunity to yank Siobhan to the far wall and closer to their would-be exit.

Aileen lumbered past, pulling a rope from the rafters. She looped it around Arthur's neck and bore down hard against his back. Gripping his hands to his throat, he hunched his shoulders and spun around to pry her loose. A deep gargling noise erupted from his throat as he broke free. He wrapped his fingers around her throat and held her down. She scratched and clawed at his hands, but he only bore down harder.

"I'll squeeze the life out of you. You bitch."

"My God!" Siobhan shrieked.

Tessie felt the breath seize in her chest. Her mother's face was turning blue, her eyes ogling up at Arthur, who only gritted his teeth. Panic surged through Tessie. Before she had time to think, she snatched up Sam's griddle pan and slammed it into Arthur's head. He slunk to the side, loosening his grip enough that Aileen pushed him off, gasping and choking for breath. Castor ran at Tessie, driving a blow to her stomach as Aileen and Arthur crawled apart on their knees.

Tessie fell hard against the back wall, and Siobhan rushed to help her as a moment of respite washed over the room. Tessie gasped for breath, hoping and praying the heat of rage and revenge was fading with their exhaustion — but there was Arthur, scrambling to his feet and glaring at her.

"You wretched bitch. Pauperess from the gutter. I should have killed you first. My son be damned." He grabbed Tessie by the throat.

Aileen, on all fours, flicked open the stove door to expose the flames burning inside.

"Arthur," she yelled, reaching for one of the torn sheets Tessie had fetched from the pantry. Lighting it in the flames, she held it up for him to see. "I'll burn the Bonnet to the ground before I let yer take it, before I let yer take me down."

She swirled the flaming fabric above her head, then launched it across the room, forcing the Angel to loosen his grip on Tessie. The fiery sheet hit the sofa in the hall, then Aileen lit another up in flames and flung it at Arthur. Then another. And another. Arthur retreated as another makeshift firebomb kicked at his heels, raining flaming embers from the ceiling.

Aileen's face flickered wildly in the light as the flames took hold of the sofa. Tessie stood back as heat filled the space and flames reached towards the rafters. She eyed the ceiling and felt the horror grip her. The entire rickety building was nothing but kindling - it would go up in flames in a matter of seconds. Grabbing Siobhan's hand, she dragged her to the front room to see Sam had almost pulled the boards free.

"What's happening?" he asked as the flames roared loudly from the kitchen.

"This whole place is going to go up." Tessie urged Siobhan towards him. "We have to get out."

Sam kicked the last of the boards free with his boot. Tessie rushed back to the kitchen to see the Angel pushed against the back door, trapped behind the burning remnants of the table in the middle of the floor. Aileen hollered over the flames.

"Come and get me now, yer mad bastard!" Aileen shimmered in the heat, tossing anything she could get her hands on, and stacking the chairs into the blazing bonfire between them. "Yer coward."

"Aileen!" His voice was hoarse. He lunged towards the flames but was forced back in a cloud of heat.

Tessie rushed at her mother. "Come on, we have to go!" But Aileen wasn't listening. She was caught in the rampage, energised by the rising flames licking at the ceiling.

"Aileen. We have to go!"

"I'm not leaving," Aileen kept her eyes triumphantly on Arthur, leaning to the side as he flung a knife through the flames.

"Come at me again, come on."

Aileen held her side, letting out a theatrical laugh as a rafter above her cracked. The ceiling clattered to the floor, a beam striking her to the head and knocking her to the ground. She didn't move. Tessie rushed forward and pushed the burning wood off her mother. The heat seared against her skin as Aileen came to. Spotting the wash bucket in the corner, she emptied its water onto the flames but it made little impact. The panic rose in Tessie's throat.

"Yer'll die! Get up. Get up."

"Where is he? He'll burn in here with me, so he will."

"Are yer crazy?"

"Where is he?"

"We're all going to die if we don't go now! Get up. Come with me now."

Aileen batted her hands away. As she grasped at her clothes, her eyes searched for Arthur through the flames. Another rafter crashed to the ground beside her. Tessie let go, helpless and urgent as the smoke plumes filled her lungs.

This was what her mother wanted. This was her choice. To die a fiery death in the city of her birth. The ashes of Aileen Fisher, the Black Bonnet, set free on the wind to wash over the Liffey and St Mary's, and traipse the Ha'penny bridge — every bit a part of this city's grit and muck.

Tessie heard Siobhan screaming for her to join them at the front door. They had run out of time. She had to go. She'd have to leave Aileen. Another beam crashed down. Tessie could barely make out Aileen's still frame laid out on the floor, now choking and spluttering into her sleeve.

Tessie lifted her skirt to cover her mouth and ran for Sam. "We have to drag her out."

"What?" Siobhan called over the roar inside. "Is she dead? Is she burning alive?"

Tessie didn't have time to answer as she cast a heavy

shawl over her shoulders and thrust a blanket into Sam's hands. "Cover yourself with this. Come on."

Sam didn't hesitate, but Siobhan clung to his arm so that he had to pull himself free. He ran after Tessie and back into the building as Siobhan cried after him.

There on the kitchen floor, Aileen had slid onto her knees, coughing and spluttering in heaves of smoky breath. Too weak to protest, she didn't fight when Sam gripped her by the shoulders. He lifted her up and Tessie held her feet. Dragging her out onto the street, the fresh air engulfed them with a piercing chill to their lungs.

Tessie took one last look at the Black Bonnet, the flames enveloping that rickety building with frightening haste. The glow from inside flickered over them in flashes. Even over the roar of the fire, Tessie could hear Arthur on the other side.

"Aileen! Aileen!" His voice boomed high over the building and echoed into the city.

"To the harbour," Tessie spluttered, stumbling under Aileen's weight. "We need to get to the harbour."

CHAPTER 43

Finn traipsed after Mickey, Madochée gripping his hand to keep pace. His body ached and a limp gripped his right side, but they were almost free of Dublin. He could feel it brewing in his bones. He wanted so badly to run but his body wouldn't let him. With any luck, all the Angel's men were still occupied behind them, and yet if he could lead them away from Tessie he would do it in a heartbeat.

Mickey marched ahead, and they followed baby Connor's cries into the evening darkness just trying to keep up.

"Yer might have told us yer plan, Mick."

"It were far from a plan, brother. Eamon forced my hand, so he did."

"And Mado. We were worried sick about yer."

"Yeah well she weren't part of the plan neither, but she sure showed up at the right time."

"I saved him from a barrel of corn," Madochée exclaimed.

"What?"

Mickey tilted his head away from Finn. "I thought we weren't going to tell him that part?"

Madochée shrugged and flashed a cheeky grin. "Well, I did. You was in the corn."

"What on earth?" Finn turned to Mickey.

"Eamon's doing. And yer can imagine what he'll do when he learns I escaped and have my son."

"Aye," Finn agreed. "Let's keep moving."

"What about Aileen?"

Finn took a deep breath, hardly having the energy or the words to describe the last two days. Could it really only be Tuesday evening? "I'll fill yer in. Let's just get on a bleedin' boat first."

The chill in the air rose in a flurry of ocean salt and brine, raising the hair on the back of his neck. Since setting foot in Dublin he'd felt they were standing knee-deep in the mire, sinking further with each and every step. Now they were so close to pulling themselves free, he hardly wanted to speak or move, lest it all collapse around them. The urgency built as the harbour peeked on the horizon. The ocean and the river-mouth called to him, as it always did, providing a way out - a way to get home.

Finn couldn't help but break into a shuddering jog as they turned the corner and the row of ships stretched out before them. Which ship would be theirs? Which one would carry them to safety? Neither he nor Madochée knew their letters well enough and he turned to Mickey for help.

"Hurry, Mick. The office," he said. "See which one is heading across." Finn gestured for them to find cover at the side of the building and Mickey passed Connor to him and rushed to the office. The young babe briefly ceased his crying though Finn patted him awkwardly on the back.

"You not hold him right, mister." Madochée reached out and plucked him up with confidence. She brought the baby's face into the crook of her neck and made a soothing 'brrr' sound into his ear. "There, baby. Stop crying now baby."

Connor's cries quieted as she rubbed his back and held him close. She looked up at Finn, shaking her head. "Like that. Just like that."

"Very impressive," Finn said. "How did yer learn how to do that then?"

"I had a little sister. Before. I did. Before they left me. She cry a lot too."

Finn managed a smile. "Yer did good, Mado. Yer did good."

Stepping out to the edge of the building, he kept an eye out across the docks for the Angel's men. The Georgian rooftops stretched all the way up the Liffey, and there, high on the corner edge of a warehouse, something caught his eye. Only the faintest line of evening light remained on the horizon, and without it, he may not have seen it all — the silhouetted figure standing out against the skyline. Finn craned his neck and squinted his eyes to be sure. But yes, there he was. The recognisable loping profile, tall and lean, his hands on his hips. The breath caught in his throat and Finn felt a sudden burst of warmth in his chest. An aching call across the sky. It was Tadhg, watching over him. Was that where he had stood all those years ago? Was that where he had watched Finn leave him behind?

This time, though, Finn saw him. He wanted to scream so loudly his brother might hear the echo carry on that briny Dublin wind across the harbour and back through all those years. Suddenly feeling every bit that twelve-year-old who felt without a choice in the world, his heart ached for all that might have been between them. For how very different their lives could have been. There was nothing that could ever bridge that gap of time now. It had been gouged out in the most brutal way and swallowed up forever. All he could do was let Tadhg know he saw him, here, in this moment.

Finn stepped out to stand directly beneath a street lantern

and raised his arm, his palm facing his brother. He held it high and proud, ignoring the pain in his ribs. It was not a wave, but a salute, to his lost brother, to a man of his own blood, to whatever time and ocean parted them. The figure across the rooftops raised his arm in return, holding it up against the fading sky. After just a moment, he turned away and disappeared once again into the cityscape.

"What are you doing?" Madochée asked, stepping up beside him.

"Nothing." Finn lowered his arm though his eyes clung to that corner of the skyline feeling a weight lift from his chest. He ushered her and Conner back into the shadows as Mickey returned.

"That one." Mickey pointed at the third ship in line.

"Alright."

"We need tickets."

"What?"

"We need tickets."

Of course, they did. Finn dropped his head and shook his empty pockets. He had a small sum still tucked in his boots, but it would not be enough. "I have enough for one. Maybe two. Yer?"

Mickey shook his head.

"I can get us on," Madochée said.

"There are too many of us, Mado, and with the baby...we can't risk being put off or draw attention to ourselves."

Madochée shrugged her shoulders and turned back to Connor, who was sucking on the corner of his blanket.

"Hey." Mickey smiled. "He likes yer, don't he?"

Madochée grinned.

"Alright. We'll wait." Finn let out a breath, trying to still the nerves buzzing in his stomach. "They should be right behind us." He turned to the alley entrance ready to take up the vantage point when there was Eamon staring back at them with a smarmy grin.

A bolt of panic struck through Finn and he instinctively squared his shoulders. How on earth did he get here? He must have slunk away from the fight the minute Tessie lowered her pistol. Finn wanted to smack that grin right off his face.

"Run back to yer folks real quick, didn't yer," he scoffed. "Left yer men out there to finish yer fight for yer?"

Eamon seemed indignant, shrugging his shoulders in a self-righteous stance. "Turncoats. Every one of them. And they'll get what they deserve for it. Just like yer about to get yours, Mickey Bell."

Mickey clenched his fists and stepped towards him.

"I got out of yer damn corn barrel, didn't I? What makes yer think anything yer can do will stop me."

"Aye. Someone's head'll roll for that." Eamon licked his lips, his eyes wide and vacant. "But if yer think yer getting out of here with that baby…well, I don't know what to tell yer."

"It's over, Eamon. It's finished," Finn warned. Where he might have felt fear or panic, now he just felt tired and fed up. This man would not get in their way. Not now. "Move. Let us pass."

"It's not finished till I say it is." Eamon pressed into the alley, stepping to Mickey who did not back down.

"Without yer precious pistol yer got nothing to stop us, brother. Yer have no men to back yer up. Step aside, Eamon. I have my boy and everything is as it should be."

"Not everything. Is it, Mick?"

"This is yer last warning, Eamon. Leave us be."

Eamon paused, lowering his eyes, a smirk settling on his lips. "Yer son will pay for yer sins." He spoke softly now, the texture in his voice silky and revolting. "Yer have forced my hand."

He pulled a large knife from his pocket and extended his arm, threading it through the gap between Mickey and Finn. He pointed the knife at Madochée and the bundled baby in her arms. The blood drained from Mickey's face.

"Yer wouldn't dare." Mickey edged towards him, a crack in his voice. "That's Ciara's boy. Yer nephew. Yer own damn blood. Yer lay a hand on him, I swear to Christ..."

The horror rumbled through Finn. What kind of madman threatened to kill a baby? To murder his own nephew? The cold glimmer in Eamon's eye rippled over them. Whatever was in this man's heart was black indeed. It sent a shiver through him.

"He is nothing to me if he goes with yer," Eamon continued. "A traitor like all the rest. Traitors will get a traitor's justice."

Eamon lunged forward, stabbing the knife into the air like a fencing sword. Finn shielded Madochée behind him as Mickey struck Eamon's arm to the side. He charged him, and they tumbled to the ground. Finn stood over them as Eamon thrashed his arms and slashed his knife like a frantic animal. Mickey cried out, straining to hold him back as Finn dodged a kick to his stomach. Eamon broke free, a mad smile sweeping his lips.

"Go Mado. Run!" Finn shouted.

But she was already fleeing, her small frame disappearing around the corner with the precious bundle in her arms.

CHAPTER 44

The smoky taste burned in Tessie's throat as she followed Sam through the back alleys with Aileen's limp body draped between them. The Angel's men would take only minutes to run the length of Capel Street and circle back to the front entrance of the Black Bonnet. They had no time to waste. Even as her chest screamed for oxygen and her throat ached for relief, she struggled with Aileen's weight and they did not stop.

If Aileen woke, she would undoubtedly try to fight her way free. Tessie let a silent prayer to St Brigid form on her lips. This very moment Finn was waiting for them at the docks. They just needed to make it there. Please, let them make it. But even as she thought the words, she knew the docks were no guarantee of sanctuary. The Angel's men could just as easily charge aboard any ship they boarded and root them out. They would need to hide or find a ship disembarking with perfect timing. That's what she prayed for — a ship slipping from the harbour just as they might slip past the Angel's men. Ships passing in the night.

As they sprung from an alley and turned into the freezing

wind, the grimy salt air hit Tessie in the face. They were close. Aileen's left leg slipped from her grasp and Tessie fell against the brick wall to her right, finally pausing to catch her breath. The evening lanterns had been lit along the walkway and dotted the remaining path towards the quay. She could see the ship masts peeking over the Georgian warehouses. Were any of them setting out this evening to cross the Irish Sea?

"She needs a coat," Tessie wheezed, breathlessly. "We need to cover her." She looked down at Aileen, her face smeared with drying blood and ash, obviously wounded, her dress soaked and stained. "They'll never let her on and someone might recognise her."

"Is she still breathing? She needs a bleedin' doctor." Siobhan touched Aileen's forehead as Tessie crouched to check her over. Her chest rose and fell steadily, though her breath rattled in her throat. Her eyelids flickered and now and then a curse word muttered on her lips. Tessie secured her makeshift bandages and wiped her face with her skirt.

"She can pass for drunk. Do yer have a bottle on yer?"

Tessie looked at Sam who shrugged his shoulders, but Siobhan dug into her skirt pocket retrieving a stout whiskey flask.

Tessie took it and sprinkled some over Aileen, dousing her hair and dress.

Siobhan snatched it back. "Steady on. I thought yer were to drink it."

"She needs to smell like a drunk."

"Alright." Siobhan took a long drink herself before tucking it into the folds in her skirt.

Tessie stood, propping Aileen up. "We'll have to make it work."

"We all look a bleedin' mess."

Sam pointed at Tessie's face; she could only imagine she

too was covered in bruises, soot and ash, just as Siobhan's cheeks were stained red from the heat, her hair in disarray. They preened themselves as Sam removed his heavy coat and covered Aileen.

She momentarily stirred, launching one arm out and tipping her head to the side. "Where is he? Where is the maggot hiding now?"

They braced, waiting to see if she'd subdue herself again, then relaxed as she quietened and sunk back beneath Sam's coat.

"I'll not be the one to tell her what we done. I promise yer that." Siobhan pointed at Tessie, but that was a problem for another day.

"Come on. Let's get her up."

They propped Aileen up by the shoulders, walking as if she were nothing more suspicious than an inebriate ready to board. Tessie scanned the area, searching for Finn and Mickey. Were they waiting close by? Already on a ship?

"I don't see them," Siobhan hissed.

It grated on Tessie's nerves, teasing the anxiety already surging through her. Where were they? Had something happened? Aileen grew heavy in her arms as Sam pulled them under a building rooftop to take stock. He shivered without his coat but didn't complain.

"Where the hell are they?" Siobhan nervously turned about.

"I don't know." Tessie bit her lip, her mind whirring. Had she missed some kind of signal from Finn? Would he have boarded a ship? "They couldn't have stood out in the open for long." She frowned, scanning the people passing by, skirting the edges for any sign of them. Every moment out here they were risking discovery. They had to move. Where on earth were they?

Sam suddenly flung his arm across them, pushing them back into an alcove and further out of the light.

"Did yer see them?" Tessie covered her face with her shawl and peeked over her shoulder.

"There are two to your right. They're waiting on us. Bloody hell."

"It's alright. We're going to get out of here." They had come this far, they couldn't get stuck now. They were getting out. Tessie took a deep breath, trying to quiet her mind. Where would Finn be? He must be here. Why couldn't she see him?

"He has to be on a ship," she said. "Whichever one is leaving first. Over there." She pointed to a clipper, and they turned to see the last of its passengers being ushered up the gangplank. "That has to be the one. Look, there on the deck."

"What is it?" Sam frowned.

"That's Mickey's cap isn't it?"

"Is it?"

"It has to be his signal. That's where they are."

"How can we be sure? Where is it going?" Siobhan craned to see.

Tessie leaned to pick up Aileen, gesturing for Sam to hurry. "Right now, it hardly matters. Come. We need to go."

"They're coming this way." Sam was focussed on the Angel's men.

"Have they seen us?"

"Not yet, but we need to hurry."

Hiking Aileen up, they turned their backs and pressed towards the clipper.

Siobhan walked ahead, gritting her teeth and dipping her eyes. "I can't bear it. They're going to see us."

"Keep going."

"They ain't blind. We're out in the bleedin' open."

"Hush, Shiv. Please. Just walk."

Tessie's heart stuck in her throat as they made it to the back of the line. "We don't have any tickets." Tessie felt the blood rush from her face. No tickets. They would never make it in time.

"Christ Almighty." Siobhan raised her voice. "Finn! Mickey! For God's sake, where are yer? Show yerselves!" Tears welled in Siobhan's eyes as she ran the length of the boat, calling up to the deck. "I swear to God, if yer get us killed I'll throttle the both of yer!"

"Shiv!" Sam rushed at her, grabbing her arm and pulling her back. "I have tickets. I have some tickets."

"What?" Tessie gasped. How could he possibly?

He rummaged in his coat pocket as it covered Aileen and produced a wad of paper sheets scrunched up together. "They're for the Atlantic line. Any ship in its charter."

"How?" Tessie asked. "How do yer have these?"

Sam dipped his eyes as he unravelled the creased pages. "Aileen had me get them for the four of yer. To set yer on these boats out of here."

Tessie's heart sunk. Of course, she did. God bless her scheming heart. "Never mind." She snatched them from Sam's hand and stepped onto the gangplank.

Turning back to Siobhan, she saw them, the Angel's men, only one ship along the dock. Her breath caught. They were so close she could hear them talking. "Don't move," she whispered and discretely gestured behind them. Tessie watched as Siobhan clenched her eyes shut, muttering a prayer.

"We have to do something," she said.

"Be quiet."

"This line is going too slow. We're stuck out here like a bleedin' sore thumb. They won't recognise me. It's yer two they know..." She suddenly pushed forward.

"Siobhan!" Tessie hissed. "Stop."

Siobhan nudged the passengers in front of them aside. "Excuse me if yer likes, let an old lady through. She's tired. She needs to rest. Have a heart. Have a heart." The waiting passengers murmured their disapproval but didn't put up a fight as she herded them aside. "Jesus'll bless yer for this mercy, so he will." She turned to Tessie and Sam and gestured for them to follow.

Sam winked as he passed Siobhan. "She'll really have yer guts for garters now."

Siobhan smiled, waving her arms to clear the remaining crowd aside. "God bless yer mercy. God bless yer mercy."

Tessie felt a pang of relief as they made the deck. Sam gave the tickets and their names to the boarding clerk, and Tessie scanned the deck expecting to see Finn or Mickey or Madochée run at her in exasperated relief. But no. There was no sign of them. There was nothing.

Tessie rushed to where she'd seen Mickey's hat hanging on the rail and picked it up. Her heart plunged in a flurry of panic. It wasn't Mickey's hat, but a stupid random hat belonging to God-knows-who.

"My God. Where are they?" She swallowed hard, sickness welling up in her stomach as she tossed the hat into the sea below. She'd really thought they'd be here. Tears stung her eyes and her throat tightened. What could have happened to keep him away? Was he lost or gone or was she simply blind? Had she walked right by them? Please. Please, show yourself. She gripped her hands to the railing.

"If he's not here, where is he? Where is he?"

CHAPTER 45

"Go with her," Mickey hollered as Finn froze with indecision. Should he run after Madochée or help Mickey fend off Eamon's blows? Jolting his aching body into action and propelling himself forward, he rounded the corner just as the last slip of Madochée's skirt disappeared behind the warehouse opposite. He lumbered after her.

"Mado," he hissed as he reached the safety of the shadows. He gasped for breath against his bruised ribcage. She did not appear. "Mado. It's me."

"Is he gone? Is he gone?" Her small voice spoke from the darkness and revealed her hiding space, crouched low beneath an overhanging window. Baby Connor was safe in her arms. "Yer were right to run, but Mickey is dealing with him. Don't yer worry."

"Some people hurt babies."

"Aye. They do. But not this baby. This baby has yer to look after him, don't he?"

She nodded and squeezed him tight. They heard crunching in the gravel and braced. Madochée pulled Finn down with her, though he was not so well obscured. With any luck, he would still go unnoticed. He tilted his head uncomfortably to the side, securing a view of the alley opening. Another scuffle crunched in the gravel nearby. And again. Surely it was Mickey. Please, be Mickey.

They waited, Finn trying to still his breath. The sound stopped. Madochée looked up at him, her eyes pleading for the answer. Was Eamon coming to get them? Were they safe here?

Finn looked around. They'd backed themselves into a corner. If it was Eamon, they were in the worst possible position. Madochée nudged him and pointed at the ground level window by their feet, indicating they should pry it open. Finn hesitated, having no idea who or what they'd find in there. The noise grew closer.

"Alright." He leaned forward, using his hand to clean the glass and peer inside. It was a basement storeroom, dark and dusty. "Can yer get yer hand in?"

Madochée, still balancing the baby on her left side, used her right to squeeze her small hand in the gap and pry it open. The window was heavy and grimy. It had not been opened for a very long time.

She passed Connor to Finn, then turned back to use both hands on the window, gritting her teeth to silence her exertion. Finally, it shifted — a little off kilter, but it shifted. She rubbed her cold hands together and tried again, managing to pry enough room to squeeze through. Finn propped the heavy pane up with a nearby stick and made sure it was secure.

"Mickey! I will get him. Yer know that." Eamon's voice boomed across the yard, ricocheting off the sides of the warehouse in thundering waves. Finn couldn't tell how far or how close he was and froze, gesturing to Madochée to wait lest any movement tip him off. No one emerged. "Mickey! Come out and face me!"

Finn shuddered. They must have been separated, and now Eamon was on the hunt. If he found them first, he could only imagine the worst.

"Go. Go." He held Madochée's hand, lowering her through the gap into the dark basement below. It was quite a drop, and he felt her legs kick out in the open air before her eyes looked up at him. She nodded for him to let go. Even in this moment, he couldn't help but marvel at her courage. For a little girl, she did not hesitate to jump into the darkness.

She plunged into the space below without a sound. He didn't hear her land. He heard nothing. Panic launched through his guts.

"Mado!" he hissed. "Mado!"

Nothing.

A scraping sound wafted up towards him, and her dark face and beaming eyes appeared. "Pass him down, mister."

She was all seriousness and business, holding her arms as high as she might. Finn took a deep breath, wedging his torso through the gap and lowering the babe into her arms. The weight of him forced Madochée to drop quickly from whatever platform she stood on so that once again, Finn could see nothing but black.

"Are yer alright? Mado?"

"Yes, mister. Come on. Hurry now."

Finn pulled back from the window and took one last look around, unsure whether to go looking for Mickey or hold to the safety of their basement hiding place.

Then the strangled sounds of another struggle came from across the yard. Two bodies slamming and wrestling. Exertion and grunting sounds. Gritted teeth and gnashing words.

"Mado..." Finn said, though his eyes held to the alley entrance.

"Go," she said, through the gap in the window.

"I'll be right back."

Finn ran towards the fighting sounds, cursing his bruised body for lagging. He rounded the corner. There they were — Mickey and Eamon, grappling against the far wall, their grip too entangled for Finn to tell if either had the upper hand. As he approached, a gargling sound emanated and Eamon broke free, staggering back. He was holding his side.

Mickey gasped for breath, and Finn to him, checking him over as he slid to the ground. Yanking at his collar, Mickey's face flushed red as he pulled himself upright. "I'm alright. I'm alright."

He struggled to look past Finn to Eamon, but they turned to find him gone. Finn jumped up, searching down the alleyway, the only sign of him a few solitary drops of blood on the ground.

"I think I got him with that damn knife. I think I got him." Mickey swallowed hard.

"He's some kind of hurt. That's for sure." Finn frowned after him, expecting to see his bright frock coat emerge from one of the surrounding alleys.

"Where's Connor and Madochée?"

"They're safe. Should we go after him?"

Mickey shook his head. "Let him go. He's done. We need to get on that boat."

Finn nodded. Tessie and the others had surely arrived. It was time for all of them to go.

BACK OUT ON THE DOCKS, Mickey and Finn held their position by the ticket office.

"I don't see them." Finn fought the sound of dread in his voice, but something wasn't right. Maybe it was the sour aftertaste of their run-in with Eamon, or maybe it was something else. Whatever it was, he just wanted out of there. Out of Dublin. Now.

"Where are they?"

"Maybe held up is all." Mickey stared down at his son - the distraught panic in his face had settled only barely, knowing Eamon was no longer bearing down.

"We still need tickets."

"Here." Madochée held up a small pouch of coins to Finn. He took it, feeling the weight of it in his hand.

"What's this?"

"My coins."

Opening it, he shook the bag around assessing how much it could be. "Where did yer get this, Mado?"

"It's mine."

Finn didn't want to contradict her but still held a question in his eyes and crouched down beside her. "Where did it come from?"

Madochée took a deep breath as if she loathed to explain herself. "Miss Ruby and Mr Kyran give me coins to buy iced buns. Every morning they do. And afternoon. Sometimes both."

"Alright."

"But the lady don't buy to me. She don't."

Finn lowered his eyes, feeling guilt creep over him. "The lady at the store won't serve yer, when yer go to buy one?"

Madochée shook her head. "She doesn't see me."

Finn swallowed, shame sticking in his throat. "Why didn't yer tell us? Why didn't yer say something?"

She reached out defensively to the purse. "Do I have to give the money back?"

Finn touched her cheek. "No. No, yer don't... but this will help a lot, Mado."

She grinned proudly.

Mickey, wasting no time, leaned in and snatched it up.

"Wait here." He dashed towards the ticket office, leaving Finn and Madochée crouched low at the corner. Surely Tessie had made it to the docks by now.

Finn's eyes darted across the scene, moving from each cluster of people to the ships being loaded behind them. Why hadn't they agreed on a meeting place? A signal. Anything! It had all happened so fast. Search as he did, Tessie's form did not appear from the crowd. What could have held them up?

Mickey reappeared clutching the tickets in his hand. He scooped Connor into his arms and pointed across the harbour. "The one on the right is leaving for Liverpool in an hour. Where is Tessie?"

"I don't know."

"Come on."

Mickey led the way. Finn's heart raced as the worry seized him. They had so little time. Pausing, he turned the opposite way. "Yer go ahead. I'll do a lap and check for them."

"Alright. Go. Hurry." Mickey's eyes scanned the crowd nervously. They needed to get out of sight. Finn knew it and forced himself into a jog as he circled the harbour. *Where are yer, Tessie? Where are yer?*

CHAPTER 46

Sam assisted Aileen to a bench as Tessie and Siobhan ran the length of the deck, searching the crowd beneath for Mickey or Finn or Madochée. Tessie couldn't imagine what had kept them, but she could hardly breathe for the dread overtaking her. Something had gone wrong.

"Where are they?" She rose to her tiptoes, desperately scanning as the icy wind whipped against her face, pushing her away.

"I'm more concerned with where this ship is going." Siobhan frowned.

"Go and find out. I'll keep watch."

The wintery bluster swept off the Anna Liffey and out to sea, lashing her hair behind her like a banner and chilling her through. She was a lone figure on the deck as the other passengers took cover — surely Finn would see her here. Surely. Where was he?

Tessie breathed in, trying to still her panic. They were on the boat. They were getting out of here. She thought back to all that had passed. To Arthur's words all those weeks ago. Pain is a language, he'd said. She just needed to learn how to speak it. How to use it. She'd thought she could turn the tide in this chaotic world of his and Aileen's. She looked down at her hands, still bloodstained, bruised and cut. She had become more a part of it than she'd ever dreamed. Was it all so hopeless? So futile? How could they ever escape it?

"It's going to New York." Siobhan returned, and Tessie heard the excitement in her voice.

"But it must go to Liverpool first? It must go by way of Liverpool."

Siobhan shook her head. "Not this one. Something about the cargo. We go straight to New York."

Tessie looked out to sea, her heart a mixture of relief and terror. "Yer were right, yer know."

"Right about what?"

"I did think I was better than yer. Of all of yer. But not in the way yer thought. I thought I could do things differently... I thought we could get through this without..." Tessie stared down at her scarred hands, now empty of Finn. She was alone again.

"Without getting yer hands dirty?"

Tessie managed a wry smile. "I don't know what I thought." And she didn't. "Just that we could do it without being like them. Like him. The Angel."

Siobhan lowered her chin to the railing, surveying the crowd below. "I don't know about him, or about anyone. I just know that it's not so easy, is it? It's not so easy to change a thing."

Tessie let a deep breath slowly release. She could only agree. Fresh starts were not so easily won. As hard as they fought, she wasn't sure they'd ever be free without the scars to show for it. Without exchanging one burden for another. "I was wrong. So very wrong."

Tessie fought back the urge to cry. She cast her eyes at her mother's injured frame curled onto the bench beside Sam. They were not so different as she had imagined. All this convincing and pleading for her mother to give up the fight and here she was on a ship for the New World. She had saved her after all - but what did any of it mean? Would anything they'd done count for anything at all? Would Aileen even survive the distance?

Tucking her hand inside her skirt pocket, she felt the hard edge of Eamon's pistol still hidden from sight. She replayed that moment in her mind. Aileen had been going to say it. She'd been going to surrender the cargo. She'd seen the anguish of it clearly on Aileen's face, the heartbreak raw in her eyes. But she'd been going to do it just the same. Tessie felt both warmth and guilt, that she had ever wanted to hear the answer. Who was Aileen going to be without the Black Bonnet? Without Dublin to call her own? Who were any of them going to be now?

"But we have survived, haven't we?" Siobhan interrupted Tessie's thoughts. "We still have a chance." She lifted her eyes as if needing to hear Tessie's confirmation.

"Aye. We do have that." Tessie patted Siobhan's hand, forcing herself to believe it. "We have a chance." They did, even if that was the only thing they had. If only she could find Finn and the others, they could take that chance together.

The engine's turbines below began to stir, erupting the ship into a hum that spilt up through her feet. My God. They were leaving. No, they couldn't leave yet. Not yet. God, where was Finn?

Tessie broke into a run across the length of the deck. She couldn't leave without him. Where? Dear God, please. Where?

Her eyes scanned the crowds for his broad shoulders, his

profile, his hair flopping at his eyes, anything. Please! And there, her heart seized. He was there below her, running in the opposite direction.

"Finn!" Her voice ripped out of her, shrill and panicked across the gap between them. Hear me! Please hear me! She saw him stop and turn, his eyes darting for her. She waved her arms and ripped off her shawl, billowing it out over the ship's edge. His eyes lit up. He'd seen her! Dear God. He ran, his loping frame darting through the crowd. Reaching the dock's edge Tessie stretched her arms down towards him as he too reached up to her, but the distance was too far too great. Her fingertips felt nothing but air.

"Tess! Tess! Dear Lord, I thought something had happened," he called up to her over the crowd.

"Finn," her voice broke. "Finn." She could barely raise her volume above the surging wind and rumbling engines.

"Did yer get her? Aileen? Are yer all there?"

Tessie could only nod and point behind her. Yes, they had all made it.

Finn broke into a laugh of pure relief. "We're over there. We're on that one!" He pointed at the clipper directly across from hers. "Come on. Come down."

Tessie's feet lurched forward as the ship beneath her moved. It was pulling away. The light faded in Finn's eyes as he realised what Tessie already knew. It was too late.

"We're headed to New York! It's going to New York!" Tears sprung in her eyes, and she stretched her arms towards him. "My God, it's too late, Finn."

"Tess! Tess!" Finn ran along the edge of the dock as the clipper pulled further away. "It's alright, Tess. Go to Boston. Boston! Go to Kyran. Find him. And we'll find yer. We'll find yer!"

"Boston." She tried to call back to him so he knew she understood, but it caught in her throat. She pushed through, clenching her fist to her chest. "We'll go to Boston."

And then she couldn't hold back the tears. She blew him a kiss as he shrunk on the docks. She folded to her knees, exhausted and heavy. They had missed each other at the very last moment. The grief fell through the pit of her stomach. How could she have let it happen?

But he was safe. Madochée and Mickey were safe. They had threaded their way through this disaster one way or another. And here on the ship to New York, Aileen had life in her yet as they sailed far away from the Angel. Far away from Eamon. Far away from it all.

She watched as Finn's silhouette shrunk against the harbour lights. She would see him again. She would see him in Boston. They would be together and their hard-fought new beginning would finally stretch out in front of them. She had to believe it. It might not look the way they had planned or dreamed, but she knew by now every fresh start came at a cost. A shedding of old skins and tattered namesakes. A casting away of all that was broken.

Turning to the sea before them, she drew the cold air deep into her lungs. Is that what they were now? Broken? She looked around at Siobhan standing strong against the railing, looking swell in the smart travelling dress Tessie had given her. She held her jawline high and embraced the wind as it beat against her.

Behind her, Sam sat with Aileen. Tessie couldn't hear them, though by their movement, Aileen was squabbling with him. Sam sat beside her, unmoving and loyal. There was nothing so cruel she could say that would make him forsake her now.

These were her companions, for better or worse. Were they broken? Hadn't that been the Angel's plan? That's not what Tessie saw when she looked at them. They might be bruised and battered. Weary and worn out. But there was life in their eyes yet. She watched as Siobhan turned her back on Dublin and looked out at the dark sea-line stretching out before them. No lights guided their way. Whatever awaited them now, they were Boston-bound, so they were.

284

The greatest gift you can give an author - is a review!

If you enjoyed this book, please leave a review for fellow readers wherever you made your purchase.

THE DEVIL'S EDGE

BOOK THREE IN THE DARKER CITIES
TRILOGY

THE FINAL INSTALMENT COMING SOON!

www.eloisereuben.com

While The Black Bonnet is a work of pure fiction, it is based in a real city, during a real historical time - the famine. The story itself doesn't revolve around factual events, but rather takes place within them, and wherever possible, I have referenced real places and streets.

Maps are one of my favourite parts of research. I use them for factual reference points and they often help me imagine life during the timeframe I am writing. How the streets are set out, and the different sections of the city organised, help me understand how far workers may have had to walk to the docks, or whether they needed to follow the river to get wherever they are going. These details anchor my imagination and can really change an entire scene.

The Vinegar Works was a real place, as was Prospects Cemetery and the North Dublin Union (Workhouse). Even the small uprising referenced by Eamon and Mickey, in Tipperary in 1848, with John Blake Dillon, really took place.

Riots did occur during the famine, though the extent of which they took place in Dublin I did not stumble across in my research. It is true that for at least part of the famine, Ireland continued to ship produce to England, however at some point this was changed.

The third and final book in this trilogy is set in America, predominantly in Boston and New York - and you can bet I am currently knee deep in maps, old photos and recipes, from the New world, this very moment!

Eloise xx